continued . . .

Also by Tracy Anne Warren

THE RAKES OF CAVENDISH SQUARE

The Bedding Proposal
Happily Bedded Bliss

THE PRINCESS BRIDES ROMANCES

The Princess and the Peer
Her Highness and the Highlander
The Trouble with Princesses

THE GRAYSON SERIES

The Last Man on Earth
The Man Plan
Mad About the Man

TRACY ANNE WARREN

Bedchamber Games

THE RAKES OF CAVENDISH SQUARE

JOVE
New York

A JOVE BOOK
Published by Berkley
An imprint of Penguin Random House LLC
375 Hudson Street, New York, New York 10014

Copyright © 2017 by Tracy Anne Warren
Penguin Random House supports copyright. Copyright fuels creativity, encourages
diverse voices, promotes free speech, and creates a vibrant culture. Thank you for buying
an authorized edition of this book and for complying with copyright laws by not
reproducing, scanning, or distributing any part of it in any form without permission.
You are supporting writers and allowing Penguin Random House to continue to
publish books for every reader.

A JOVE BOOK and BERKLEY are registered trademarks and the B colophon
is a trademark of Penguin Random House LLC.

ISBN: 9780451469243

First Edition: March 2017

Printed in the United States of America
1 3 5 7 9 10 8 6 4 2

Cover art by Aleta Rafton
Cover design by Katie Anderson

Bedchamber Games

Chapter I

WITHDRAWN

London, England
May 1821

Rosamund Carrow's heart gave a single heavy thump as the coach drove up Chancery Lane and came to a halt before the main entrance to the Honourable Society of Lincoln's Inn. She glanced through the vehicle's small window at the gatehouse, with its pair of great oak doors. Above, set into the sixteenth-century brick, lay the coats of arms of Henry de Lacy, the Earl of Lincoln; King Henry VIII; and Sir Thomas Lovell—an illustrious grouping for an illustrious institution.

"Are you certain I look all right?" she asked her brother, Bertram, who sat across from her in the dark, quiet confines of the coach.

He swept her with a quick glance. "Course you d-do. W-wouldn't have let you out of the h-house if you d-didn't."

She tugged at the unfamiliar black men's jacket and

white waistcoat to make sure the garments were straight, then smoothed a damp palm across one leg of the black summer-weight woolen breeches she wore. In keeping with the sartorial requirements of tonight's dinner for attorneys-at-law, she had also donned a black robe, black stockings and flat-black shoes with broad silver buckles, all of which she'd borrowed from Bertram, then altered to fit. The shoes had proven the most challenging, but she'd managed by stuffing the toes with cloth.

As for the way she felt in her new masculine attire, she couldn't quite decide. On the one hand, it seemed odd to move about without the protection of a dress, as if parts of her were exposed in the most unseemly manner. After all, she wasn't used to displaying her legs, and most particularly not her calves, even if they did happen to be encased in black stockings. Yet the novel sensation of wearing breeches was curiously liberating, her body no longer burdened by hard whalebone stays and the cumbersome layers of petticoats and gown. Still, she couldn't say she enjoyed having her breasts bound flat against her chest or that she savored the restrictive sensation of her neck being trussed up like a goose in the cravat Bertram had aided her in tying.

The most emotionally unsettling part of her disguise, however, had come from the necessity of having to cut her long, straight brown hair. She'd balked and very nearly changed her mind about going along with Bertram's scheme when her maid—who was in on the identity switch, as were the rest of their staunchly loyal and reliably discreet household staff—approached her with a pair of scissors to do the deed.

Yet after much debate between herself and Bertram, some of which had become uncharacteristically heated, Rosamund had allowed her hair to be cut to shoulder length. Although it was not at all in keeping with the current style, they'd agreed that she would leave her hair a bit long and wear it secured in a queue like men of the previous century. Curiously enough, the old-fashioned style suited her long face and silvery gray eyes, making her look more serious and mature— a good thing, considering how much younger than her eight and twenty years her whiskerless cheeks made her appear now that she was pretending to be a man. And not just any man, but a practicing barrister.

"Just r-remember to keep your v-voice lowered like we p-practiced," Bertram said in his familiar soft stutter.

"I will," she replied, testing out the deeper cadence that somehow still felt comfortable to her when speaking. Had it not, she knew there would have been no chance of her keeping up the deceit.

She let Bertram step down from the coach first, then took a deep breath and followed after him.

The courtyard was cast in lengthening evening shadows as they made their way onto the grounds, the imposing Tudor-style brick buildings rising up around them.

She'd been to Lincoln's Inn on only one other occasion, more than a decade earlier, when her father, prominent barrister Elias Carrow, had stopped to handle a quick matter of business. He'd admonished her to stay in the coach, but she'd snuck out after he left and walked around the grounds with their footman trailing behind her. She hadn't been allowed inside the buildings, of course, and had gotten nowhere near the members' rooms. But tonight her curiosity would finally be rewarded.

She did her best not to gawk through the lenses of her spectacles as she and Bertram moved past paintings and portraits, and the armorial bearings of distinguished members both past and present. Instead she concentrated on keeping her shoulders squared and her stride direct and confidently authoritative so as not to reveal any feminine softness.

"C-can't have you walking like a g-girl and giving the whole thing away," Bertram had warned during one of their practice sessions at home.

A congestion of voices reached her ears as she and Bertram entered a drawing room. Lawyers in dark robes stood in loose groupings, drinks in hand as they conversed.

Bertram leaned in close. "Everyone ch-chats for a bit before we m-move into the hall to d-dine. Come. Let's f-find Stan P-Partridge so I can make the necessary i-intro-d-ductions."

Rosamund swallowed, her throat tight. So far none of the men around them seemed to have noticed her. But when they did, what then? Would they see her and Bertram as the male cousins they were supposed to be? Or would the others realize that a feminine interloper was in their esteemed midst?

Her pulse thundered between her ears. Despite all their careful preparations, had she and Bertram miscalculated? He had so much confidence in her, certain she would succeed. If only she had that selfsame composure. Then again, it had been Bertram's plan from the start. *His* wild scheme that she act as his cocounsel so she could help him handle their recently deceased father's remaining cases without everything turning into a disaster.

Not that her brother was a bad lawyer.

He wasn't.

He was actually quite good.

It was only that, because of his stutter—which always worsened under stress—he'd never performed well in court. In fact, until now he'd handled all the in-chambers work while their father had been the one to appear at trial.

Of course, it had been their father who pushed Bertram to be a barrister in the first place despite the fact that he had never been comfortable speaking in public and would much rather have chosen another profession. Just as it had been their father who educated and trained her in the law, taught her how to analyze, develop and present written and oral legal arguments. She'd even participated in moot courts. Sadly those had been conducted only in private with Bertram and their father, since women weren't permitted to practice law. Had they been, she would have become a barrister and been called to the bar years ago. She found the law fascinating, and it would have been her pride and delight, as the elder sibling, to step into their father's shoes rather than forcing her brother to do work that had never been suited to his nature.

Then, one evening three weeks previous, she'd discovered Elias Carrow dead at his desk; a sudden aneurysm, or so the doctor had said. And in an instant, she and Bertram had found themselves parentless and alone, their whole world turned upside down.

So now here she was, disguised as a male barrister in order to gain official admittance to one of the Inns of Court. Bertram had thought of "borrowing" their elderly cousin Ross's legal credentials and his place on the Law List, which luckily provided no personal specifics about the attorney other than his name and that he was qualified to practice law. It was an idea that would still never have worked had it not been for the fact that Cousin Ross was a country barrister who detested London and never ventured farther south than his home in Yorkshire.

"There's not a soul here in the city who will recognize him or his name," she remembered Bertram assuring her. "And Cousin Ross will never know a thing about it. As for the Inn, the head of membership, Stan Partridge, has agreed to let you come along to d-dinner Friday night, or rather agreed to let *Cousin Ross* come along. You're required to attend three d-dinners before you can be admitted, but he says you can make up the other two later. He's not the sh-sharpest knife in the box, but he's a capital fellow nonetheless. He won't give us a spot of trouble."

Not a spot of trouble . . .

She only prayed he was right, her pulse racing at a Derby-worthy clip.

She glanced back toward the entrance, doing a few quick calculations in her head. It wasn't too late to beat a hasty retreat. All they needed to do was turn around and slip quietly away with no one the wiser. She reached out to stop Bertram, words of apology on her lips, but he was already striding forward, intent on locating Partridge. Before she had time to catch up with him, a pair of older men moved into her path, blocking her way. Determined not to lose her brother in the crowd, she shifted sideways and, without intending to, bumped into another man she hadn't even realized was there.

She looked up, then up again, as he swung around to face her. At five foot seven, she was tall for a woman and usually didn't have to lift her eyes more than an inch or two in order to converse with a man. But this man towered above her, topping her height by at least half a foot.

She drew in a quick breath, heart leaping, and not just from the collision. He was quite simply the handsomest man she had ever seen. One might even describe him as beautiful, with his thick golden brown hair, eyes that were a stunning blend of gold and green, a straight, elegant nose, strong chin and refined yet boldly masculine cheeks and jawline. As for his mouth, it was as if nature had formed it expressly for kissing—though why she would think such a thing when she had almost no experience in such matters, she hadn't the slightest idea.

At the moment, however, that attractive masculine mouth was thinned into a line of rueful annoyance as he shook a few red droplets from his fingers, then reached for a handkerchief. Their collision, she realized, must have caused him to spill some of the wine from the glass in his hand.

"I beg pardon," she said, remembering at the last second to deepen her voice. "I am afraid I did not see you."

He flicked her a glance as he dried his hand. "It's of no matter. Accidents happen."

Tossing back the remaining inch of wine in his glass, he set the vessel on the tray of a passing attendant, then calmly folded his handkerchief in quarters before returning it to his pocket.

She noticed that it was made of white silk and not the linen that her brother always used. His clothing was also elegant and finely tailored, though understated in a manner only those of substantial wealth could afford.

"And you are, sir?" the beautiful man asked, the question spoken in a mellifluous baritone that made her body tingle in a most surprising and inconvenient way.

It took her a long moment to even compute what he'd said. "Me? Oh, I'm Ros . . . Ross Carrow." She clenched her fingers at her side, relieved that she'd managed to stop herself in time from uttering "Rosamund," which had unthinkingly danced on the tip of her tongue.

"Carrow, is it? How do you do? I am Lord Lawrence Byron."

Byron? He was Byron?

She recognized the name, her father having mentioned it on more than one occasion over the years. As she recalled, Lawrence Byron was known for winning lawsuits, his formidable reputation in legal circles earned through hard work and keen insight rather than via any reliance on his aristocratic connections. If she remembered right, his eldest brother was a duke.

Good heavens.

Lord Lawrence scrutinized her with a look. "Are

you new to Lincoln's Inn? Can't say as I recall having made your acquaintance before."

"Yes, I am new." She strove to keep her voice low and masculine—or at least what she prayed sounded masculine. "I've just lately arrived here to the city from the north country."

Bertram had made her recite the made-up details of her life as Ross Carrow so many times that the words came easily.

Lord Lawrence's well-groomed eyebrows drew together. "You don't have the sound of a north country man."

"I spent my early youth here in London before my family moved," she explained. "Guess I never lost the Town accent."

He nodded, then narrowed his eyes.

What is he looking at? She fought the urge to squirm.

God above, he doesn't suspect me, does he?

She held steady, careful not to lower her gaze.

"Carrow?" he said slowly. "Any relation to Elias Carrow?"

An odd combination of relief and pain arrowed through her, the abrupt reminder of her father hard to take. Her hands trembled as she fought a fierce wave of grief, for try as she might, she still had trouble accepting that he was gone. Even now it seemed impossible that she would never again hear the commanding persuasion of his voice or have the pleasure of debating history, politics, literature and the law with him.

She nodded, swallowing hard. "Yes, Elias Carrow was my . . . cousin."

Lord Lawrence's gold-green eyes filled with compassion. "My sincere condolences for your loss. I didn't know him well, but he was a fine man and an excellent barrister. His death was a dreadful shock to us all in the legal community. He will be sorely missed."

Something inside Rosamund softened, touched by the genuineness of his words. For many, such an expression of sympathy would have been perfunctory at best, but she sensed that Lord Lawrence truly meant what he said. "Thank you, my lord."

She was thinking he was about to say more when Bertram appeared at her elbow, along with a tall beanpole of a man whose berobed arms flapped around him like a crow when he walked. The man smiled hugely at her as he took in the sight of her and Lord Lawrence standing together in conversation.

"Oh-ho," he said in a booming voice that seemed at odds with his scrawny build. "Finding your way already, I see. Good, good. I'm Stanley Partridge, by the by, and you must be Ross Carrow, or so your cousin here tells me."

He didn't offer to shake hands, since it was against tradition for barristers to do so. Instead he grinned again and awaited her reply.

To her profound relief, he seemed to accept without hesitation that she was precisely who she said she was—namely, a man. A tiny contrary part of her wondered if she ought to be offended that her transformation was being so easily believed. How could they not see that she was female? Then again, perhaps it was as Bertram said—people saw what they expected to see.

"How do you do, Sir Stanley?" She bowed—another bit of male etiquette on which Bertram had instructed her. "It is a pleasure to meet you. Allow me to thank you for inviting me to join you here at Lincoln's Inn. You are most hospitable, particularly given that I only lately arrived in the city."

"Oh, we barristers are a brotherly sort, as I'm sure you well know." Partridge hooked his thumbs into his waistcoat pockets and leaned back on his heels. "Bertram here speaks most highly of you. Course he would, seeing as he's your cousin." Sir Stanley took a moment to laugh at his own joke. "But clever newcomers are always welcome within our ranks, whatever their origins. Is that not so, Lord Lawrence?"

Byron, who had looked on silently until now, nodded solemnly. "Indeed they are. Particularly when there are liberal libations to be had in honor of the occasion."

For a moment, no one spoke.

Then Sir Stanley let loose a booming laugh. "Just as you say, my lord. Just as you say. What man doesn't relish a good tipple, particularly when someone else is footing the bill?"

Byron's expression remained stoic, yet she couldn't help notice the irreverent twinkle in his eyes. It made her wonder all the more just what sort of man lived behind his smoothly urbane facade. Clearly he was shrewd and knowledgeable, with a flair for subtle drama. She suspected he was unpredictable as well, in a manner that most likely regularly threw his opponents off their game. She abruptly decided she was glad she would never have occasion to oppose him in court. He must be the very devil to defeat.

"But come, come, we must continue with your introductions, Carrow. Won't do to monopolize His Lordship indefinitely. Lots of people to meet before the night is done." Partridge gestured around the crowded room with a swipe of his long black-clad arm in a way that reminded her of a bat this time.

Rosamund surveyed the assemblage of men and swallowed against a fresh rush of nerves. She exchanged glances with Bertram, who gave her a bolstering look of encouragement, then away again. As she did, she found Lord Lawrence's gaze on her.

Her natural instinct was to lower her own. But she knew that among men, such an action would signal weakness. And in this circumstance, she couldn't afford to seem weak.

Be a man, she told herself. *Do what a man would do.*

And so she stared.

He stared back.

Subtly she lifted her chin.

He arched an eyebrow.

She forced herself not to blink.

He didn't appear to require blinking.

"If you will excuse us, my lord," Partridge said, unaware of the silent duel going on.

Lord Lawrence stared a few moments more, then angled his gaze toward the other man, his demeanor as easy and in control as if the past few seconds had never occurred.

"Of course, sir. Pleasure as always." Byron inclined his head toward Partridge, then Bertram, who nodded back. Then he looked at her again. "Carrow. Good meeting you. I'm certain our paths shall cross again. London may be a big city, but the legal community is surprisingly small."

"As it ought. Until then, my lord." She bowed shallowly.

He returned the courtesy.

Before anything more could be said, Partridge was herding her onward, while Bertram followed in their wake.

As for Lord Lawrence, she knew better than to look back at him. Then she forgot him altogether as another round of introductions began.

Lawrence watched Ross Carrow walk away, uncertain exactly what it was about the man that provoked his curiosity. Carrow seemed intelligent and well-spoken, but then, barristers generally were as a breed—with the unfortunate exception of his cousin Bertram, whose reputation for awkward silences and stuttering preceded him wherever he went. Must be the reason he'd asked Ross Carrow to join him here in London. Undoubtedly he was trying to fill the great void left by his late father.

Lawrence had been rather surprised by the flash of intense sorrow that had appeared on Carrow's features when Elias Carrow was mentioned. Not that the other man shouldn't be saddened by the death of his relation; it just seemed rather extreme for a relationship that must surely have been conducted at a great distance and between men of such disparate ages.

Then again, what did he really know about the Carrow family? Nearly nothing, having met Elias fewer than a handful of times in passing and once when standing opposite him in court.

Still, this new Carrow seemed curiously different from his cousin. Maybe it was his obvious youth and fine-boned features that set him apart. God knew the boy couldn't need to shave more than once a week, his cheeks were so smooth. Nor could he be much past twenty, though considering the fact that he'd already completed his apprenticeship in the law and been called to the bar, he must have another two or three years on him at least.

One thing for which Lawrence could not find fault was Carrow's nerve. When he'd caught Carrow's eye there at the end, something in him rose in challenge. In his experience, most men would have quickly looked away, defeated. But not Ross Carrow. Instead he'd stood his ground, assertive and unyielding and something more . . . something on which Lawrence couldn't quite put his finger.

And perhaps it was that quality alone that intrigued Lawrence the most, leaving him to wonder how formidable an opponent the younger man might be. Not that they were likely to have occasion to find out. Nevertheless, it might be amusing to go toe-to-toe with him in court and find out exactly how far Carrow's nerve could take him.

Smiling wryly at the idea, Lawrence turned away, intent on locating a fresh glass of wine before he made his way into dinner.

Chapter 2

"Where are you off to? It's barely six o'clock—not time yet to leave for a ball."

Lawrence paused in the act of drawing on a pair of tan leather driving gloves and turned to look at his twin brother, Leopold, standing in the entrance hall of their town house in Cavendish Square.

The two of them were identical, possessed of the same tall, athletic physique, golden brown hair, bold, masculine features and green-gold eyes—although in Lawrence's case his eyes were more gold than green.

"I'm not going to a ball," Lawrence said as he resumed donning his gloves. "If you must know, I'm promised for dinner with a colleague." Finished with the gloves, he reached for his beaver top hat and set it on his head.

Leo raised an eyebrow. "A colleague, hmm? I'd have thought you'd had more than your fill of dry legal talk after that dinner at Lincoln's Inn last night. *Gah*, what a bore that must have been."

Lawrence smiled softly. "It wasn't so bad. Unlike

you, I like so-called dry legal talk and do not find it boring in the slightest. Amazing to think you actually studied law alongside me at university."

"Had to study something, now, didn't I?" Leo grinned. "No, I far prefer my life these days—spending time with my wife, seeing to our estate and working on my new novel. Thalia says it's even more fiendishly frightening than the last one."

Much to everyone's surprise, except perhaps to Leo's wife and Lawrence himself (they were twins, after all), Leo had put his previously unused talents to work at novel writing. Last year, he'd completed his first book, a lurid tale of intrigue, murder and mayhem that sent chills along the spines of everyone who read it. He'd even managed to find a publisher—although as a concession designed to keep from adding more notoriety to the already infamous Byron family name, he'd adopted a pseudonym. So far, Mr. B. Ron Delpool had made a tidy little profit in book sales with more apparently to come.

Lawrence smiled. "If it's half as good as the last, you'll have another rousing success on your hands. So, when are you going to let me read it?"

"When it's finished and not a day sooner. She's a far kinder critic than you are, you know."

"Only because she sleeps with you, dear boy. I'm under no such constraints." Lawrence laughed.

Leo shot him a dirty look, then joined him in laughing a few moments later.

"Sure you can't get out of your dinner tonight?" Leo said. "I promised Thalia I'd take her to the theater. Why don't you join us?"

"I'd love to, but it will have to wait for another occasion, I'm afraid. The man I'm meeting has some information he thinks might come in handy for an upcoming case of mine. Can't afford to put him off."

"God, it's a working dinner. That sounds even duller than I'd imagined. What's happened to you, brother mine? You used to be so much fun."

"I'm still fun," Lawrence said defensively.

"No, you're not, and if you aren't careful you're going to turn into a stodgy old man." Leo shook a finger his way. "What you need is something to shake you out of your seriousness, some spot of trouble that will breathe new life into your soul."

"The last thing I need is to find myself in the basket like the pair of us used to do. It's taken three bloody years, but I've finally managed to put talk about my arrest for public brawling behind me. I'm certainly not about to start it all up again and tarnish my reputation over some new peccadillo."

"Oh, your reputation was tarnished long before that, and yet you're still regarded as one of London's finest barristers. I shouldn't worry overmuch about a new scandal causing you any great difficulty."

"I'm not going to be involved in any scandals. I'm done with such things."

"Done with scandals?" Leo gave a dismissive laugh. "But you're a Byron. It's what we do. Are you quite sure you're my brother? Here, let me check to make sure you haven't been replaced by a changeling in the night."

Before Lawrence could stop him, Leo reached out

and pried one of Lawrence's eyelids wider apart as if he was searching for signs of demonic possession.

Irritated, Lawrence batted his twin's hand away. "Stop that. You're acting like an ass."

Leo snickered unrepentantly.

"Who is acting like an ass?" asked a lilting female voice.

Lawrence turned his gaze toward the stairs and the beautiful dark-haired woman descending from the landing above. The sapphire silk skirts of her evening gown whispered softly with each graceful step she took. As Lawrence watched, his brother's eyes brightened with unconcealed love and pleasure. Lawrence was forgotten as Leo moved forward to take his wife's hand and draw it to his lips. Thalia smiled back with a warm intensity that was almost too intimate to witness.

No one looking at them could doubt the abiding depth of their devotion. Certainly not Lawrence, who knew firsthand the trials they'd faced in order to be together and how nothing short of death would ever be able to part them again.

Lawrence averted his gaze in order to give them a few moments of privacy. On the occasions when Leo and Thalia came to London, they all lived here together in the spacious town house on Cavendish Square. Even so, that didn't mean he liked playing the voyeur. Besides, it was strange sometimes seeing a man who looked exactly like himself exchanging amorous glances and more with a woman who was as near a sister to him as one of his own.

Leo whispered something into Thalia's ear and she

laughed before swatting his chest with a playful hand. He dropped a brief, though thoroughly passionate kiss on her mouth before the two of them came back to their less than solitary surroundings and turned again toward Lawrence.

"So, which one of you is the ass? Or need I ask, Leo, my love?" Thalia said, a smile still dancing on her lips.

"Why, Lawrence, of course," Leo declared with a mischievous wink. "Says he's going to some deadly dull legal dinner tonight. Maybe you can convince him to change his mind."

Thalia shook her head. "Since I know he's every inch as stubborn as you, I won't bother trying. Although it would be lovely to have you join us, Lawrence. Charles Mayne Young is performing at Covent Garden this evening and is sure to be excellent."

"Much as I would enjoy accompanying you, I have important business tonight that cannot wait," Lawrence replied. "I'm surprised some of our other siblings aren't coming along with you to make a party of it. Esme and Northcote are still at Ten Elms with little Kyle, and Cade and Meg won't come south from Northumberland until next month, but nearly everyone else is here for the Season, including some of the cousins. I suspect at least a few of them could be talked into a night of theatrical entertainment."

"Actually we begged off our invitation to the Packham soirée, to which I know Edward and Claire and Mallory and Adam are promised," Thalia volunteered, referring to more Byron siblings and their spouses. "Leo and I are having dinner here and then joining my friend Mathilda Cathcart and her husband at the theater afterward."

"Drake and Sebastianne said they might join us," Leo added, "but Drake is working on some new experiment, so I wouldn't lay odds on them showing up."

"Nor I." Lawrence smiled, thinking of his brilliant but absentminded older brother and his clever and infinitely patient wife.

"Maybe we shall see you tomorrow night, then, or the next?" Thalia ventured.

Lawrence shook his head. "I'll still be preparing for a case. Then, later this week, I have dinner scheduled with Justice Lord Templestone at his house in Kew."

Leo frowned. "Baron Templestone, you mean? Phoebe Templestone's father?"

"Yes, the very same," he answered, a note of challenge in his voice.

Lawrence was quite familiar with his twin's thoughts on the subject of Phoebe Templestone and Lawrence's recent attentions toward her. After being introduced to the pretty blonde at the start of the Season, he'd danced with her at various balls and taken her driving once in the park. He knew rumors were circulating about the two of them and that more than one wager had been entered into the betting book at White's Club. But then, he was generally linked with some debutante or other each Season, so it was nothing out of the common way.

The surprising truth this time, however, was the fact that he was actually considering asking her to be his wife. It was no secret that Phoebe's father harbored hopes of a match between them. After all, a marriage alliance with the Duke of Clybourne's only remaining unwed sibling would be a prized feather in Temple-stone's cap.

Yet the advantages of a union with Phoebe Temple-stone would not be all one-sided. Her father was a high court judge, a powerful man in the field of law, who many thought would one day become the Lord Chief Justice of England. In the meantime, Carlton Templestone would serve as a valuable ally, able to aid Lawrence in his goal of becoming King's Counsel and a Serjeant-at-Law, then later ascending into the judiciary himself.

Up to this point, however, Lawrence had taken great care not to display more than a polite and respectful interest in Miss Templestone. Until he was firmly decided whether to offer for her, he didn't want to find himself caught in a matrimonial trap he couldn't escape.

As for the girl herself, she was young and sweet, a biddable eighteen-year-old with good manners and a moderate amount of talent playing the pianoforte. She would make a fine wife, especially for a barrister. Yet he was under no illusions as to his feelings for her.

He did not love her and knew he never would.

And therein lay the basis for his brother's disap-proval. It wasn't Miss Templestone in particular of whom Leo disapproved; it was the fact that he knew Lawrence felt nothing warmer toward her than a mod-est liking.

At first, Leo had paid scant heed to Lawrence's attentions toward the girl, assuming he was just being kind because of her father. But when Lawrence had continued seeking her out at dances, Leo's disregard turned to confusion, then concern, and more recently alarm.

"You aren't actually courting that girl, are you?" Leo had said confrontationally the day Lawrence returned from taking Miss Templestone out for a drive in Hyde Park at the height of the Fashionable Hour.

"Possibly. I haven't fully decided," Lawrence had said as he sat in his favorite chair in his study. "Would it be so bad if I took a wife?"

He wasn't sure which of them had been more shocked in that moment—Leo for having his suspicions confirmed or Lawrence for admitting to the possibility.

Over the next half hour, Leo had treated him to a highly uncharacteristic lecture on the subject of marriage, counseling that there was only one reason—and one reason alone—to wed, and that was love.

Lawrence had listened quietly, making no great effort to disagree. He was fully cognizant of the fact that all seven of his siblings were madly in love with their spouses and had wonderful marriages. He knew too that they all believed he ought to wait and find a woman he genuinely loved. Yet always at the back of his mind was the question . . .

What if there is no great love waiting out there for me? No perfect, fated mate who will someday fill my days with joy.

His siblings' matrimonial success was mostly the result of luck, and Lawrence didn't put much stock in such things, especially not when it came to himself.

He far preferred relying on solid facts and unbiased reason. And the fact was that in the whole of his nearly twenty-nine years, he had yet to meet a woman with whom he wanted to spend more than a few weeks, let alone his entire life. Considering this Season's new crop of debutantes and all the ones who had come before them, he didn't believe that situation was likely to change.

Not that he suffered from a lack of feminine companionship. Quite the contrary. His reputation as a rakehell was more than justly deserved. This year alone, he'd kept company with an amazingly limber ballerina, a lusty young widow who enjoyed having intimate relations in public locations, and one memorable night with a pair of opera singers who had wrung sounds from him he hadn't realized he could make. But as pleasurable as those experiences might have been, he was no more in love with those women than he was the cloth-headed Society girls who made his eyes glaze over two seconds after they started to speak. So he'd decided with the same unemotional logic he employed as a barrister, if he wasn't likely to marry for love, he might as well do so for convenience.

When he first chose to train in the law, he'd done it as a bit of a lark, along with Leo, who'd seen no useful purpose in either of them joining the military during a time of peace or in entering the Church—an overly pious prospect that would have run in direct opposition to their lusty, irreverent natures. So rather than entering one of the usual professions for younger sons, they'd gone into the law. Unlike Leo, however, Lawrence had been instantly taken with the discipline.

The law provided intellectual complexity and an ever-evolving challenge that he found fascinating. So by the time he'd earned his credentials, he knew he'd found his life's calling. He'd also known that ultimately he would want to advance in the field, and what better, more satisfying means of achieving such a goal than to become a judge?

And so his sights had turned to Justice Templestone's pleasant and pretty daughter. He didn't love her, but she would suit his needs and objectives.

Even so, something held him back from making a firm commitment, some niggling awareness that told him to wait just a little while more. So he did, reassured that with the end of the Season still weeks away, there was plenty of time yet to decide.

Lawrence looked at Leo, who appeared as if he wanted to say more.

Before he could speak, Lawrence gave the wrist of one of his gloves another tug. "If you'll both excuse me, I really do need to be on my way. Have a most enjoyable evening. You can regale me with the details of the play tomorrow over breakfast."

Thalia smiled gently, while Leo scowled at him with frustrated concern.

Setting a finger to his hat brim in farewell, Lawrence went out the door.

Chapter 3

Three days later Rosamund strode into the busy courtroom alongside Bertram, her arms filled with legal books and papers, her dark robes whispering around her trouser-clad legs. On her head sat a tightly curled white barrister's wig that had arrived only that morning from Ede and Ravenscroft. Her own queue of dark hair was tucked neatly inside the back of her jabot-style collar, the two rectangular white bands of which trailed down her shirtfront. Bertram was dressed in an identical style, the stark black-and-white lawyer's attire serving only to heighten the peaked quality of his complexion.

At least he'd stopped looking green, the way he had at the breakfast table before he'd hurried abruptly out of the room to be sick. She supposed she wasn't faring a great deal better, her own stomach in knots.

What if we're caught? she kept thinking. *What if someone discovers the truth?*

Then again, she'd spent an entire evening at Lincoln's Inn, conversed at length with her tablemates over a four-course dinner, then stood before the entire company of barristers to recite the words necessary for her admittance to the Inn and no one had guessed. No one had pointed an accusing finger, unmasked her as a fraud and had her dragged away. Of course the barristers assembled at Lincoln's Inn weren't the same as a court that had the power to do far worse than kick her out of the building should her real identity become known. But she was already in too deep to turn coward now.

And then there was Bertram.

One look at him, as they found the way to the defense side of the advocates' table, was enough to convince her that she was doing the right thing.

Was he turning a little green again?

If he stuck to the trial notes they had prepared and practiced with over the past two days, he ought to manage well enough. She only prayed he made it through the necessary witness testimony. There was no telling who the prosecution might call since they were not required to share such information. Nor were they required to provide copies of sworn depositions or even to provide evidentiary details that had been gathered against the defendant.

Personally she took issue with the current legal notion that a "spontaneous defense" was the best way to ascertain the truth. But until the law could be amended so as to grant more rights to a defendant, they would have to work with what they had. At least it wasn't a criminal trial, so Bertram didn't have to worry he might be sending someone to their death if matters did not turn in their favor. And she would be here to help him in whatever way was useful, but most especially as moral support.

She and Bertram took a seat at a large rounded table, their books and papers arranged before them. Clerks and court note-takers were making their own preparations nearby while the bailiff stood at the ready, waiting to call order to the court.

With a few minutes yet to spare, Bertram reviewed his notes for the dozenth time, mumbling quietly under his breath, while she picked up an already sharpened quill pen and began to sharpen it again. As she did, she heard footsteps approach and stop on the opposite side of the table. When she looked up, her eyes widened as she gazed into the unforgettable face of Lord Lawrence Byron.

She dropped the quill.

"Good morning, counselors," he said.

Bertram's head came up, his cheeks turning even paler as he registered the presence of their opposing counsel. He swallowed, his Adam's apple bobbing beneath his neck cloth. "G-good m-m-morning."

Inwardly Rosamund groaned. Bertram was even more anxious than she'd imagined.

That did not bode well.

She kept her own features as emotionless as possible and gave a short, though amicable, nod. "My lord. Good to see you again."

"And you as well, Mr. Carrow."

His robes, she saw, were of the finest quality, as was his wig. The tight white curls emphasized the powerful lines of his facial bones and turned his eyes an even more arresting hue of gold and green.

She glanced away, forcing aside her reaction with a stern reminder that it wouldn't do to be caught staring at him with an admiring feminine eye. Luckily he didn't seem to notice.

"I didn't realize when we met the other evening that we would be facing each other across the advocates' table today. Did you?" She added the last, curiosity getting the better of her.

"No. Interesting, is it not, how these matters play out?" He laid down a thin sheaf of papers, a quill and what appeared, at least from an upside-down vantage point, to be a copy of the brief.

Had he brought nothing else? Of course, with his notable record of winning cases, perhaps he didn't feel the need for more. He had no cocounsel either, she noticed.

"At least we have a sunny day for the proceedings." He leaned back in his chair, looking completely at his ease. "This courtroom turns gloomy as a grave when the weather is inclement no matter how many candles may be lit."

At her side, Bertram nodded absently, his pallor even more pronounced. Lord Lawrence studied him for a moment, a hint of pity in his eyes.

Rosamund's shoulders stiffened at the look, her natural sense of protectiveness leaping to the fore. Bertram might not be as smoothly polished and glib of tongue as Lawrence Byron, but what he lacked in poise, he more than made up for with hard-fought determination and perseverance.

Bertram would show him.

So would she.

"Your clients, I believe." Rosamund gestured toward the public gallery above and the trio of elegantly attired gentlemen who had just entered with great fanfare. A pair of liveried footmen cleared the two front benches for their employers' use, shooing off the others gathered so they were forced to squeeze into the rear seats or to stand. And then there was the silver-haired old matron, the late Mr. Vauxley's great-aunt, who had accompanied them. Her expression was as stiff and uncompromising as her back was ramrod straight. The ostrich feathers on her elaborate bonnet obstructed what little view remained for those unfortunate enough to find themselves seated behind her.

As Rosamund knew from her case preparation, the Vauxleys were a wealthy gentry family with connections to the peerage. They had brought suit against the young widow of the matron's late son claiming that she was illegally in possession of several very valuable pieces of jewelry, two paintings and a racehorse, who was a favorite to win next month's Derby—thus the interest from the public. The Vauxleys insisted that the items and the horse were part of the entail on her late husband's estate and therefore belonged to the family. But Bertram and Rosamund's client, Patricia Vauxley, insisted that they were all jointly held as personal property given by a husband to his wife. "It's all rightfully mine," she'd told them. And she would not relinquish any of it—not without a fight.

Lord Lawrence turned his attention to Bertram. "There is yet time to settle, should your client agree. Young Mrs. Vauxley is waiting in the corridor to testify, I believe. I can wait if you wish to confer with her."

Bertram stared for a moment, then shot a sideways glance at Rosamund. She could read the mix of panic and longing in his eyes, knowing he wished to accept. The case, as they were both aware, was not going to be an easy one to win and a settlement, even at this late hour, would spare him the necessity of appearing in open court. But he knew as well as she did that the widow Vauxley wasn't going to agree.

Rosamund gave Bertram a barely perceptible shake of her head and watched his shoulders sink with resignation.

"No, my lord. We shall p-proceed as planned," Bertram said.

Lord Lawrence graciously inclined his head. "As you wish." His eyes returned to Rosamund. "Good luck, then, and may the best man prevail."

Or woman, she thought with a hint of inward satisfaction.

For here *she* was in court, acting as cocounsel in a real legal proceeding. For a woman, it was a notable achievement, even if she and Bertram were the only ones aware of it.

The bailiff called for order. The noise in the room abruptly died down, chatter ceasing so that only the rustle of clothes and a nervous cough disturbed the hush. Everyone stood as the judge entered from an antechamber and took his seat in a heavy wooden chair set high behind the bar. She, Bertram and Lord Lawrence bowed to the judge as a sign of respect to king and country before resuming their seats.

Given the nature of the civil suit, there would be no jury. Instead the outcome would be decided by the judge, so it behooved the attorneys on both sides to remain in his good graces. She only hoped His Honor was a patient, receptive sort of man rather than the intolerant kind who might take a dim view of Bertram's stutter.

The trial began.

Lord Lawrence stood and addressed the judge and those gathered, his smooth baritone voice carrying into the farthest reaches of the courtroom at an effortless pitch and volume. With cool, concise logic, he laid out the basic elements of the dispute and the legal justification for his position that the property in question ought to be returned to the possession of his clients.

He began to call witnesses, starting with the solicitor, who had drafted the last-known revision to the Vauxley family entail; the family's man of business, who had an intimate knowledge of the Vauxley Estate, its property and contents; and the head trainer for the racehorse. All three men testified that the valuables in question were part of the entail and that despite the sad and tragic demise of young Mr. Vauxley, whom everyone had admired and loved, his widow was not entitled to keep the property under dispute.

When Bertram was given a chance to cross-examine the men, he declined on each occasion. "N-no q-questions, Y-Your H-Honor," he said, voice quavering.

With a stoic yet clearly confident expression, Lord Lawrence rested his case. The mood in the courtroom was quite plainly on his side.

Then it was Bertram's turn. Hurriedly he glanced through his notes one last time, including the two points that Rosamund had slid his way in reaction to the testimony just concluded. He rose to his feet, trying to hide his shaking hands within the folds of his robes.

Rosamund sent him a bolstering look, willing him to be confident, as he began to call his own set of witnesses. He started with the widow Vauxley, whose dark eyes were wide and round with anxiety as she made her way into the witness box. She glanced around, clearly as uncomfortable as Bertram himself as she was sworn in.

He had to start twice before he managed to make himself heard, the judge barking out a gruff order to "Speak up, man. Can't decide on this case, if I can't hear anything you say."

People in the gallery tittered, and a pair of onlookers catcalled rude remarks that sent color rushing into Bertram's cheeks.

The judge called for order and the room fell silent once more.

"Good m-morning, Mrs. Va-Va-Vauxley. Thank you for appearing t-today. I o-only have a f-few qua-qua-qua-questions, so this sh-shouldn't t-take long."

"It'll take forever if ye keep stammering like that," someone jeered from the gallery.

Rosamund bristled, waiting for the judge to reprimand the miscreant. Across from her Lord Lawrence frowned, his jaw tight as he stared up into the crowd as if in search of the speaker.

But the judge offered no chastisement. He simply

waited for the outburst to die down before nodding to Bertram. "Counselor, you may continue."

Bertram's extreme pallor had returned. Swallowing hard, he took a deep breath, then reached out for the leather-bound case that contained the jewelry.

The set consisted of five pieces: necklace, bracelet, ring, earbobs and a tiara. They were all fashioned from gold, diamonds and sapphires and were valued at a substantial sum. During the earlier testimony, Lord Lawrence had entered the items into evidence together with the paintings—one a well-done oil of Mr. Vauxley, the other a landscape with a view of the grounds at the Vauxley country house and, of course, the racehorse.

With the disputed property—all except the horse that remained stabled in Surrey—having been taken into safekeeping by an officer of the court prior to the trial, it was the first time Bertram or Rosamund had been able to see any of it firsthand.

"M-Mrs. Vauxley. A-are these your j-jewels?" Bertram asked.

"Objection," Lord Lawrence said. "Ownership of the jewelry has not yet been established and is what we are here today to decide."

"Sustained," the judge agreed. "Pray rephrase the question, Mr. Carrow."

Bertram wiped shaking fingers across his damp forehead before facing Patricia Vauxley again. He held out the case. "Are these ja-ja-jewels th-the o-ones that were in your possession p-prior to this t-trial?"

She took a moment to study them. "Yes. Those are my jewels."

"Objection," Lord Lawrence said. "The witness is once again asserting a right of ownership that has yet to be determined."

"Sustained." The judge directed a look at Patricia Vauxley. "Madam, please refrain in future from saying you own the items under consideration. As the prosecution has stated, that is what we are convened to determine. Mr. Carrow, you may continue."

Bertram swallowed nervously and moved back to the advocate's table to consult his notes. He shuffled through the cards and dropped two to the floor. Clearly flustered, he dove down to retrieve them.

"Any time now, Counselor." The judge tapped impatient fingers on the table in front of him.

Bertram popped up again, his face the color of a sunset, pink all the way to the scalp. And he was sweating. Badly. "S-sorry, Y-Your Ho-Ho—" The word stuck in his throat, refusing to come out. "Y-Your Ho-Ho-Ho—Ho-Hon—"

Rosamund's heart broke inside, anguished for him, especially when amused whispers and outright laughter sounded from the gallery above. The testimony was quickly becoming the nightmare that Bertram had feared it might become. And as she knew, the more uncomfortable and embarrassed he became, the worse his stutter would get until he wouldn't be able to speak at all.

The judge sighed loudly. "We all know what you are trying to say. Do get on with it, Mr. Carrow. Assuming you can, that is. Are you certain you are a barrister? You are barely able to string two coherent words together."

Bertram's color shot even higher and he said nothing. Rosamund wasn't sure he could.

Before she thought better of the impulse, she leapt to her feet. "Your Honor, if I might seek the court's indulgence, I would ask for a five-minute recess."

The judge's gaze was steely as it locked on her. "And you are, sir?"

"Carrow, Your Honor. Ross Carrow."

"Another Carrow, is it? Well, I hope you are better able to articulate your sentences than your—what relationship is the other counselor to you?" The judge waved a hand toward Bertram, who stood mute, his shoulders stooped in acute misery.

"My cousin."

"I hope your tongue is less tied than your cousin's. Very well. Five minutes, Counselor. I suggest you put them to good use."

Noisy reaction broke out across the courtroom; Mrs. Vauxley was left standing in the witness box, looking around uncertainly, not sure what she should do.

But Rosamund had no time to worry about Patricia Vauxley, her full attention focused on her brother as he dropped down into the seat beside her.

"Ra, Ra," he whispered, bending close so no one else could hear. "I'm s-sorry. I c-can't d-do th-this. I d-don't kn-know wh-what I-I w-was th-thinking. It's a-all a b-bloody ca-ca-catastrophe. Y-you're g-going t-to h-have t-to t-t-t-take o-over."

Her eyes widened. "Take over? Bertram, I can't."

"Y-you c-can. Y-you h-have t-to. O-otherwise—"

Otherwise, we are going to lose.

With his confidence shattered, Bertram would never

be able to regain his composure in time to get through the rest of the witness testimony and cross-examination. Worse, he'd reverted to using the shortened, phonetic form of her name, which he only ever did when he was utterly distressed. It was a habit that went back to the darkest days of his childhood, when saying her entire name had been an exhausting impossibility for his then-seven-year-old self. When at a mere two years his senior she'd been his only true lifeline after their mother died, a lifeline he needed again now.

He swallowed hard again, the desperation and defeat clear in his eyes.

Yet how could she agree to step into the role of lead counsel when she'd never planned to do more than sit quietly at his side? It was one thing to accompany Bertram to court, quite another for her to take over the entire case. Besides, she wasn't a barrister, not even if she did have more than a solid grasp of the law. It would be sheer misguided hubris to even consider proceeding. If Bertram wasn't capable of continuing, they would simply have to withdraw as acting counsel; there was no other way.

What, then, of Patricia Vauxley?

Rosamund's eyes turned to the young widow where she waited in the witness box. She seemed a decent enough person, brave beyond her years as she dealt first with the grief of losing her husband, then next with the strain of going to war with her relations over valuables she unquestionably believed to be hers.

The items under dispute were only things, true. Yet somehow it didn't seem right that she should lose them because her legal counsel wasn't able to satisfactorily represent her. Of course, she could always seek a new trial on the basis of inadequate counsel, but trials cost money, and money was something Patricia Vauxley no longer had in excessive amounts.

Then there was the issue of Bertram himself and his reputation—or what little of it would remain if he withdrew from the case. Word would get around. How he'd been rendered nearly speechless and been unable to proceed. How he'd had to withdraw in disgrace because of his stutter. He'd be ruined as surely as if he'd committed some disbarrable offense. Their solicitor would most likely withdraw his support as clients refused to retain Bertram on their behalf. In short, his law career would be over.

But not if she stepped up and took his place.

Yet could she? Should she?

Suddenly she looked up and met Lord Lawrence's gaze where he stood a few feet distant, talking idly to one of the clerks. Up to now, she realized he'd been doing his best to afford her and Bertram some semblance of privacy. But he had to be curious. Had to know there was some pivotal decision afoot.

He arched a single golden eyebrow as if to say, *"Well, what's it to be?"*

Before she had time to react, the bailiff called the court to order again. Lord Lawrence resumed his place across from her and Bertram at the advocates' table. All of them stood as the judge reentered the courtroom.

He settled into his chair, then looked at her and Bertram. "Well, counselors. Are you prepared to proceed?"

Bertram sent her a quick sideways glance, visibly pleading.

She considered for another moment, then drew a breath and squared her shoulders. "Yes, Your Honor. The defense stands ready."

"Then the floor is yours."

Praying she didn't make a sorry mess of things—or worse, get herself caught—Rosamund approached the witness box and resumed the questioning that Bertram had begun.

Chapter 4

"After careful consideration of the evidence and the testimony provided," the judge intoned nearly three hours later, "I find for the defense. The assets in question shall herewith be returned to the defendant, Mrs. Patricia Vauxley, for her sole and unquestioned use. That will be all. This case is closed."

A cacophony of reaction flooded the room. The widow Vauxley, who had been escorted into the courtroom to hear the reading of the verdict, was clearly jubilant. She exchanged a heartfelt embrace with the older woman at her side, who Rosamund suspected was her mother or perhaps an aunt.

Meanwhile, up in the gallery, members of the Vauxley family looked as if they had been poleaxed, their astonishment and displeasure unmistakable. Old Mrs. Vauxley's eyes snapped with such fury, in fact, it was a wonder she didn't set the courtroom ablaze with nothing but the expression on her face.

Rosamund paid them scant heed, however, as she turned to Bertram, her features wreathed in a smile of exultation. Remembering herself at the last second, she refrained from flinging her arms around her brother to give him a congratulatory hug. Instead she clapped him on the shoulder in a way she hoped looked appropriately masculine and did her best not to crow—or not excessively at least.

"We won, Bertie. We actually won," she said, hardly able to believe it despite having heard the judge's verdict with her own two ears.

"No, *you* won." He smiled back, his eyes alight with triumph. "You were s-splendid, just as I always knew you would be. Sorry I b-botched things so badly earlier. If not for you, we would be enjoying a f-far d-different result, I fear."

"You were nervous, that's all. You'll do better next time."

"Oh no," he said, shaking his head, "there won't be a n-next time. I've more than learnt my l-lesson." Before she could ask him exactly what he meant by that, his eyes wandered toward something behind her. "We'll t-talk later when there aren't so many ears to hear," he said. "Looks like one of the clerks has n-need of me. I'll just n-nip off and see what he wants. I'll make certain too that a-arrangements have been taken care of to deliver our client's v-valuables into her possession. Shouldn't take too long, I expect. Twenty minutes at most."

"Very well, then, go on. I'll meet you at the coach."

With a nod, Bertram walked away.

Despite the significant number of people still milling around inside the courtroom, she suddenly felt quite alone. With an inward sigh, she began to gather up her and Bertram's papers and books. As she did so, a little of her buoyant good humor evaporated. Celebrating, she found, was never half as satisfying when one tried to do it by oneself. But Bertram would be back soon enough and they would resume the festivities—and their discussion of his plans for the future. If there was time, perhaps Cook could make one of Rosamund's favorite sweets for pudding—fresh berry pie or raisin and treacle tart. Either one would be delicious.

The idea helped revive her spirits.

She was stacking one last set of papers together when she became aware of someone standing behind her. Glancing over her shoulder, she discovered Lord Lawrence Byron, his height such that she had to look up to meet his eyes.

She straightened. "My lord."

"Mr. Carrow."

"Is there something I can do for you?"

"Not at all. I merely wanted to offer my congratulations on your win today. You argued a deft and persuasive case. Most impressive."

A jolt of surprise went through her coupled with feelings of pleasure and pride. From everything she knew of Lawrence Byron, he wasn't the sort of man who gave compliments lightly, not unless he thought them deserved. For her to best him was one thing. For him to praise her for it was quite another.

"Thank you, my lord. That is most generous of you to say."

He shrugged. "It's nothing more than the truth. I realize now that I ought to have paid more attention to the hallmark on the jewelry in particular, since it played such a pivotal role in determining that portion of the case. Then again, since jewelry doesn't generally carry hallmarks, I suppose the oversight can be understood, if not excused. Believe me, it is an omission I will not make again."

"I only thought of checking the pieces myself because of a previous case on which I worked," she confessed.

In fact, the evidence had not been turning in her favor until she'd had a spark of inspiration and thought to look on the tiara for the marks, which could tell not only the maker but the date of assay.

"As for the letter about the Thoroughbred, I won't ask where you came by that. It was a stroke of luck indeed." Lord Lawrence smiled wryly. "It will be interesting, though, to see if your client comes to regret winning that portion of the suit. Racehorses are notoriously expensive and can eat their way through a man's, or woman's, pocketbook with scarcely any effort at all. She had best hope the stallion takes the Derby as promised or she may find herself having to sell the rest of what she gained today."

"Well, if the crowd's interest today is any indication, he's going to make her rich. Are you a gambling man, Lord Lawrence?"

A light sparkled deep in his gold-green eyes. "I've been known to indulge on occasion. And you?"

Up to a week ago, she would have told him she was one of the least daring people he would ever meet. But considering the fact that she had just won a lawsuit—and not just any lawsuit but her very first—all while pretending to be a man and a barrister, she supposed she ought to revise her former estimate of herself.

"Of course I take risks," she said. "How else do you think I managed to prevail against you today, my lord?"

Lord Lawrence's eyes momentarily widened. Then he laughed, the sound a warm, rich thunder that made her senses hum with pleasure.

"No, Carrow, you definitely don't lack for nerve. Come round to my club tomorrow night. Brooks's in St. James." He reached into his pocket and withdrew a card. "Give them this and they'll show you in. Nine o'clock, shall we say?"

Nine o'clock? She was usually getting ready to retire at nine o'clock. And had he really just asked her to join him at a gentlemen's club?

Without waiting for her agreement, he turned and walked away.

She stared after him until he'd gone, then looked down at the rectangle of stiff white paper in her hand. It contained a single line of text printed in an elegant black script. *Lord Lawrence Byron.*

She ran her thumb over his name.

"What were you and Byron talking about?"

She started and looked up to find Bertram at her elbow. "Where did you come from? I thought we were meeting at the coach."

"Got done s-sooner than expected. So? What did Lord Lawrence want?"

She slipped the calling card into her pocket. "He was just congratulating me on winning the case."

"Really?" Bertram frowned skeptically. "Rather g-generous of him, considering. He h-hardly ever loses a case, so he can't be terribly happy about this one."

"Doubtless not, but he's too much of a gentleman to show it."

"Hmm, he is that. So, are you r-ready to go home? We have some celebrating to do."

She smiled at the reminder. "Right you are."

It wasn't until later that evening, long after Cook had cleared away the last of the empty berry and custard tart plates, that Rosamund remembered the calling card. Inside her bedroom, she fished it out and studied it again, wondering why Lord Lawrence had extended the invitation. Was he just being collegial or had he some other motivation in mind?

She also wondered why she still hadn't told Bertram.

Probably because she knew he wouldn't approve. Despite the fact that she was presently pretending to be a man in public, as her brother he was naturally protective of her. She doubted he would relish the idea of her traipsing around London on her own, particularly at night, even if she did so in the guise of Mr. Ross Carrow. Then again, she was an adult woman, who was fully capable of taking care of herself. At eight and twenty, she was quite firmly on the shelf, her chances of finding a husband long since past.

Once, when she was a fresh-faced girl of eighteen, she'd not only had a beau but had even thought to wed. Tom had been a smart, dashing young lieutenant whom she'd met at an assembly. On that first night he'd asked her twice to dance, taken her in to supper, then begged to be allowed to see her again the following day. With breathless excitement, she had said yes. For improbable as it might seem, she had tumbled head over ears in love with him in the course of a single evening, and to her profound delight, he had done the same with her.

Those few all-too-brief weeks of summer had been the best of her life. During that time, she and Tom had shared long walks and lively conversations, taken carriage rides and attended readings and concerts as they'd quietly begun planning their future together. But even then it had seemed too much like a dream with halcyon days that had been far too wonderful to last.

There'd been a chill in the air on the first day of September 1811 when Tom received orders to leave for the peninsula. With only a week left before he had to depart, he'd begged her to marry him. She'd wanted to agree, but her father had said no, telling her she was too young to take such an important step, especially with a man she had known for only a few weeks.

So she'd let Tom go with an impassioned kiss and promises to write every single day. He'd said he would return as soon as he could get leave and that he would find a way to convince her father to let them wed. They'd sworn their love and fidelity to each other, and then he'd been gone.

By January, Tom was dead.

She'd known the worst had happened when his letters abruptly stopped. Her fears were confirmed nearly a month later when a friend of his, a Lieutenant

Friars, wrote to tell her the tragic news that Tom had been killed during a raid on a Spanish town. The lieutenant had sent back the letters she'd written to Tom. They were neatly tied inside a length of red ribbon, each one worn and dog-eared, as if they'd been read dozens of times. He said Tom had spoken of her often—the girl he loved and couldn't wait to marry. She'd tucked them inside the bottom of a trunk, next to his letters to her, then locked them away, together with her heart.

She'd gone on living her life, throwing herself into running the house and assisting her father, and later Bertram, with their practice of the law. But there had been no more suitors. For a long time she hadn't even noticed the occasional overtures of interested young men until one day they had stopped asking altogether. By then she was three and twenty and considered an old maid before she'd emerged from her grief long enough to realize that her chance to marry and have children had passed her by. Never one to dwell on regrets, she'd closed the doors on that loss as well and thrown herself even more deeply into her work for her father and brother.

So now here she stood, contemplating the invitation of a brilliant attorney who wished to meet with her, even if he didn't know who she really was. Bertram would tell her to send her regrets to Lord Lawrence. But Bertram had also told her tonight that he needed her to continue pretending to be a barrister for a while longer. They couldn't afford to toss aside their father's last cases, he'd said, especially not until he managed to transition his practice toward solely offering legal opinions and scholarship and handling matters that didn't require him to appear in court. Until then, he wanted her to go on being Ross Carrow.

But even if he had wanted her to go back to being herself, she wasn't so sure that she wanted to anymore.

Not after today.

Not after getting a taste of what it was like to argue a real case in a real courtroom before an actual judge and have a chance to pit her mind and her talents against a skilled barrister like Lord Lawrence Byron.

Once she'd gotten over her initial nerves and started to relax, she'd begun to enjoy herself. What's more, she'd begun to enjoy the freedom granted to her by posing as a man. As well as the respect.

She'd wondered on occasion over the years what it must be like to be a man and have the right to take up a profession. How it must feel to be admired for one's mind instead of constantly coming up against society's narrow strictures that confined a woman to home and hearth rather than allowing her the freedom to exercise all of her God-given interests and talents.

But now that she was literally walking in men's shoes, she had firsthand knowledge of the differences between the sexes. When she expressed her thoughts and opinions as an educated woman, she was all too often ignored by anyone outside her family. In her brief time as a man, she could tell that people listened and took note. They cared what she had to say, even if it was about nothing more important than the weather.

It was a heady distinction and one she wasn't ready to give up. And if she wasn't going to stop being Mr.

Ross Carrow, barrister-at-law, then it only made sense for her to accept the invitation from Lord Lawrence.

Besides, how could she pass up an opportunity to see inside one of London's most exclusive gentlemen's clubs? Not even Bertram had ever managed to wheedle an invitation to the lofty environs of Brooks's.

I'm going, she decided. *Or rather Ross Carrow is going, tomorrow evening at nine.*

Now all she had to figure out was how to get out of the house without Bertram's being aware.

Padding over to her bed, she sat down and began to plot. She'd won a lawsuit today against one of the city's most respected lawyers, so surely she could find a way to sneak out of her own house without getting caught.

She hoped.

Chapter 5

"Another brandy, my lord?" asked one of the footmen at Brooks's Club.

Lawrence looked up from the comfortable chair in which he sat, a copy of the *Times* in hand. "No, nothing more at present. I'll wait and have another once my guest arrives."

"Very good, my lord." With a bow, the servant withdrew.

Lawrence glanced at the clock across the room.

Five minutes past nine.

Carrow was late.

He turned a page, refolded the newspaper, then resumed reading. But as he started what promised to be an interesting article on the economy, his thoughts turned inward.

Even now he wasn't entirely certain what had prompted his impromptu invitation for the other man to join him here tonight. Curiosity, he supposed, since it wasn't often that he lost a case, especially not one that ought to have been quick and easy to win. But

Ross Carrow had turned all his carefully considered legal arguments on their head, presenting unexpected evidence and convincing testimony that had swayed the judge to his side. He'd given a damned fine defense, something that was no simple trick in a legal system in which the prosecution nearly always had the advantage.

So just who was this upstart country lawyer of whom no one had heard even a week before? Lawrence always found it useful to take the measure of the men with whom he dealt, and what better way to do so than over friendly conversation and a few drinks?

Assuming Carrow showed up, that is.

Lawrence looked at the clock again and saw that it was now ten minutes past the hour. He would give him a while longer before he gave up and called for his carriage. Truth be known, he could do with an early evening. He had a new legal brief to review as well as a case he was preparing that was scheduled to be heard Tuesday next. And tomorrow night he was committed to attend a ball at which he had promised to dance and have supper with Miss Templestone. He was, as his sister-in-law Thalia had noted recently, too busy for his own good.

After downing the final swallow of brandy in his glass, he returned to his paper.

Ross Carrow arrived five minutes later, escorted into the room by one of the footmen. The barrister's cheeks were flushed and he wore a slightly harried expression. Despite the spectacles Carrow wore, Lawrence found himself struck once again by the other man's youthfulness and the curiously delicate cast to his features. In fact, when viewed in the room's mellow candlelight, one might even say he was rather pretty.

Lawrence blinked, wondering from where that bewildering and unexpected thought had come. He brushed it aside like an unwanted speck of lint and got to his feet.

"My lord, good evening," Carrow began. "Pray forgive my lack of punctuality. I had some difficulty finding a hack and it set me behind times."

"Could you not take your own carriage?"

"No, I . . . my"—Carrow broke off with a sudden frown—"cousin has use of it tonight."

Lawrence wondered at the hesitation, but if there was trouble between the cousins, it was none of his business. Considering Bertram Carrow's poor performance in court the previous day, it wouldn't be surprising if words had been exchanged afterward.

"The streets are always crowded this time of year and the hackneys along with them," Lawrence said in an understanding tone. "But no matter. It gave me a few extra minutes to catch up on the day's news." He gestured toward an armchair opposite his own, silently inviting the other man to be seated.

Carrow sat, but rather than leaning back, he perched carefully on the chair's edge with his spine straight, knees together and hands folded neatly in his lap. Lawrence eyed the unusual posture but made no comment as he settled comfortably into his own chair.

"What would you care to drink?" Lawrence asked.

"Oh, um, tea sounds welcome."

Lawrence arched a quizzical brow. "Tea? At this hour? You're not a Methodist, are you?"

"No. I'm Church of England," Carrow said, looking mildly puzzled.

Lawrence studied him for another moment, then turned to address the waiter, who stood a discreet distance away. "A bottle of your best claret and two glasses." He met Carrow's bespectacled eyes again, noticing as he did what a luminous silvery gray they were. "You do drink wine, I presume. Unless you really would rather have that tea?"

A tiny line creased the skin between Carrow's eyebrows. "No, the wine sounds excellent."

The waiter left to retrieve the order while another servant stepped forward and soundlessly removed the empty brandy snifter that sat at Lawrence's elbow.

"So, how are you finding the city?" Lawrence settled back again. "I recall you mentioning that you've only recently come south. From York, was it not?"

"Near York, yes."

"And how are you finding London so far?"

"A great deal larger than York," Carrow said in a flatly ironic tone.

Lawrence paused, then laughed. "Touché. Perhaps I ought to have asked instead if you like it. The city can put people off at times."

Something sparkled in Carrow's gray eyes, a gleam that shone through the lenses of his spectacles. "Not me. There's a vitality here that I find almost electrifying. Each morning I awake, eager to begin anew. In a city as filled with life as London, one never knows what the day ahead will hold."

"Particularly after a day like the one you had yesterday, I expect."

A slow smile curved Carrow's mouth. "Yes, particularly so."

Lawrence felt something shift inside himself and without conscious intent he smiled back. He was oddly relieved when the waiter returned just then with the wine, giving him an excuse to turn away.

Rosamund drew a silent breath as Lord Lawrence attended to the wine, taking advantage of the respite to steady her frayed nerves.

Mercy, but he certainly knew how to keep her on her toes, even if they were just making small talk. Yet despite the anxiety her masquerade naturally invited, she couldn't help but enjoy the back-and-forth between herself and Lord Lawrence. It reminded her a little of their earlier sparring in court. Although at least there she'd had the law and rules of procedure to rely upon. Here she was strictly on her own.

She was also on his home turf, Brooks's Club every inch as exclusive and elegant as she had imagined. As the daughter and sister of middle-class lawyers, she wasn't used to breathing the same rarefied air as members of the aristocracy. Yet tony as it undoubtedly was, the place wasn't nearly as exciting as she'd been led to believe in the gossip rags. Really it was just groups of well-dressed men sitting around drinking, talking and, if she wasn't mistaken, playing cards in one of the adjacent rooms. It rather reminded her of what her brother and his cronies got up to in the neighborhood pub, just fancied up a bit.

She watched as Lord Lawrence sampled the wine, reminding herself again that she needed to be doubly careful about everything she said and did. She could still kick herself for ordering tea. With the exception of breakfast, tea was a woman's drink. She ought to have asked for something manly, such as whiskey or port, but considering that she'd never tried either, she didn't suppose this was a wise time to experiment. At least he'd offered her an unexpected olive branch by selecting wine. Claret had never been her favorite, but at least she wouldn't disgrace herself—or worse, give herself away—with a small draft of that.

After the wine was duly approved, the servant filled two glasses set on a silver tray, extending the first to Lord Lawrence, then the other to her. She accepted with a murmured thanks that was stoically received before the man withdrew.

Lord Lawrence leaned back in his chair once more and raised his glass in a toast. "To victories large and small."

She repeated his gesture. "To victories."

To her surprise, the wine tasted smooth yet refreshing with notes of oak and fruit that reminded her of autumn blackberries.

She loved blackberries.

She took another drink, deciding she might need to revise her opinion of claret.

"Of course I'll be waiting for another opportunity to best you, you know," Lord Lawrence said.

Not sure there would be one, Rosamund applied herself to her wine again rather than respond.

"So," he mused in a deceptively mellow voice, "just how long do you intend to carry on with this?"

She sputtered and the wine went down wrong.

She began to cough.

And cough.

When she didn't stop, unable to fully catch her breath, Lord Lawrence rose, came forward and whacked her once on the back. She gasped from the force of the blow and drew a wheezing inhalation, wondering whether that breath might be her last. Then suddenly her throat opened up and she was breathing again, her lungs blessedly filling with air.

"Better?" he asked after a moment.

She nodded, coughing a couple more times. "Yes," she said on a raspy croak.

Carefully she set her wine aside.

"That's a relief." Lord Lawrence dropped back down into his seat, apparently satisfied that the danger had passed. "Only imagine the trouble it would cause were you to drop dead here in the middle of Brooks's Club. The old-timers would likely have apoplexy over their evening being disrupted."

Indeed a few of the other men in the room were watching her, their expressions ranging from curiosity to barely veiled irritation. One elderly man huffed, restraightened the pages of his newspaper and disappeared behind them again.

She coughed one last time. "Far be it from me to discompose any of your acquaintance, my lord."

His lips curved, eyes gleaming with shrewd amusement. "Oh, I have the feeling you regularly discompose any number of people, both in and out of the courtroom." He took up his glass again, swirling the wine inside. "Now that you've recovered, what have you to say to my question?"

Her heart pumped in the quick, terrified beats of a trapped animal. Did he know? But how could he? Unless he'd guessed. Had he asked her here so he could corner and humiliate her as he revealed the fact that he'd seen through her disguise?

"What question is that, my lord?" she asked with apparent innocence. If he wanted the truth out of her, he was going to have to accuse her point-blank.

"The one I asked before you were unfortunate enough to go off on a paroxysm. I'm just curious to know how long you plan to carry your cousin's weight. After today, it's clear which one of you is the better barrister. Yet you allowed him to take the lead . . . at least until he started making a mare's nest of things."

Relief rushed through her, tension melting from the clenched muscles in her shoulders and back. But then his words sank in completely and she stiffened anew for an altogether different reason this time. "I beg your pardon?"

"Come, now, everyone in legal circles knows Carrow's father took care to keep his son employed behind the scenes so he wouldn't have to try any cases. Obviously Elias Carrow can't shield him anymore. I presume that's where you come in. I only wonder why you let him open his mouth at all when he can barely manage a coherent sentence in public. Deferring to him based on some misguided sense of loyalty does neither of you any good."

Her hands turned to fists. "My—cousin—is a fine attorney with an excellent grasp of the law."

"I'm not saying he isn't a competent lawyer. I'm merely pointing out, as we all observed today, that he isn't suited to the courtroom. You, however, are. Just how old are you anyway?"

"I fail to see what my age has to do with anything."

Instead of answering, he waited, his gaze patient yet unwavering.

"Four-and-twenty," she grudgingly admitted.

She and Bertram had agreed that since she looked younger as a man, she'd be well-advised to shave a couple of years off her real age of twenty-eight should anyone inquire.

"Precisely my point." Lord Lawrence swirled the wine in his glass. "You can't be more than three or four years beyond your apprenticeship, yet you performed as well as or better than many a seasoned barrister of my acquaintance. That fact alone has me intrigued."

Warmth replaced her irritation. She didn't know him well, but she felt certain that Lord Lawrence Byron never bestowed praise unless he thought it genuinely warranted.

"Is that why you asked me here? I did wonder."

A little smile teased the corners of his mouth. "I like to know my competition and befriend them when I can."

"What makes you think we would ever be friends?"

"What makes you think we wouldn't?"

She gazed into his striking eyes, then looked away, aware of her pulse beating at a disturbingly erratic pace. Honestly it wasn't fair that he should be so handsome. Being here tonight, talking with him, was a bit like sitting down for a chat with Adonis.

"Do you play billiards?" Lord Lawrence asked.

"Billiards?" She blinked at the non sequitur.

"You know. Cue sticks. Felt table."

"I know what billiards are, my lord. But no, I've never played."

He slapped a hand against one thigh, then got to his feet. "Good. That'll make it that much easier for me to beat you. Come along. The room's just down the passage."

"Sorry, but I couldn't possibly."

"Course you could. I won't take no for an answer."

Fighting down a fresh case of nerves, she stood, realizing that Lord Lawrence had no intention of being gainsaid. Mutely she followed.

A pair of white billiard balls clacked inside Lawrence's hand as he set them up for a new game.

So far, he and Ross Carrow had played twice. After handing the younger man a wooden cue and explaining the basic rules of the game, he'd allowed him a few practice shots, and then they had set to.

Predictably Lawrence had won the first game, taking control of the table after Carrow failed to score with an easy shot early on. Lawrence had put away ball after ball, making repeated cannons as he sank the white and red balls into the six pockets with practiced skill and quick precision.

Without waiting to see if Carrow wished to continue once they were done with the first game, he'd set up again and recommenced play. He'd also shrugged out of his coat, tossing it over the back of a nearby chair. Despite his suggestion that Carrow do the same, the other man had stubbornly refused, a decision that was not helping his game, considering how his tight sleeves impeded his range of motion. Still, the more Carrow played, the more he improved. He'd even managed to sink a few shots that weren't too poorly done, especially for someone with less than an hour's experience.

Lawrence crossed to a dark wooden sideboard that held his glass of wine, picked it up and drank what remained. Reaching for the bottle of claret that had been carried in earlier by the waiter, he refilled his glass and topped off Carrow's.

He held Carrow's glass out to him.

Carrow accepted but took only a single swallow before he set his glass aside.

Not much of a drinker, Carrow, he thought. Far too serious as well, although he did have a sense of humor, which seemed to make an appearance at the unlikeliest of times. Still, for a young man of twenty-four, he could do with a bit of loosening up. The tension in his shoulders—beneath the coat he refused to take off— gave him away. Maybe it was simply a matter of Carrow being in unfamiliar surroundings, since it was plain as the slender nose on his face that he'd never been inside a private gentlemen's club before. But Lawrence suspected there was more to it. It was almost as if he were hiding something, which made no sense whatsoever. After all, what could an obviously talented young attorney only recently removed from the country have to conceal?

Whatever it might be, Carrow was an odd duck; there was no denying it. Even so, the more time he spent in his company, the more Lawrence liked him, regardless of any misgivings he might harbor. Carrow was . . . unusual to say the least. Clever of mind and nimble with words, able to turn a phrase to interesting and amusing purpose.

He was extremely knowledgeable as well.

While they'd played billiards, they talked, veering away from the law to discuss such varied topics as history, literature, the arts and enough politics to spark an energetic debate or two. Yet even though they'd hit on several points of disagreement—Carrow, it seemed, was even more of a Whig than he, his views verging on the radical—they'd found a surprising amount of common ground between them.

When he'd invited Carrow here tonight, he really had just been interested in seeing what made the man tick. He'd never imagined he might end up genuinely enjoying his company.

"What say you to a wager this time? Nothing large, mind, just a little something to add some flavor." Lawrence took up his pool cue again.

Carrow glanced at the clock on the fireplace mantel. "An intriguing idea, but another time perhaps. It's late and I ought to be going."

"It's not even midnight. Surely you aren't still keeping country hours? This is London, where people often don't seek their beds till dawn."

"Society people, you mean, my lord. You'll find I hail from different stock."

"Perhaps, but I am acquainted with many a so-called professional who is known for burning the candle at both ends. Live a little, Carrow. If you don't now, when will you ever?"

A shadow of indecision darkened Carrow's silvery gray eyes. Lawrence recognized the look as temptation, an impulse with which he was well acquainted.

"It's only a game of billiards," Lawrence said.

Carrow was silent while he considered. Then he sighed. "Very well, I'll stay, but for no longer than an hour. Considering your own professional commitments, I wouldn't think you'd want to carouse all night either."

"This? Carousing? Hardly." Lawrence laughed. "We'd need harder liquor, deeper play and a few willing wenches to move it into that territory. In fact, when I was younger than you, my brother Leo and I spent a rather unforgettable night on the town. Each of us drank two bottles of whiskey apiece, gambled for high stakes at three different gaming hells and shared the services of a quartet of frisky little whores who we fucked so long and hard we could scarcely crawl into our carriage to return home the next morning. Now, that, Carrow, is carousing."

But rather than laugh and make some ribald remark, Carrow just stared. His eyes were round, lips parted, with flags of color staining the ridges of his cheekbones. Abruptly he turned away and busied himself chalking up his cue.

Lawrence looked on, perplexed. If he wasn't mistaken, he'd shocked the other man. But surely Carrow wasn't so sensitive he was put off by a bit of plain speaking? Not even a country-born lad could be that inexperienced.

"Certain you're not a Methodist, after all?" Lawrence teased, unable to resist the impulse.

Carrow ground the small wedge of chalk harder against the tip of his billiard's stick, then set it down with a soundless snap. "Let's play, my lord. The hour isn't growing any earlier."

"As you wish." Lawrence sent him another quizzical look.

Carrow picked up his white cue ball and walked to the end of the table. "To be honest, though, the effort seems pointless, considering you'll only best me again. As for wagering, I'd have to be a fool to agree, given the inevitable outcome."

"Oh, I wouldn't be so sure about that. You're not bad for a beginner," Lawrence said. "Who knows, you might even surprise yourself, especially if you took off that blasted coat. What is it precisely you're trying to hide under there anyway?" he joked.

Something flashed in Carrow's eyes, a glimmer of unease so brief Lawrence would have missed it had he not been looking directly at him.

Carrow straightened his shoulders, eyes down. "Since you're so certain my lack of a coat will improve my aim, then by all means, I'll give it a try."

Without waiting, he put his cue aside, then worked his arms out of his jacket. Rather than toss it aside as most men would have done, Carrow took a few moments to neatly fold the garment and drape it over the back of a chair.

Lawrence quietly shook his head. Honestly Carrow never failed to surprise.

"Ready, my lord?" Carrow asked.

"Nearly. We haven't decided on the terms of our wager yet."

"No, we have not," Carrow said in an unencouraging tone.

"Since this is a friendly bet, we should play for something other than money." Lawrence drank more wine while he considered. "I know. Loser treats the winner to an outing of his choice. And although I don't generally make concessions when it comes to games of skill, I'll spot you fifty points, given how new you are to the sport. First to three hundred wins."

Carrow frowned. "You're still virtually assured to win."

"Never say you're afraid, Carrow?"

"Course not," the younger man retorted gruffly.

Lawrence smiled slowly. "Well, then, shall we?"

For a second, Carrow looked as if he might still refuse. Abruptly he walked to the end of the long table and set his ball in place. Leaning forward, he slid the wooden cue back and forth between his fingers to loosen his muscles, carefully lined up the shot and took aim. He struck in a firm, smooth motion that sent the ball racing over the green baize. Exactly as it was supposed to, it hit the cushion at the far end, then rolled back again.

Both men watched as it came to a stop.

"Good shot. See how much easier it is in shirt-sleeves?"

Carrow agreed with a nod. "Your turn, my lord."

"Lawrence."

"What?"

"Call me Lawrence. All the 'my lords' get old after a while."

Carrow regarded him. "As you wish . . . Lawrence."

"Now move aside, Ross, so I may commence battle."

Chapter 6

"Here ye are, gov'nor," announced the hack driver as he came to a halt in front of Rosamund's town house nearly two hours later. The windows were dark, everyone having long since retired to bed.

She counted out the fare and handed the coins to the man, watching for a moment while he set the horses in motion and disappeared up the street. She shivered despite the warm wool of her coat, the night cold even for spring.

A dog barked in the distance, reminding her that she had best get inside. The neighborhood was a respectable one with little crime, but London was still London and one never knew who might be lurking in the shadows.

Rather than going to the front door, though, she opened a low gate set off to one side of the house and hurried down a set of stairs. Taking out a key, she unlocked the kitchen door and let herself inside.

Gentle warmth radiated from the banked stove, the rest of the darkened room dominated by a large wooden table that was scrubbed clean in preparation for making tomorrow's meals. Briefly Rosamund considered lighting a candle to help guide her way upstairs. But dressed as she was, she wanted no one to awake and find her only now returning home.

She turned and was starting in the direction of the rear staircase when she noticed a large shape seated in one corner of the room. A scream rose to her throat.

"Where in Hades' name have you been?"

Her cry cut off as recognition set in. She laid a hand on her chest, her heart racing so fast it was a wonder it didn't beat its way out of her ribs. "Good God, Bertram, you scared me nearly to death."

He struck a flint and tinder and touched it to a candlewick. A small golden pool of light spread between them. "If I did," he said in a hard voice, "you've only yourself to b-blame. Have you any notion of the time?"

She met his gaze, guilt rising. "I realize it's late—"

"Late? It's nearly t-two o'clock in the morning. Ever since I discovered you gone, I've been frantic. Much longer and I was going to contact the night watch and ask them to dr-drag the Thames for your corpse."

Rosamund crossed her arms. "There was hardly cause to do that."

"I wouldn't have had cause to do anything if you hadn't snuck out of the house in the first place. Where did you go?"

She smothered a yawn. "Could we do this in the morning? As you pointed out, it is quite late."

"No, we cannot *do this* in the m-morning. We'll do it now."

"Very well, but let us at least go upstairs to the sitting room where we can be more comfortable. I would like to get out of this greatcoat."

Without waiting for his agreement, she picked up the candle he'd lit and headed for the stairs.

Bertram followed, grumbling unintelligibly under his breath.

After pausing to hang up her coat in the front hall, she went into the nearby sitting room. She added a log to reignite the dying fire, then took her usual seat in an adjacent wing chair.

Bertram dropped into the chair opposite.

It was only then that she noticed his disheveled appearance, his hair standing up in tufts as if he'd spent the last few hours raking his fingers through it. Guilt set in again. "I am sorry for worrying you," she said.

He made a hmmphing noise under his breath, clearly not ready to forgive her quite yet.

"You wished to know where I've been."

His eyes went to hers.

"Brooks's Club," she said.

"Broo—What?" His mouth dropped open. "What were you doing there?"

"Lord Lawrence Byron invited me to join him."

"Byron?" he said, his eyes narrowing. "What did he want? And when did this invitation even occur?"

She picked at a spot of lint on her trouser legs. "Yesterday, after we won in court."

"You mean when I saw the t-two of you talking? I thought you said he'd just come to offer his congratulations."

"He did. He also invited me to join him at his club."

Bertram's jaw tightened. "And you didn't think it important to m-mention that to me?"

"I wasn't sure if I was going to accept or not."

"And when you *did* decide, you still said nothing?"

"I knew you would likely object, so I—"

"D-damned right I object," Bertram said, his generally easygoing veneer cracking beneath the force of his anger. "Byron may be an excellent attorney, but in all other respects, the man is an unprincipled libertine."

"Unprincipled hardly seems fair," she protested. *As for libertine . . .*

"Fair or not, you are to stay away from him."

"On what grounds?"

"On the grounds I just described. He's an unrepentant rakehell with a highly unsavory reputation when it comes to women. Why, if you were pr-privy to some of the stories I've heard, you'd be upstairs locking yourself in your room right now, thanking your st-stars you made it home with your chastity intact." He narrowed his eyes again. "It is still intact, isn't it?"

"Bertram!" she said, shocked to her bones for the second time that evening. As for the lewd stories to which Bertram was alluding, she'd already heard at least one of them—and from none other than Byron himself.

"In case you've forgotten," she said, "he thinks I'm a man. Believe me, nothing untoward happened tonight."

Bertram stared at her for another few seconds before some of the tension eased from his shoulders. "Then what did the pair of you find to do all evening?"

Briefly she considered telling him to go stuff himself, particularly considering the base accusation he'd just made. But then she reminded herself that he was only concerned for her welfare, as a brother watching out for a sister he loved. Some of her anger melted away. "We had drinks—wine. Then we played billiards."

"Billiards?"

"Yes, he taught me the game."

"Did he, now?" Bertram said, a sarcastic edge to his voice.

"Yes. I was ham-fisted as a baby at first, but I seemed to catch on after a couple of games. I very nearly won the last one, came within twenty points, although he spotted me fifty to start, so I suppose it wasn't all that close after all."

He'd also won their bet.

She frowned, wondering if she ought to divulge that last bit of information to Bertram. Generally she didn't keep secrets from her brother—not that she'd really had any to keep until recently. But it was quite plain that he didn't approve of her striking up a friendship with Lawrence—or rather *Lord Lawrence*, she forced herself to think. For in spite of the fact that he'd given her permission to use his first name, she wasn't entirely sure she should. It seemed almost too intimate somehow, as if they really were friends.

"Good Christ, you like him, don't you?" Bertram said with a dawning amazement.

"Language, Bertram. You've obviously forgotten you're speaking to your sister despite my sitting here dressed in your clothes."

He looked momentarily mollified. "My apologies."

She inclined her head, hoping her expression of affront had put him off the trail. But once Bertram got his teeth into something, he didn't let go, not until he was satisfied.

"Well?" he asked.

"Well what?"

"You know what. Byron. Do you like him?"

She lifted her gaze to her brother's, then shrugged. "Honestly, how should I know? I'm scarcely acquainted with the man."

"You know him enough to have formed an opinion, and from what I can see, it's a positive one."

"I wouldn't say that necessarily. He *is* a wealthy, overly indulged aristocrat who lives in a world quite different from our own, even if he does happen to be a barrister. But yes, he's intriguing. Smart, well educated, sophisticated. And he seems genuinely interested in what I have to say. Of course I enjoyed an opportunity to converse with him."

Yet would he still have felt that way had he known he'd spent an evening with Miss Rosamund Carrow— pretend barrister and spinster rather than the male colleague he thought she was?

She masked a sigh, less than happy with the response that came to mind. "I shouldn't worry, Bertram. Despite tonight's invitation, I doubt Lord Lawrence Byron will bother spending any more of his precious time with the likes of me. He was curious, that's all. I'm unknown in London legal circles, and after I beat him in court, he wanted to see if he could figure me out."

"And has he?"

"No. He thinks exactly what he's supposed to think, and now that his curiosity has been satisfied, that will be the end of it. My guess is the most I'll see of him is an occasional glimpse in the halls at court."

Unless they had another case against each other, but the chances of that happening weren't good. For, despite her decision to continue handling her father's outstanding legal work, it would last only so long, and then she would have to fade quietly away and return to her life as it used to be.

Of course there was the bet she'd lost to Lord Lawrence and the excursion she—or rather Ross—owed him. But it was unlikely he'd actually want to collect. A busy man like him had probably forgotten about it already.

She ran her fingers along the crease in her trouser leg and fought down another sigh.

Bertram studied her for a few seconds more. "I suspect you're right and I'm making too much of it."

"Yes, you are, rather."

A log shifted in the fireplace, sending up a quick plume of red-gold sparks before settling down again.

"I'm just glad you got back home safely," he said.

She smiled. "I am too. But, Bertram, I will have to go out on my own from time to time if we're to make this deception work. People will begin to wonder if you're forever escorting me everywhere. Men don't do that."

He scowled. "I suppose, much as I don't like leaving you on your own. I trust in future that you'll keep evening engagements to a minimum."

"I doubt I'll have any more."

"And you'll tell me when you are going out, p-particularly at night," he continued. "No more sneaking out."

"No more. I promise."

Satisfied, he leaned back in his chair.

She did as well, her eyes watering as a yawn surprised her. She lifted a hand to cover her mouth. "It really is late. We should both get some rest."

"So we should." He met her eyes, his own suddenly twinkling with an almost boyish light. "But first, tell me about Brooks's. What is it like?"

With a grin sliding over her lips, she told him.

Chapter 7

Two weeks later Lawrence helped himself to eggs, sausage and toast from the buffet in the morning room before he took a seat at the dining table. Brilliant June sunshine glinted off the silver coffeepot as a footman filled his cup, steam wafting upward in a fragrant curl. Once the servant withdrew, Lawrence opened a freshly pressed copy of the *Morning Post* and began to read while he enthusiastically applied himself to his meal.

Leo joined him ten minutes later, murmuring a quiet good morning as he crossed to the buffet to fill his own plate. He sat down opposite Lawrence and took a grateful swallow from his cup of hot coffee.

"Thalia having breakfast in her room this morning?" Lawrence asked as he turned a page.

"Still asleep," Leo said around a mouthful of bacon. "We didn't get home from last night's ball till the wee hours, so I doubt she'll be up before noon."

Since Leo and Thalia's marriage, her once sadly tattered reputation as a notorious divorcée had largely been forgiven so that she was once more being received by most of the Ton. There were still a few sticklers who refused to acknowledge her, and likely never would, but with the Byrons having closed ranks to demonstrate their approval of her, the invitations had begun pouring in once again.

As for Leo, Lawrence knew his twin was pleased by his wife's renewed acceptance within Society but only because it made Thalia happy. Otherwise, he couldn't have cared a jot. So long as he had Thalia, that was all that mattered to him, reputation be damned.

Leo smothered a yawn and reached for the jam pot, spreading liberal amounts of strawberry preserves on two triangles of buttered toast. He ate one in two bites, then downed more coffee before he applied himself to the healthy mound of eggs on his plate. "What time did you get home? Can't recall seeing you after Thalia and I went in for supper at midnight. Did you even stay to eat?"

"No, I left just before. I'm due in court tomorrow and need today to prepare, so I thought a full night's sleep would do me good."

Actually Lawrence had nearly skipped last night's ball altogether, but he'd given his word he would attend and so he had. He'd danced a few sets with a variety of young ladies, including the lovely Miss Templestone. She'd smiled with pleasure when he asked her to stand up not once but twice. He'd disappointed her, though, by not escorting her in to supper, a demerit on his mainly unblemished record.

But maybe it was for the best at present, given the

shy yet inviting looks she often gave him. He knew that she was expecting him to ask for her hand in marriage. Just as he knew that's exactly what he should do. So why didn't he just pop the question and get the deed done? She and her father would certainly be pleased by an engagement between them. Yet whenever he thought about taking that final step, he hesitated.

Quite likely it was an instinctive resistance to the idea of losing his bachelor's freedom and nothing more. He only needed a little more time to reconcile himself fully to the idea of taking her for his wife. Once he did, his qualms would disappear. In the meantime, he had professional obligations to meet, such as the case he would be arguing tomorrow.

Thinking of court, he wondered if he might bump into Ross Carrow. He hadn't seen or heard from the younger man since their billiards match at Brooks's Club. He'd thought Carrow would have contacted him by now to satisfy the wager he owed him. He was probably busy too, though, and just hadn't gotten around to it. Perhaps he needed a bit of reminding.

"Something have you vexed?" Leo asked.

"What?" Lawrence looked up, surprised to have been caught woolgathering.

Leo nodded toward the paper. "Something in there annoying you? You're forever reading politics and the opinions of Tory idiots with whom you don't agree. Sometimes I think you do it just to make your own blood boil."

"No, I do it to keep up with the facts on both sides of an argument so I have a thorough understanding of the topic at hand. Always better to know what one's adversaries are thinking rather than to remain ignorant. I find it easier to beat them that way when the opportunity arrives."

"I suppose, but if you aren't careful, you're going to give yourself an ulcer."

Lawrence patted his stomach. "Me? Impossible. My stomach is steel-plated."

"The only thing steel-plated about you is your hard head."

Lawrence laughed and Leo joined him.

While Leo finished his meal, Lawrence returned to his newspaper, skimming over a few articles before settling on one that did indeed make his stomach muscles clench with anger.

After downing the last of his coffee, he tossed aside the paper and got to his feet. "I'm off to work in the library. See you anon."

Leo glanced up from his perusal of the latest racing results. "Oh, before I forget, I've been told to remind you about the surprise anniversary party for Ned and Claire next week. Mallory has already tasked me with the job of making sure you remember to buy a gift."

"I should think you'd be the one in need of reminding about that."

Leo grinned. "Not a bit. That's what I have Thalia for."

Lawrence snorted. "Don't let her hear you say that."

Leo's grin widened, unrepentant.

"Yes, well," Lawrence said, "tell our dear sister Mallory that I am perfectly capable of managing my affairs, including the purchase of gifts. Now, if that's all, I need to get on with my work."

Leo chuckled and returned to his newspaper while Lawrence left the room.

"I find for the claimant—all costs to be paid by the defendant. This court is adjourned."

Rosamund let out a sigh of relief at the judge's decision, a smile moving across her lips. She had won again—this time on behalf of the claimant.

Her client, a robust man with a chest like a boxer's that strained the buttons on his waistcoat, ambled forward. He pumped her hand with an enthusiastic shake, even more exultant at his win than she. "Excellent work, Mr. Carrow. Excellent. I cannot thank you enough."

"You are most welcome, Mr. Chipsbury. Hopefully this will be the end of your difficulties with your competitor."

Mr. Chipsbury was a successful tea merchant who had been battling a rival merchant over lies the man had been spreading about his product, falsely claiming that Chipsbury used old, inferior tea leaves that he dyed to look new by using a mixture of vegetable peelings and manure. The talk had cost Chipsbury a great deal of business, plus customer goodwill Rosamund hoped would now be restored.

"It ought to shut his big gob, that's for certain," the older man said, "seeing he's to pay not just the damages sought and punitive costs but my legal bill as well. Make sure you charge him extra so every penny hurts."

Rosamund resisted the urge to laugh. "I'll do my

best, given the ethical constraints. Congratulations again, Mr. Chipsbury. I know you must be pleased that His Honor ordered the defendant to issue a public apology to you as well."

"Dead thrilled, I am." Chipsbury beamed, thumbs tucked into his waistcoat pockets. "I'm going to make sure each and every one of my customers sees that apology if it's the last thing I do."

"As you should, Mr. Chipsbury, as you should."

"What kind of tea do you favor, Mr. Carrow?"

"Tea?"

"You do drink tea, I presume." His thick eyebrows gathered with sudden suspicion. "Don't tell me you're one of those coffee men?"

"No. I love tea. Drink it every day."

Chipsbury's smile returned. "Then I'll send round a crate of my finest. Only the best will do for a great man like you." He clapped her on the back with a force that nearly sent her stumbling forward. She caught herself against the table and somehow conjured up a smile. "Thank you for the kind offer, but it isn't necessary."

"Course it is and I won't take no for an answer. Green or black?"

She met his determined look, wondering what he would think if he knew the truth—that his "great man" was actually a "great woman" instead.

"Green or black?" he repeated.

"Black."

"Right you are." He smiled widely. "Well, I'll quit chewing your ear, since I know how busy you are."

"As are you, Mr. Chipsbury."

She met his eyes again, then tensed, afraid he was winding up for another manly clap on the shoulder. Instead he shook her hand one more time—crushing it in a powerful grip—then departed, whistling under his breath.

After flexing her aching hand to restore the normal flow of blood, she reached up to make sure her wig hadn't gone askew, gathered her belongings from the barristers' table and left the courtroom.

She was alone today despite Bertram's not so subtle hints about wanting to accompany her. But as she'd told him earlier, her deception would be more believable if he wasn't always trailing after her like some hovering duenna. Besides, he had work of his own to do. Over the past two weeks, the pair of them had settled into a new rhythm of sorts with Bertram seeking out noncourtroom work that their father would have rejected without a second thought, while she handled the rest. Bertram was happier, and if truth be known, she was as well. She loved the law and relished a chance to practice it.

Of course, she would have to give it up sometime, but with each passing day she worried less about being caught. From ordinary hawkers on the street to the professional men with whom she now rubbed elbows, each one of them believed her lie. To them she was a man, regardless of her fine features and occasional less-than-masculine gestures. But she was getting better at pretending, having taken to observing the actions and habits of the men around her, then doing her best to mimic them. Even Bertram had commented recently on how convincing she had become.

She turned a corner in the hallway, her thoughts on her empty stomach and the nuncheon awaiting her at home, when the door of a nearby meeting room opened. Two men exited and joined the cluster of people milling about in the corridor. She paid them scant attention and walked on, weaving between a pair of gossiping clerks and a lawyer with his nose buried in a handkerchief.

"Carrow?"

She turned her head, her step slowing at the sound of her name. Her pulse stuttered when she saw that the speaker was Lord Lawrence Byron. For a fleeting instant, she considered pretending not to have heard him and hurrying on. But since he was now looking directly at her, she guessed it was too late for that.

Not that she'd been avoiding him precisely, but after her talk with Bertram, she'd decided that maybe it would be prudent to put a bit of distance between herself and Lord Lawrence. Oh, not for the reasons her brother had outlined—a notorious womanizer like Lawrence Byron would never be interested in an old maid like her. Were he to meet her as her real female self, she was sure, he wouldn't give her a second look. But that didn't mean that she hadn't noticed him or that she was immune to his considerable charms. She liked him already after spending only a single evening with him. Just imagine how she might feel were she to give their nascent friendship a chance to deepen. Nothing good could come from getting to know him better, especially not when Ross Carrow would have to "disappear" one of these days, never to be seen again.

Yet here was Lord Lawrence, walking toward her after having bade a quick farewell to his bewigged colleague. "Carrow," he said in greeting, looking handsome and refined in his own lawyer's garb. "This is a happy accident running into you today."

"Just so," she said, regulating her features so they didn't reveal her suddenly churning emotions. "How are you, my lord?"

"Quite well. And you? Have you just come from court?"

"Yes. Another case concluded."

"Successfully, I trust?"

She couldn't keep from smiling. "I won, if that's what you're asking."

"Well, then, congratulations. *Again.* I seem to say that to you every time we meet, do I not?"

"It's early days yet in my London career. Most likely you'll have the opportunity to offer your condolences at some point."

"I'm not so sure about that. Let's just say I'm thankful not to have been the one on the receiving end of a drubbing from you this time. I had my own case to handle today." He inclined his head in the direction of the room from which he had come. "That was the opposing counsel with whom I met. We just reached a settlement."

"In your client's favor, I trust?"

It was his turn to smile, a boyish grin that did funny things to her stomach. "Very much in my client's favor," he said.

"Then congratulations in return and well done. I am pleased to hear that your winning streak has resumed."

"As am I. Speaking of winning things, I've been thinking about our billiards match the other evening."

Some of her buoyancy fell away. "Ah, the bet, you mean."

"Yes, the bet." He arched a golden eyebrow. "I trust you have not forgotten?"

"Of course not!" she said, hating how defensive she sounded.

In truth, she had thought frequently about their bet, hoping against hope that he would be the one to forget and let it go. But considering that men viewed gaming debts as matters of personal honor, she'd known it wasn't likely. Duels had been fought over far less.

"I've just been overly engaged," she said. "I meant to contact you earlier, but the time got away."

"Exactly as I presumed." His tone was as smooth and agreeable as his words. "To save us both the bother of corresponding later, why do we not settle this now? In fact, I know just the thing. There is a mill in Watford this Saturday. Supposed to be a real bruiser of a battle."

He waited, watching as though he expected her to crow with excitement.

Instead her stomach churned. "A mill?" she repeated. "Boxing, you mean?"

Amusement glinted in his eyes. "Yes, that is generally what happens at mills. Don't you like boxing?"

Her? Like boxing? Not that she'd ever actually witnessed a bout of fisticuffs, but she'd certainly heard enough to know that it involved a pair of grown men punching and bloodying each other in some ridiculous contest of male stamina and strength—usually until one of them either gave up, passed out or died. No, she couldn't say she liked boxing.

But most men loved it, including Lawrence Byron apparently.

"Of course I like boxing," she said with false enthusiasm, wondering when she'd turned into such a natural liar. "Sounds excellent. Saturday, did you say?"

Lord Lawrence sent her another quizzical look before his expression cleared. "Yes. And since you don't always have ready access to a carriage, why don't we take mine?"

"That would be most agreeable." She decided not to mention that she wouldn't have been able to use Bertram's carriage even if she'd wanted to, considering the fact that she couldn't drive.

"Capital." Lawrence reached for his pocket watch and checked the time, closing the heavy gold case with a small snap. "Look, I've got to be back in court in a few minutes. I'll drop round Saturday morning, say about eight? It's going to take a couple of hours to get to the field where the mill is being held, and if we're not early, we won't get a view of anything worth seeing."

She swallowed past the lump in her throat. "Eight it is, then."

After she provided him with her home address, the two of them parted ways.

Her body was stiff with anxiety as she left the courthouse, wondering how in the world she'd landed herself in such a fix.

Chapter 8

Rosamund was still puzzling over the bind she'd put herself in as Saturday dawned sunny and warm. She dressed in the fresh set of black men's clothes she'd sewn for herself in the evenings after work, wondering how she was going to break the news to her brother about the day's outing.

She'd considered telling him earlier, but hadn't been in the mood to endure the displeasure she knew he'd unleash. Better to leave it to the last, she decided, so he wouldn't have the time or opportunity to convince her not to go. For as nervous as she was made by the prospect of accompanying Lord Lawrence to a boxing mill, she found herself equally excited and intrigued as well. Then too it would be a chance to spend time with him again, something even prudence couldn't convince her to avoid.

She ate breakfast—or tried to at least, since she was too nervous to choke down much more than half a slice of plain toast and a few sips of some of the delicious black China tea that had arrived courtesy of Mr. Chipsbury.

Bertram entered the dining room just as she decided to give up on her meal. He took a seat at the table across from her, then quietly told a housemaid what he wanted for breakfast. Once the girl had hurried off to the kitchen, he turned his sights on Rosamund, his brow creased with inquiry.

"Why the trousers? I thought you were going to relax and wear a dress here at home on Saturdays and Sundays. Unless you've an appointment with someone today."

She picked at the remaining toast half on her plate, slowly breaking it into pieces. "Actually I do."

Bertram reached for the teapot and filled his cup. "Oh? With whom?"

Rosamund hesitated, then drew a breath and plunged ahead. "Lawrence Byron."

He scowled. "Byron? What does he want now? This isn't another visit to his c-club, is it?"

"No, we're going to a mill."

"A boxing mill?" Bertram's eyes widened.

"That's what *I* said when he mentioned it. I'm glad I'm not the only one who needed clarification."

"You are *not* going," he said flatly.

"We've been through this already. Appearances, Bertram, remember?"

"Appearances be d-damned. A boxing mill is no place for a woman."

"Which he doesn't know I am. Nor will anyone else. I'll be fine. Besides, this excursion is my way of settling the wager I lost to him."

"What wager!"

"I told you I lost to him at billiards."

His eyes darkened like thunderclouds. "But not the fact that it left you in his d-debt. Goddamn it, Rosamund. T-two minutes in that scoundrel's company and he's g-got you in his clutches."

"Don't be absurd. It's a day out of the city where we'll be surrounded by dozens and dozens of people."

"*Men*, not people."

"One of which I'm supposed to be."

"And what do you mean 'out of the city'? Exactly where is this mill taking place?"

"Watford."

Below in the street came the sound of horses' hooves and carriage wheels drawing to a halt in front of the town house. Rosamund darted a quick peek through the window and caught sight of a now-familiar head of thick golden brown hair, broad male shoulders and the smartest sporting phaeton she'd ever seen.

She leapt to her feet. "He's here."

"And he can go away again," Bertram complained sullenly.

"I'll be back in a few hours, well before nightfall, so you've no need to worry."

He tossed down his napkin. "You're right, since I'm coming with you."

"No, you are not." She hurried around the table and laid her hands on his shoulders to press him back into his seat. "There isn't room for you in the phaeton. It's a two-seater. And anyway, you weren't invited."

"I'm inviting myself."

"Bertram, stay. Please. I'll be fine. Lord Lawrence will look after me."

His scowl deepened. "Lord Lawrence thinks you're

another b-bloke, so he won't bother to look after you. Particularly not if he decides there's something else he'd rather do instead."

"He's hardly going to strand me somewhere. Despite your opinion, he is a gentleman."

Bertram snorted. "That remains to be seen."

Downstairs, a knock came at the door.

She bent and pressed a kiss against her brother's cheek. "Have a good day. I shall see you for dinner."

Before he could begin another round of objections, she rushed out of the dining room and down the stairs, praying he didn't follow. She deliberately slowed her step on the last few treads, not wanting to be caught hurrying—or worse, tripping.

She'd just reached the final step when the footman opened the front door.

And there stood Lord Lawrence, framed in the entrance. He looked even more dashing than usual in a coat and trousers of dark bottle green, a color that brought out the clear forest tones in his golden green eyes. She liked his silk waistcoat too with its subdued geometric pattern of tiny gold keys on a warm ivory background.

She schooled her features into what she hoped was an expression of calm welcome, uncomfortably aware how fast her heart was beating beneath her cloth-bound breasts.

She drew a deep breath and reached up a hand to push her spectacles higher on her nose. "My lord, good morning. You are very prompt, I see."

"Good morning to you, Carrow," he said as he moved inside. "And I'm only here to the minute because I'm hoping if we leave now we'll be able to avoid the worst of the traffic on the turnpike. If nothing else, we have a good day for the journey. Should make for easy travel at least. Are you ready?"

"Indeed. Just let me get my hat and gloves."

Moving quickly, she retrieved the items, wanting to be gone before Bertram decided to put in an appearance. But then suddenly he was there, looming above them on the upstairs landing.

She watched as Lord Lawrence's gaze moved upward to fix on her brother. He sent him a friendly smile. "How do you do today, Carrow?"

"My lord." Bertram stared balefully, his hands fisted at his sides.

Tension filled the space.

Good God, she thought, *is he deliberately trying to ruin everything? If he isn't careful, he's going to get both of us caught.*

"We're just going, cousin," she said in a purposely cheerful voice.

"Yes, so I see. Cousin." Bertram met her eyes, his own filled with a concern he couldn't quite conceal, not from her anyway. "I trust you'll remember what we discussed."

"Of course. Now, we'd best not keep His Lordship's horses standing any longer. I'm sure they're anxious to be on the road."

Bertram opened his mouth and for an instant, she feared he was going to outright refuse to let her leave. But then he obviously thought better of it, his shoulders sinking in defeat. "I'll see you this evening."

"Until this evening," she agreed, sending him what

she hoped was a reassuring look. Quickly, before he had time to change his mind, she hurried out the door.

Lord Lawrence followed after.

"What was all that about?" he asked once the two of them were settled in the phaeton.

"What do you mean?" she said, feigning ignorance.

"Between you and your cousin. I couldn't help noticing an undercurrent there. That and the fact that he didn't seem too keen on you going out."

Blister it all. Much as she loved Bertie, sometimes he made her hands itch with the temptation to give him a good ear boxing.

"It's nothing. Just some family business," she said.

"Ah, I know all about family business. I shall say no more."

But Bertram had roused his curiosity, and curiosity from Lord Lawrence Byron was the last thing they needed.

"He's worried about me gambling at the mill today," she said. "I told him that our outing is in repayment for a wager I lost to you and he's concerned that I'm getting in too deep, now that I'm in London."

She waited, watching to see if he believed her story.

"Sometimes it's good to have protective relations, annoying as they might seem." He sent her a sideways glance. "You aren't getting in too deep, are you?"

"No. You're the only one I've wagered against. Just my bad luck to have lost first time out."

Byron laughed. "Well, the bookmakers will be in Watford today, but there's no need to bet unless you want. If you do, I'll make sure you don't lose anything greater than pocket change."

"How obliging of you, my lord."

"That's me. Always obliging."

"Why do I find myself doubtful of that?"

Lord Lawrence laughed again and set the horses in motion. "You're buying drinks and nuncheon, by the by. Just a friendly reminder in case you do decide to wager."

"Duly noted. Now, tell me about this phaeton. It's cracking. How many miles an hour have you done?"

Leaning back in the well-sprung seat, she let Lord Lawrence talk, enjoying the sound of his voice, the warm summer breeze and the thrill of the adventure ahead.

Chapter 9

"Give 'im wot for," shouted a man from somewhere within the roisterous crowd.

"Put 'im in the ground, ye bastard," another called.

"Keep yer dukes up and go fer 'is gut. That's right, mate. Ye'll have him back on the ropes in a tick—just don't give up."

Punches flew between the two heavily muscled, bare-chested opponents who circled around each other in the center of the ring. Sweat and blood sheened their skin, damp hair matted close to their skulls. Cuts and bruises bloomed across their swollen faces, along torsos and across two pairs of cloth-bound knuckles. Each man was waging a battle of stamina and dominance as the all-male crowd that was packed shoulder to hip roared out its frustration and encouragement.

From a place disturbingly near the front, Rosamund watched in horror, cringing every time a new punch was landed. Instinctively she edged closer to Lord Lawrence, whose attention was riveted on the action along with the rest of the crowd.

So much for a fun adventure. When she'd agreed to accompany him, she'd never imagined it would be so raw and brutal.

And they called this sport.

When she and Lord Lawrence first arrived at the open field that had been selected for the bout, she'd been fascinated and intrigued by the spectacle of it all. More than a hundred men were gathered for the event. They came from all classes and walks of life—farmers and laborers mingling with soldiers, shop clerks, merchants and nabobs. There were gentlemen mixed in as well, local landholders hobnobbing with their tenants for an afternoon as well as aristocrats like Lord Lawrence who had made the trip from London for a few hours of entertainment.

Every one of them was in a boisterous good humor—joking, laughing and telling tall tales while they laid bets and imbibed spirituous liquors, with the scents of warm male sweat, tobacco smoke and yeasty beer redolent in the air.

It was a side of life from which she was normally excluded. A slice of freedom forbidden to the fairer sex.

She'd even dared to purchase two foamy pints of dark stout for herself and Lord Lawrence. True, she'd ended up leaving most of hers untouched, since she didn't really care for the bitter, grainy flavor, but it was an experience all the same. She'd also placed a bet, a very small one, on the outcome of the boxing match—a bare-knuckle bout that had the crowd wild with anticipation.

Then everyone had assembled around the make-shift ring, jockeying for the best view. Lord Lawrence, of course, hadn't had any trouble commandeering a prime spot, his height and natural aura of authority allowing him to cleave a path without his having to utter a single word. They simply parted for him as she walked along in his wake.

Then the fight started, her earlier enjoyment vanishing after the first jaw-crunching punch. Yet as much as she'd wanted to hide her face behind her hands and close her eyes, she'd known she couldn't. She'd even managed to grin a time or two when Lord Lawrence glanced her way, as she pretended she was having the time of her life.

But her time of pretending had long since come and gone, as the fight dragged on and the competitors waged a battle of endurance rather than decisive, one-sided skill. She crossed her arms over her chest, holding tight as her stomach rolled like a storm-tossed ocean wave, beer sloshing uncomfortably inside.

God above, will it never end? she thought as the pummeling continued, the groans and grunts and slick, wet sounds of flesh pounding flesh audible even over the raucous noise of the crowd. A fresh round of cheers and catcalls rang out, offering encouragement and deprecation on both sides.

Suddenly one of the men, more wiry and compact than his beefy competitor, stumbled backward a couple of steps as he endured a volley of blows to his head and face. When he teetered, the crowd quieted in an abrupt hush as they all waited to see if he would fall. He moved back, shaking his head as if he couldn't quite clear his thoughts.

The bigger man advanced, grinning past a mouth

of bloody teeth as he prepared to land a last, decisive blow. Up went his arms, fists balled for maximum power.

And that was when the leaner man struck, laying into his foe's unprotected stomach and ribs with a series of cunning blows that drove the air straight out of his lungs. His eyes were wide with pain and shock as he tried to recover. But it was too late, the wiry boxer winding up for a solid one-two punch to his opponent's jaw.

There was a terrible crunching noise, and then blood and spittle flew from the big man's mouth, arcing in a wide stream that splattered across everyone in its path. A pair of teeth followed, flying through the air before bouncing like dice across the rough wooden stage.

Numbly Rosamund watched them roll to a stop. Only then did she notice the glistening red drops of blood on her boots. She whirled, one hand clutched to her mouth as she fought her way free of the crowd. A crash reverberated somewhere behind her, and a roar exploded from the crowd, but she barely heard it, too intent on escaping the fray.

She made it out and around to the far side of a stand of bushes before her nausea overcame her. Everything came up. She was still gagging and gasping for air, hands braced on her knees, when a handkerchief appeared in her line of sight.

Lord Lawrence waited, making no comment on her embarrassing display.

She trembled, grateful at least that she hadn't broken into tears. "I've got my own," she croaked, her strained voice even deeper than usual. She fumbled for her pocket, but it eluded her in her distress.

"Take it." He moved the handkerchief another inch closer.

This time she accepted, pressing the soft white silk against her mouth before folding it over to wipe her perspiring face. It smelled wonderful, like him.

"Thank you," she said, straightening. "I'll have this laundered and returned to you."

"Keep it. I've plenty more." He cast her an inquiring look. "You all right?"

She nodded, reluctant to meet his eyes. "The beer must not have agreed with me."

He arched an eyebrow. "Stout can do that to a man sometimes."

But they both knew the stout had nothing to do with it.

When he said nothing further, she had yet more reason to be grateful. She'd never thought so before, but apparently male pride could be a good thing after all.

Her eyes landed on the spots of blood drying on her boots and she swallowed convulsively. Gathering up a handful of leaves from the nearby bush, she leaned over and quickly scrubbed them across the leather before tossing them away. When she straightened, it was to find him holding out a silver flask.

"Have a drink," he urged. "It'll calm your stomach, believe it or not."

She thought to refuse at first, then reluctantly did as he suggested, swishing the unfamiliar alcohol around in her mouth before swallowing. She coughed, the whiskey burning like fire.

But he was right. It did help, some of the shock to her system easing. Without giving herself time to consider the ramifications of what she was about to do, she took a second swallow before handing him back the flask. Her tense muscles relaxed with a kind of pleasant inner sigh, the last of her nausea fading away.

He gave her a measuring look as he tucked the flask back into his coat pocket. "Why don't you go to the phaeton while I collect our winnings? Shouldn't take me more than a few minutes."

"What winnings?"

"From the fight, of course." He grinned, the gold in his eyes gleaming like newly minted coins in the bright sunlight. "Our man won—or didn't you realize?"

She shook her head, having rushed away before she could see the end of the fight.

"Should be a tidy sum, considering we both bet against the favorite," Lord Lawrence said. "I'll have to remember to order the house's best wine at nuncheon."

"In celebration?"

"No. Because you're paying."

Three hours later, Lawrence leaned back in his chair as the inn's serving girl cleared away the last of the meal. By way of the owner—whose palm he'd made sure was well greased—he and Ross Carrow had managed to acquire one of the inn's two private parlors. The common rooms beyond were noisy and filled with smoke, packed to bursting with overflow from the after-mill crowd.

Throughout the service, the comely serving girl had

made a point of showing off her more than ample bosom, taking care to bend low each time she set a dish of food on the table or refilled their glasses. She left no doubt as to what she was offering, careful to give himself and Carrow a fine view of the bountiful flesh inside her shirt.

She'd paid particular attention to Carrow, flirting with him in the most shameless way. But rather than taking the bait, Carrow had mostly ignored her, which had only made her try harder. By the end of the meal, Lawrence felt rather sorry for the poor thing. He was almost of a mind to offer to tup her himself out of pity, but considering the way she'd flounced out of the room a moment ago, he wasn't sure she'd appreciate his sacrifice.

He smothered a laugh and regarded Carrow over the rim of his glass. Despite his having imbibed barely half a bottle of wine—and the two swallows of whiskey he'd taken from Lawrence's flask—the fellow was clearly foxed. Lawrence couldn't recall any man of his acquaintance with a lower tolerance for drink. It was rather amusing actually and not something Carrow probably liked to share with his fellows.

Lawrence, on the other hand, had a very hard head and could drink virtually anyone under the table—with the possible exception of his brothers, that is. Oh, and Esme's husband—Northcote had not one but two hollow legs.

He supposed he ought to get Carrow up, into his carriage and safely home.

At least the other man had regained his appetite after casting up his accounts at the mill. To both their surprise, Carrow had managed to eat a fairly substantial lunch, even more proof that he had no head for alcohol; by now the food ought to have ameliorated the effects of the liquor they'd drunk.

He obviously had no tolerance for the sight of blood either, Lawrence mused with a silent chuckle. Whoever would have imagined Carrow to be so squeamish? Good thing he'd chosen a career in the law rather than opting for medicine or the military. He'd have had a rude awakening with either of those.

Across from him, Carrow slumped in his chair, his color high, his eyes owlish behind the lenses of his spectacles. The thin metal frames shone silver in the late-afternoon sunlight, their color nearly a match for the pure silvery gray of his eyes, though in no way its equal. He had pretty eyes, Carrow did, with long, dark, luxuriant lashes that were lovely enough to be the envy of any woman. His skin was smooth and translucent as well, cheeks rouged in the most becoming of ways. In the right light, he really was quite attractive. Some might even say beautiful.

Beautiful?

Lawrence blinked and shook himself, wondering where in the hell that thought had come from.

I obviously need a rest.

"Time to go," he said gruffly, tossing his napkin onto the table before getting to his feet. "We have a long drive back and the afternoon traffic is sure to be heavy."

Carrow stared blankly, clearly trying to orient himself in light of his inebriated condition. "Oh. Yes. All right."

Carrow fumbled for his coin purse, opening it to count out the proper amount to cover the bill. He didn't get far, though, staring with some confusion at the small hillock of farthings, pence, shillings and crowns he'd upended onto the table.

Lawrence gave him another minute, then let out an exasperated breath. He pushed aside Carrow's hands, noticing how long and delicate the other man's fingers were. "Leave off. I'll do it."

Without waiting for Carrow's agreement, he selected the proper amount, slid the rest back into his coin purse and handed it back to him. "You ought to be damned glad I'm not the dishonest sort. I could rob you blind and you'd never even know."

"Rob me? Why would you do that, Lawrence?" Fumbling, Carrow somehow managed to return his purse to his pocket despite its taking nearly three tries.

"God, you really are pickled, aren't you?" Lawrence rolled his eyes. "Can you stand?"

"Course I can stand." With an ear-jarring screech of wood against wood, Carrow shoved back his chair. But when he got to his feet, he stumbled. Just barely he managed to catch himself against the edge of the table. "Oops."

Carrow giggled; there was no other word for it.

Lawrence raised his eyes skyward again, then moved to Carrow's side. Taking hold of one arm, he wrapped it around his shoulder and hoisted the smaller man upright, Lawrence's other arm locked around Carrow's waist. Carrow sagged against him, his body surprisingly light.

"The room's spinning," Carrow said. "Why is the room spinning?"

"Because you're off your head with drink, Ross. Now, let's get you out to the carriage."

"Ross?" Carrow mumbled. "That's right, *I'm* Ross. Ross. Ross. Ross." He giggled again, then tipped back his head. "And you're Lawrence."

"Indeed." With a slight shove, he propelled the two of them forward.

"You sound so serious, Lawrence. So stern but very lawyerly."

"Then it's a good thing I'm a lawyer, isn't it?"

"Like me, but don't tell anyone." Carrow made a loud shushing sound.

Lawrence chuckled. "Don't worry. Your secret is safe with me."

"Bertram says I shouldn't like you, but I do. He says you're a bad influence."

"Bertram might be right."

Carrow dragged them both to a halt. "No, he doesn't know you like I do. You're good. A good man." Reaching up, he patted Lawrence's chest.

"Only on occasion, but I appreciate the vote of confidence."

Carrow looked into his eyes, staring deep. "You'll always have my vote, though I'm not allowed to do that either."

Lawrence decided not to pursue that odd non sequitur. "Come along, let's get you to the phaeton."

"Yes, your glorious phaeton. But aren't you coming too?"

Lawrence repressed a laugh. "Of course I am. Who else do you think will do the driving?"

"Certainly not me, that's for sure." Carrow snickered.

Somehow the pair of them made it down the stairs and outside into the stable yard, where Lawrence signaled for his carriage to be brought around.

Carrow swayed, humming softly to himself as they waited.

When the phaeton arrived, Lawrence helped the other man up into the seat, half pushing as Carrow stumbled his way upward. As he did, Lawrence's eyes fell on Carrow's rounded buttocks, their shape dramatically outlined by the snug cloth of his trousers. As far as buttocks went, they were far more shapely than most men's—not that he had ever spent a great deal of time looking at other men's rear ends, but with Carrow's literally in his face, it was hard not to notice.

Oddly discomfited nonetheless, he gave Carrow a harder push than he might have otherwise and sent the other man sprawling onto the far side of the seat. Suddenly concerned that Carrow might tumble out the other side and do himself injury, Lawrence leaned across to straighten him up.

After he got him settled, he looked over to find Carrow studying him. "You're rather gorgeous—did you know that, my lord?"

"Gorgeous, am I?" Lawrence said, half-amused.

"Hmm, far more so than me. Really, it isn't fair, all things considered."

"Oh, I don't know. You're not so bad."

Without his meaning to, Lawrence's gaze moved across Carrow's face, taking in the lithe curve of cheekbones, the straight sweep of a nose and the lips that were lush and gently parted, as rosy as any woman's.

He wondered how they'd feel, those lips. Were they really as soft as they looked?

Abruptly Lawrence came back to himself and jerked away, putting as much room between him and Carrow as the seat would allow. His heart thudded in his chest, his breath quickened far more than normal.

Hell and damnation, what was that?

Never in all his years had he experienced even the slightest hint of attraction for another man. Not that he condemned men who had that proclivity—what consenting adults did in their own private lives was strictly up to them and nobody else's business, whatever the law might say on the subject.

But he was a man who liked women.

Only women.

So what in the hell had that been?

Up to this instant, he'd never even imagined he could feel something of an amorous nature for a member of his own sex. To him, it was impossible. Yet there it was.

He darted another glance at Carrow, relieved to see that the other man had sunk into a doze in the opposite corner. God, he hoped Carrow hadn't noticed anything untoward when Lawrence was looking at him.

It would be mortifying to say the least.

He looked back toward the inn, thinking suddenly about the serving wench and the ample breasts she'd so brazenly displayed during their meal. She'd be happy to accommodate him, he was sure. Briefly he considered leaving Carrow here in the phaeton and going back inside. Twenty minutes. Ten, if they were especially quick and he could get this . . . whatever *this* was out of his system.

But in Carrow's current condition, Christ knew what might befall him if he were left alone. Besides, it was nothing. Just an aberration likely brought on by too much drink. Trouble was, he hadn't had all that much to drink today, not for him anyway.

With a sharp tug to his driving gloves, he leaned over and took up the reins. Ahead of him, the horses perked up their ears, stamping against the ground with an eagerness to be on their way. After another quick glance at Carrow to make sure he was still asleep, Lawrence flicked the reins and set the phaeton in motion.

He drove fast, even faster than his usual hell-for-leather speed, determined to reach London as quickly as possible. As for Carrow, he didn't look at him again.

Rosamund startled awake as the phaeton came to an abrupt halt.

"We're here," Lawrence said.

She ran a hand over her face and sat up, a shot of pain twinging her back muscles from being slumped in the seat for so long. She barely remembered climbing into the vehicle, her memory hazy about a great many of the things that had happened after she and Lawrence left the grounds of the boxing mill and headed for the inn.

There'd been a meal and a serving girl who'd needed to tighten up the loose bodice on her dress. And wine. More wine than Rosamund generally permitted herself to drink. Good heavens, but she'd gotten tipsy. Actually, a lot more than tipsy, if she was being strictly honest.

Luckily the long nap she'd enjoyed seemed to have cleared the worst of the cobwebs from her head. She only hoped Bertram didn't notice her muzzy-headed state when she went inside.

"Can you make it down on your own?"

She glanced up at Lawrence and saw the dark glower on his face. He looked . . . angry. Why was he angry? Had she done something wrong? Or worse, said something wrong?

Rather than answer, she levered herself into a standing position, still a bit unsteady on her feet as she calculated the distance to the pavement. Normally she wouldn't have had any difficulty climbing down, not even if she'd been wearing a dress. But with her balance less than optimal, she hesitated, one hand gripped along the edge of the vehicle.

She must have made some sound of distress, since Lawrence suddenly huffed out an impatient breath, tied off the reins and leapt to the ground with an athletic ease that put most men to shame.

He looked up—or rather glared up—at her. "Go on. If you stumble, I'll make sure you don't hit the pavement and crack your head in two."

"Don't worry," she said, taking offense at his tone. "I can see to myself."

Without giving herself more time to consider, she began her descent, aiming for the narrow metal step set along the side of the phaeton. Her boot heel landed correctly at first, but she misjudged the angle on her opposite leg as she came down. She teetered and would surely have sprained an ankle, or worse, if not for the hard hand that wrapped around her upper arm to steady her. Lord Lawrence let go seconds later.

Heart racing, she turned, intending to thank him despite his inexplicably foul humor, but he had already leapt back up into the carriage.

"I trust you can see yourself inside?" he asked coldly.

"I can."

"Then good day to you, Carrow." With a flick of the reins, he set the horses in motion.

She stared after him, her chest frozen by a sensation as icy as his parting words.

Behind her, the front door of the town house opened. "You all right, miss—I mean Mr. Ross," the footman corrected, casting a worried look around to make sure no one else had heard.

But they were safe; the street was empty.

With a sigh, she turned, and went up the steps into the town house. Her head was still swimming, a dull ache beginning to form behind her eyes. "Tell my brother I'm back and have gone to my room."

"You can tell me yourself." Bertram emerged from the hallway that led to his study in the rear of the house. He must have been listening for her to return, she realized. "You look pale. What's happened?"

"Nothing has happened. I have a touch of the head-ache, that's all. I'm going to take a hot bath and lie down for a while."

He frowned. "You're sure nothing untoward has occurred?"

"Quite sure."

He gave a sniff. "You smell like alcohol and tobacco smoke."

"I was at a mill with more than a hundred men. Of course I smell like alcohol and tobacco smoke."

Bertram crossed his arms. "So? What did you think?"

"About the mill? It was brutal and bloody. I didn't like it."

He looked somewhat mollified at her pronouncement. "So you won't be accompanying Byron on any-more jaunts, then?"

She thought again about Lawrence and how he'd acted before he'd driven away. She still had no idea what she could have done wrong. Perhaps she'd annoyed him at nuncheon? Maybe he hadn't liked having a friend who turned into a stumbling drunk on barely a thimbleful of spirits—assuming they were still friends. She wasn't so certain anymore.

"I can safely say I've seen my first and last boxing match," she said. "As for anything else, I don't know. Now, I really would like to go upstairs. I'm feeling rather unwell."

Bertram's expression changed to one of concern. "I'm sorry. I'll send the maid up to you. Shall I have Cook send d-dinner up as well?"

"I'm not hungry. I think I'll just go to bed if it's all the same to you."

"Of course. Sleep well. I'll see you in the morning."

With a nod, she made her way upstairs and into her room. After stripping off her coat, she sprawled wearily across the bed. Two minutes later, she was asleep.

Chapter 10

"Shh, do be quiet. They'll be here any minute."
Mallory, Lady Gresham, flapped her hands in
an effort to hush the nearly thirty family members
and close friends gathered in the drawing room of her
and her husband, Adam's, London residence. Among
their number were all but one of Lawrence and Mallory's siblings, who included Edward, Duke of Clybourne; lords Cade, Jack, Drake and Leo; and the
youngest sister, Esme, Lady Northcote. All the siblings' respective spouses were in attendance as well.
As for their growing multitude of offspring, the children had been left safely at their various homes this
evening while the adults gathered to celebrate the
tenth wedding anniversary of the family patriarch,
Edward—or Ned, as he was more familiarly known—
and his duchess, Claire.

Bottles of fine French champagne waited on ice,
presents were stacked on a large table in an adjoining
room, while downstairs the kitchen staff was laboring
to prepare the lavish meal Mallory had planned for

the special occasion with the help of the Greshams' excellent chef.

Lawrence leaned back in his chair and sipped his glass of whiskey, doing his best to pay attention despite his preoccupied frame of mind. He'd been like that for nearly a week, ever since he returned from the boxing mill he'd attended with Carrow.

He scowled and took another drink.

"Ned and Claire think they're arriving for a quiet family dinner," Mallory continued, "so everyone needs to hide except for the people I told them I'd invited. Which includes Drake and Sebastianne, Leo and Thalia, Adam, Lawrence and Mama, of course. Mama, you're fine exactly where you are."

"Well, that's a relief, my love." Ava, Dowager Duchess of Clybourne, smiled, amusement dancing in her gentle green eyes. "I'd just gotten comfortable in this chair. I would hate to have had to leave it again so soon."

Lawrence was grateful he didn't have to move out of his spot either. Despite the festive occasion, he wasn't in the mood to indulge in silly games.

"What about the rest of us?" Cade said, standing behind his wife, Meg, where she sat on the sofa, one hand cradled over her shoulder. "Where is it exactly we're supposed to hide? I, for one, am not squatting behind the sofa, and Meg most certainly is not, considering her delicate state."

Mallory rolled her eyes at her older brother while Meg smiled and reached up to give Cade's hand a reassuring pat. Ever since he found out she was pregnant again after a nearly nine-year gap, he'd been hovering over her like a mother hen. He'd nearly refused to make the long trip south from their estate, but Meg—and her doctor—had convinced him that she was in excellent health, and in no appreciable danger, considering she was only four months along.

"No one is expecting either of you to squat anywhere," Mallory said.

"Thank God for that," quipped Jack. "Last time I squatted somewhere it was to—"

"Jack, don't," his wife, Grace, warned in a quiet voice.

"Don't what?" Jack asked. "I was only going to say that the last time I squatted it was to help make mud pies with the girls." He paused, a devilish twinkle in his eyes. "Why? What did you think I was going to say?"

"With you, one is never entirely certain." A tiny smile hovered on Grace's lips, softening her words.

He leaned toward her and whispered in a voice that was still loud enough to carry, "Worried it was going to be something naughty? I'm saving that for later tonight when we're alone."

His mother sent him a stern look while Esme's husband, Gabriel, Lord Northcote, and her cousin India's husband, Quentin, Duke of Weybridge, laughed aloud. Esme, India, Claire's sisters and their husbands and several of the others chuckled under their breath. India's youngest sister, Poppy, who was in Town enjoying her first Season, giggled nervously, looking slightly scandalized. As for Grace, a still-youthful-looking mother of five, she blushed like a schoolgirl; Jack laughed merrily and dropped a quick kiss on her lips.

Even after all their years together, it was clear that he still had the power to make her weak in the knees.

Lawrence smiled briefly and took another drink.

"Enough," Mallory said with an impatient clap of her hands. "I need all of you to wait behind the Chinese screens that I've set up at the end of the room or behind the draperies for those who are game."

"We are," some of the younger cousins volunteered, practically dancing with excitement.

Before anyone else had time to react, a footman appeared at the door. "My lady, you asked me to inform you of the duke and duchess's arrival. Their carriage just pulled up."

"Did you hear that!" Mallory pointed toward the adjoining room. "Go! All of you, now. And hurry."

A great commotion ensued while everyone who was supposed to hide rushed to do so.

A strange quiet fell over the drawing room, with the remaining Byrons doing their best to act as if nothing extraordinary was going on. Mallory hastily took a seat next to her husband and smoothed the skirts of her elegant purple silk gown. Adam reached over and squeezed her hand, waggling his dark brows in a way that made her smile.

"Someone say something," Mallory whispered when the silence continued. "They'll know something is afoot if we're all sitting here quiet as a gathering of Benedictine monks."

"I don't believe anyone would ever accuse us Byrons of being monks, silent or otherwise," her elder brother Drake remarked smoothly.

"Most particularly the *otherwise*." Gabriel caught

Esme's hand and brought it to his lips as light laughter spread around the room.

Lawrence swirled the last of the alcohol inside his glass and wondered whether he might have time for a refill before dinner began.

Just then the butler appeared at the door to announce the Duke and Duchess of Clybourne before standing aside to admit them.

"Ned, Claire." Mallory rose to her feet and gave her brother and sister-in-law hugs of welcome. All of the others stood as well to offer greetings. Edward gave his mother a kiss on her cheek; then Claire warmly did the same.

"You sound like a merry party," Claire said, looking around at them. "Have you all started without us? You did say eight?"

"I did," Mallory confirmed. "And of course we haven't started without you. But before you sit, there's something I have to show you."

Edward gave his sister a curious look. "Oh? And what might that be?"

"*This!* Everyone," Mallory called.

"Surprise! Happy anniversary!"

The whole room erupted into a roar of noise and movement as all the assembled guests burst from their hiding places. Claire visibly startled while even Edward looked momentarily astonished.

Then he laughed and moved to wrap an arm around his wife's waist. "See? I told you they hadn't forgotten us."

Claire flushed with obvious pleasure and a little embarrassment.

And despite Edward's usual reluctance to display affection in public, he kissed her. "Happy anniversary, my love. Here's to ten years of truly wedded bliss and many more to come."

"Yes. Many, many more to come," Claire murmured before kissing him back.

The rest of the evening progressed splendidly, in part because of the spirited company, but mainly because of Mallory's exceptional skills at planning parties.

Lawrence did his best to join in the festivities, pushing aside his own brooding thoughts in order to celebrate the enduring union of his eldest brother, Edward, and his beloved wife, Claire. Lawrence was genuinely happy for them both.

Wine flowed during dinner as course after sumptuous course was served by an attentive staff. From caviar to lobster patties, cream of leek soup, tender lettuce salad, fresh green peas with tiny onions, butter-poached turbot and crispy roasted quail, veal medallions with tiny mushrooms and a never-ending array of side dishes, no one could do anything but rave. The pièce de résistance of the evening, however, was a towering cake made of almonds, fruit and whipped cream that had everyone exclaiming with delight.

Lawrence thoroughly enjoyed the meal, yet as the evening wore on, his earlier preoccupation crept back upon him. Like a ghost intent on haunting him, his last encounter with Carrow refused to go away. More than once, he'd told himself that he must have imagined his reaction to the other man. He was attracted to women—and *only* women—so whatever he'd felt, it could not have been real.

To prove that to himself, he'd paid a call on one of his old lovers, a beautiful, voluptuous widow who had been more than delighted to welcome him back to her bed. They'd engaged in a mutually satisfying all-night marathon that left him in no doubt of his sexuality. He'd assumed that would be the end of it.

Yet in spite of his own certainty on the subject, he found himself thinking about Carrow, usually at the most inconvenient times. Like now when he ought to be celebrating with his family and friends rather than ruminating over things best forgotten. At least he hadn't run into the man at the courthouse this week. But at some point, of course, it was inevitable that their paths would cross again.

But he was done thinking about Carrow.

For tonight anyway.

Determined to put Carrow out of his mind, he threw himself into the festivities. After dinner, everyone returned to the drawing room, where they proceeded to laugh, tell jokes, drink and reminisce about old family stories, particularly ones concerning Edward and Claire.

Once Lawrence and Leo got started, he and his twin fell into a familiar old rhythm as they each sought to outdo the other. They began talking in tandem, one starting a sentence while the other finished it. It was a game in which they hadn't indulged for a long time.

"Wait, wait," Leo said, holding up a hand. "I've got an even better one. Remember Claire's first London

Season and how determined she was to convince Ned that he didn't want to marry her after all?"

"Please. Do not remind me," Claire groaned with an embarrassed little laugh.

"I've never seen Ned so befuddled—" Lawrence said.

"Or so mesmerized," Leo finished.

"That's because I was falling in love." Edward smiled indulgently at his wife. "Despite the hell you put me through, my darling."

"Watching you two circle around each other—" Lawrence began.

"It was more entertaining than a Sheridan comedy," Leo said.

"And remember the time he nearly flayed a strip off the pair of us?" Lawrence asked.

"On which occasion?" Leo answered.

"Which occasion is right. The both of you were absolutely incorrigible," Edward said.

"And still are." Thalia sent her husband a teasing smile, her eyes filled with love.

"All part of our charm." Leo winked. "But in this case, I'm referring to the time Lawrence and I snuck Claire into Brooks's Club."

"You did what!" Sebastianne exclaimed. At her side, her husband, Drake, merely smiled, plainly unsurprised.

Gabriel looked between Lawrence and Leo before his amused gaze alighted on the duchess. "And here I always thought you were above reproach, Your Grace. I'd nearly forgotten you were once known as Claire the Dare."

Claire shrugged. "I was young and foolish. What can I say?"

"Why have I heard nothing of this before?" Esme leaned forward, obviously hurt at being left out of this particular family scandal.

"Because you were young and still in the schoolroom, sweetheart. But really, it was nothing." Claire waved a hand as if to brush it all aside.

Esme, however, was not about to be put off. "Yes, but how did you manage it? As everyone knows, ladies are not allowed inside gentlemen's clubs."

"You're right; they are not," Lawrence began with a mischievous smile.

"Not unless they go in disguise, that is," Leo continued, an identical grin on his face. "Which is why she went with us dressed as a man."

Dressed as a man . . .

In disguise . . .

The words hit Lawrence like a splash of icy water and spun around in his head in an endless taunting refrain. The conversation around him faded into mere background noise, as a mental picture of Ross Carrow came into focus.

Ross Carrow with his delicate features and winsome good looks.

Ross Carrow with his long eyelashes and beautiful silver eyes.

Ross Carrow with his lush pink lips, curiously lyrical voice and full, rounded bottom that Lawrence had yet to completely eradicate from his memory.

Impossible as it might seem, all the puzzle pieces suddenly began to fall neatly into place, snapping together into a single coherent whole. The odd incon-sistencies and peculiar reactions.

Like the way Carrow sat.

How he couldn't hold his liquor.

The uncomfortable look on his face whenever he heard a casual bit of profanity.

And most illuminating of all—how he'd turned white as a sepulcher and dashed off to cast up his accounts over a few drops of blood at a boxing match. Lawrence had always sensed there was something not quite as it ought to be about the other man.

And now he knew what it was.

Because Ross Carrow wasn't a man at all—he was a woman!

"Great bloody Christ!" Lawrence hit a fist against one thigh.

Around him the room fell silent, every eye turning his way. Only then did he realize he'd spoken out loud—and at some volume apparently, since everyone was staring. Even Leo was giving him the eye—a silent *"what the hell was that?"*

"Your pardon." Lawrence sent them all a self-deprecating smile. "Just woolgathering about a . . . case I've been working on."

"Must be quite the case to elicit that kind of reac-tion," Jack remarked.

"If you aren't careful, Lawrence, you'll rival my record for least attentive person at a party." Drake smirked, for once without his usual mathematician's pad and pencil in hand.

As for Leo, Lawrence's twin was studying him with open speculation, clearly unconvinced. That was the trouble with having once shared a womb—it was usually damned near impossible to get away with a lie.

But this was a secret Lawrence intended to keep, for now anyway. Not because he didn't trust his twin brother—or any of his other brothers. He would trust each one of them with his very life. No, instead it was because he was still absorbing the full import of his revelation.

For now that he knew that Ross Carrow was a woman, he had to decide how to proceed. After all, there was a fraud at large, one who was most definitely in need of unmasking.

Chapter 11

Rosamund finished scribbling a last few notes, then closed the heavy leather-bound law book she'd been reading. She placed it atop a pile of other books that she'd searched through already. She'd been here in the members' library at Lincoln's Inn since midmorning, having claimed a table at the far end of the room where she could have maximum quiet for the case she was preparing.

Over breakfast earlier that day, Bertram had raised no objections when she told him where she was going and that she would likely be there well into the afternoon. Apparently he had decided she would have little chance of getting into trouble if she spent the day surrounded by dry legal tomes and archival texts, maps and papers.

She—or rather Ross Carrow—was now a fullfledged member of the Inn after her brother had accompanied her to the last of her required member dinners only a few evenings earlier. She'd hoped she would see Lawrence Byron there, but she'd been doomed to disappointment, far more than she cared to admit.

A full ten days had passed since their outing together, yet the memory of his gruff behavior and hurried departure remained sharp in her mind. A part of her worried that he was avoiding her, but it was far more likely that he'd simply forgotten her.

He was an aristocrat and even she knew that Society's fashionable elite were in the midst of what was known as the London Season. Quite probably he was far too busy rubbing elbows with his rich, powerful friends to bother spending time with a middle-class lawyer who had owed him a gaming debt. Well, that debt was paid now, so she supposed he had no further reason to seek her out. Other than by means of sheer happenstance, she would probably never see him again.

She frowned as she slid a new volume forward and opened the book, wishing she could drive thoughts of Lord Lawrence Byron from her mind.

Half an hour later, she'd nearly succeeded, her thoughts focused squarely—or almost squarely, since he still slipped in from time to time—on the case law she was analyzing. So she didn't even notice when footsteps approached and came to a halt next to her. Without warning, a firm hand clapped her across the shoulders, hard enough to jolt her forward in her seat.

Her pencil jumped from her fingers and rolled halfway across the table. She looked up, her irritation falling away when she recognized the man towering above her. "Lawrence!"

He grinned, his eyes very gold against the green today. "Ross Carrow. Toiling diligently as ever, I see."

"Just doing a bit of research."

"Something interesting, I hope?"

"Rather. I'm working on a property dispute case with a history that goes back some decades. It's proving far more intriguing than I would ever have imagined."

"I congratulate your good luck. Or are you the sort, like me, who only accepts cases that promise a measure of intellectual entertainment?"

"Sadly no, my lord." She shook her head. "Some of us haven't the luxury of being able to pick and choose with no consideration for mundanities like financial gain. Most of us have to work for a living."

Lawrence set a hand on the table and bent near. "You aren't implying that I am lazy, are you?"

"Not at all. You're an exceptional attorney. Some might even say brilliant. You're just spoiled like all of your kind."

His eyes flashed and she held her breath, wondering suddenly if she'd gone too far.

He held her gaze, long enough for her pulse to pick up speed. "And what exactly is *my kind*?" he drawled softly.

"Rich and aristocratic, of course."

"Careful, Carrow. Republican talk such as that could land you in trouble with certain people. Not me, mind, since I've always been of a Whiggish persuasion. But the walls, especially around here, have big ears."

"Duly noted, my lord. And forewarned."

As if to prove his point, a sudden, indignant shushing came from a man seated at one of the nearby tables. He glared at her and Lawrence from beneath a pair of gnarled white eyebrows, his eyes blazing with such heat she was surprised the two of them weren't turned to pillars of ash on the spot.

She exchanged a look with Lawrence and found his lips twitching with suppressed humor. Her own twitched in reply and she hurriedly glanced away, fighting against a rising tide of laughter that threatened to escape her mouth.

Lawrence dropped into the chair next to her and leaned close. "Better not or you'll get us into even more trouble."

Her stomach tightened at his proximity, the delicious scents of citrus, linen starch and clean man teasing her senses. "Me?" she whispered. "You're the one who started it."

"I fail to see how. I was only making friendly conversation at a reasonable volume. Can I help it if you're loud?"

"I am not loud," she said, her register rising slightly before she got her deepened voice back under control.

The old man's eyebrows twisted dangerously as he shot them another venomous glare and hissed again. This time two more men looked up from their studies to see what the disturbance was about.

Rosamund busied herself by reaching out to retrieve her wayward pencil, but despite her attempt at silence, Lawrence wasn't finished.

"You are so." He taunted with a smirk. "But I'm sure you can't help it. Must be one of the reasons you're so good at trial."

"My loudness has nothing to do with my success in the courtroom and you know it."

"So you admit you're loud. Good of you to agree."

Her mouth dropped open, the logical part of her brain admiring the neat way he'd lured her into his verbal snare. No wonder he was such a skilled barrister. As for the emotional part of her, she wasn't nearly so sanguine. "I did *not* agree."

"I beg to differ." He crossed his arm. "But we can debate this on another occasion, since you are supposed to be quietly doing research."

"And what of you, Lord Lawrence? What are you doing here, other than plaguing me?"

"I came in to collect a book, what else?"

"What else indeed. Go get your book and leave me in peace before both of us are ejected from the room."

"You've got a point about that. The crotchety old man who keeps hissing at us like an enraged goose happens to be a very distinguished senior bencher."

"He's not," she said, horrified. She'd just gained her membership to the Inn—however fraudulent the circumstances—and didn't need to jeopardize it over something as foolish as being reprimanded for talking in the library.

"He also has virtually no sense of humor," Lawrence added.

"Then why on earth do you keep talking? Are you deliberately trying to get me told off?"

He met her eyes again, his gaze direct yet strangely enigmatic. "Now, why ever would I do that?"

Yes. Why would he?

An uneasy shiver chased over her skin, but she

quickly brushed it aside. Lord Lawrence simply liked to tease, that was all, and she was an easy mark.

"I have work to do, Lawrence," she quietly admonished. "As I'm sure you must too."

She bent her head and turned a page in the book she'd been reviewing before he arrived.

"Actually there is something I need to discuss with you," he murmured. "It won't take long. Why don't we step out into the corridor where we can speak freely?" He stood, his chair scraping against the wooden floor in a way that drew fresh scowls from the white-haired old bencher who slammed one book closed before reaching for another.

With a nod, Rosamund put down her pencil and followed after Lawrence.

Once outside the library, he led her to a bench and sank down. She sat beside him and waited, careful to keep her knees spread slightly apart with her hands on her thighs rather than folded together in her lap as she normally would have done.

He relaxed back, regarding her in a way that made her wonder if he was going to bring up the last time they'd met. Although whatever it was that had caused his ill humor when he'd driven off that day, he seemed past it now.

"We're both busy, so I'll get straight to it," Lawrence said. "I've been asked for a legal opinion on a matter of some import and I find that I could do with a fresh perspective. I was wondering if you'd be willing to bat it around with me, debate the finer points, as it were, before I come down on it one way or the other."

He wants my counsel on a point of law?

Although she'd argued legal tenet with her father many times over the years, Bertram was really the only one who'd ever actually sought out her advice. Not that Lawrence Byron would necessarily agree with her on whatever it was he wished to debate, but still, it was a compliment just to be asked.

Her chest swelled with undeniable pride. "Yes, of course, I'd be happy to."

He smiled, his mouth curved in a way that never failed to set her pulse aflutter.

"Grand," he said, getting to his feet again. "Why don't you drop round for dinner tomorrow night? Seven thirty, shall we say? That way we won't be rushed."

She stood as well. "Dinner where?"

"My town house in Cavendish Square." He rattled off the number. "I'll tell my butler to expect you."

"Oh, but—"

"Yes?" He arched a dark golden brow, his eyes gleaming in that unfathomable way again.

Bertram wouldn't like it. In fact, he'd likely refuse to let her out of the house. But as she'd reminded him on more than one occasion, it really was none of his business anymore.

She was supposed to be Ross Carrow—and men went out for dinners with friends and colleagues all the time. Beside, Bertram was wrong about Lawrence. Despite his supposed terrible reputation, he'd never been anything but decent to her. Nor had he led her into a world of depraved iniquity. One might point to her having gotten drunk in his company, but really that had been her own fault. How was he to have known she had no head for drink?

No, she would be safe with Lawrence just as she had been every time before. As for Bertram, he would simply have to abide by her decision. Then again, perhaps she could convince him to go out for the evening with some of his cronies. Since their father's death, he'd been staying in far too often. But if he left the house, it would be an easy enough thing for her to slip out as well.

"Nothing," she said, offering Lawrence a smile. "Seven thirty tomorrow, it is."

"I look forward to it."

She nodded, then turned to retrace their steps to the library, expecting him to follow. "Coming along? You needed a book, did you not?"

"I did, but it would seem I've lost track of the time and must be elsewhere. I'll stop back for the book later."

"Oh, all right. Good day, Lawrence."

"Good day, Ross."

Lawrence watched him go—or rather watched *her* go—not moving an inch until Carrow disappeared back into the law library.

It had all gone exactly as planned, easy as child's play.

Initially he'd considered going to her home and confronting her outright about his suspicions. But she was smart and wily enough to simply deny it; she and Bertram Carrow, that is, whoever the man might really be to her. Was he actually her cousin . . . or something more? Her lover perhaps, since the two of them lived together and the other man was clearly in on the scheme?

No, if Lawrence wanted the truth, he needed to get Miss Carrow—or whatever her real name might be— onto his own turf. Needed to lull her into a false sense of security, and then, when her defenses were sufficiently lowered, pounce with the deadly quickness of a cheetah to shake the honesty out of her.

He fisted his hands at his sides, the anger and incredulity that had been simmering inside him these past few days boiling up again. Even now he couldn't believe she'd fooled him—fooled them all!

Every time he looked at her now, he saw a woman, marveling that he'd ever believed her to be anything else. In the full light of the truth, her femininity was so obvious as to be laughable. For despite the masculine clothing and short queue of hair, her features were softly drawn rather than boldly angled, her skin baby smooth and free of the rough grain caused by shaving, her movements lithe and graceful rather than heavy or loping.

As for her gestures and reactions, he'd always known something essential about her didn't add up. He'd had a hard time keeping the smirk off his face minutes ago as he watched her settle onto the bench and let her knees loll apart in a deliberate attempt to sit like a man.

Only she wasn't a man and now that he knew it, he couldn't see her any other way. Nor could he stop his body's intuitive attraction to her. At least he understood now why he'd always found her appealing despite his mind's natural refusal to accept what his senses were telling him. An instinctual part of him had always recognized her true essence, like an animal sensing a potential mate.

And duped though he might feel, both personally and professionally, he couldn't deny his desire for her. Her sweet scent alone had been enough to drive him mad as he'd lounged next to her at the library table. It was one of the reasons he'd teased and baited her—enjoying their verbal games, yes, but needing the distraction as well—as thoughts of kissing and touching her flooded his mind, images of all the ways he wanted to take her racing past in a kaleidoscope of need.

But seducing the cunning little minx would have to wait. First, he needed to expose her deception. He would see about exposing the rest of her later.

As for her illegal practice of the law, he would have to put a stop to that as well. Although on that score he couldn't fault her for her obvious wish to be a barrister. Clearly she had talent—more than most of the lawyers of his acquaintance—as well as the education to excel in the profession. The only barrier to her being an attorney was her sex, unfair as that might seem.

But he couldn't let himself get caught up in sympathy for her, not now. She'd played him for a fool, and if there was one thing he could not abide, it was a liar.

"Ross Carrow" needed to be taught a very valuable lesson, and Lawrence had decided that he was exactly the man to do it.

So let the games begin.

Chapter 12

The following evening, the hack rolled to a stop in front of Lord Lawrence's Cavendish Square town house with precisely one minute to spare.

Rosamund had had to race not to be late, the task of getting Bertram out of the house proving far more difficult than she'd ever envisioned. But after a great deal of subtle and not-so-subtle coaxing, he'd finally admitted that it might be a good idea to accept some of his friends' frequent invitations and join them for a night out.

And so he'd departed—leaving her, once she knew for certain he was gone, with barely enough time to hurry from the house, locate a hackney cab and make the trip across town.

After stepping down from the vehicle and paying the driver, she took a moment to gaze up at Lawrence's grand, three-story Palladian town house. The front door was painted a fine, glossy black with a polished brass knob and knocker that looked elegantly

sophisticated against the building's white-gray Port-
land stone.

The door opened as she started up the steps, the
butler waiting to receive her. "Mr. Carrow?"

At her nod, he took her hat and gloves and laid
them on an exquisite Louis XIV table that looked
quite at home in the beautifully appointed entry hall
with its black-and-white marble floor, fine white col-
umns and wall niche. A grand staircase swept down
one side with majestic grace.

She tried not to make a show as she studied the
elegant refinement of the place. Everything was done
with a sense of taste and understated sophistication
rather than a need for ostentation. This was old aristocratic money at its best, she mused, more aware than
ever of her own middle-class upbringing.

The butler gestured politely. "His Lordship is
expecting you. If you would care to follow me."

"Of course."

He led her a short distance down the hall, then into
a beautiful drawing room that, to her surprise, bore
a decidedly feminine touch with gracefully turned
furnishings and appointments done in cheerful hues
of ecru and apricot. She loved everything about it,
including the airy draperies, gilded mirror, large fireplace and tall Sèvres vase filled with an arrangement
of fresh flowers whose sweet perfume filled the air.

Still, the room made little sense, given that this was
a bachelor's establishment. Or at least she'd always
assumed that Lord Lawrence was a bachelor. After
all, he'd never mentioned a wife. Then again, consid-

ering the circumstances of their acquaintance, why would he?

Her heart lurched strangely in her chest at the idea, and she realized she was far more troubled by the possibility than she cared to admit. Not that it mattered, she assured herself. Even if there were a Lady Lawrence lurking about, it changed nothing. Lawrence believed she was a man. They were colleagues and friends, nothing more.

Yet even if he was unmarried and circumstances between them were entirely different—if she'd never disguised herself and he'd met her as a woman, and if by some improbable chance she'd caught his eye— there could still never be anything between them; their worlds were simply too far apart.

Before she had time to consider further, the butler opened the door to another room, then stepped aside to admit her.

"Mr. Carrow, my lord," the servant announced in politely rounded tones.

Lord Lawrence glanced up from where he sat in a comfortable-looking armchair, then set down the book he'd been reading and got to his feet. As he walked forward, he shot her a dazzling smile that sent her heart into a fresh ricochet. His gold-green eyes were brilliant in the late-evening sunlight, his dark golden hair gleaming in a nimbus that reminded her a bit of a crown. For God knew, he was certainly handsome enough to be a prince.

"Good, Ross, you've arrived. And right on time."

She swallowed beneath the snug confines of her

neck cloth and worked to keep the emotion off her face. "Yes, I didn't want to be late again and give you the impression that I'm incapable of punctuality."

"I knew that already, since you're never late to court. Then again, I don't fine people for tardiness like some of the judges do."

"Or bellow at them, thank the heavens," she said, returning his smile.

Lawrence chuckled. "Old Judge Morely, do you mean?"

She nodded.

"Yes, he is a terror. Half-deaf too, which only makes it worse. But don't ever shout back at him, trying to be heard. He'll call you out on it, ask why the hell you're yelling, since he can hear you just fine, then roast you over hot coals for the rest of the testimony." He crossed to a small bar. "Drink?"

"No." She shook her head, remembering vividly what had happened the last time she partook of alcohol in his company.

He sent her an amused look out of the corner of his eye. "Perhaps you're right. This way you can enjoy wine with dinner."

She wasn't sure it would be wise to do that either, but she didn't openly disagree.

While he busied himself pouring his own drink from one of the finely cut crystal decanters, she took a moment to look around the room.

Clearly it was his study. Everything exuded an unapologetic masculinity, from the massive mahogany desk that stood at the far end of the room to the spacious wooden table and deep armchairs situated in a comfortable arrangement near a set of tall windows. Bookshelves lined the dark-painted walls, every inch filled with leather-bound volumes whose scent bore traces of fine-quality paper, ink and age. A pair of excellent horse paintings, by an artist she didn't recognize, hung in positions of prominence over the fireplace mantel, while a large globe of the world sat suspended at a safe distance inside its wooden cradle.

She resisted an urge to approach the globe and give it a testing spin.

"I thought we would take dinner in here tonight." Lawrence resumed his seat, drink in hand, motioning with the other for her to take the seat across from him. "It's far more comfortable than the dining room."

She lowered herself into the chair. "So it will just be the two of us, then. Your wife won't be joining us?"

"My wife?" His eyebrows shot high. "Whatever gave you the notion that I'm married?"

"Nothing I've heard. I only wondered after seeing the room your butler led me through on my way here." She nodded in the direction of the drawing room. "Apricot and cream don't strike me as your sort of colors, not to mention the huge vase full of fresh blooms."

He stared for an instant, then tossed back his head and laughed. "No, I don't suppose they do. But you may put your mind at rest about my being married. I'm not—not yet anyway. The drawing room was decorated by my sister-in-law, Thalia. My twin brother and I own this town house together, and he and Thalia stay here when they're in London. They departed yesterday for their country estate but left the flower arrangement behind."

A quick sense of relief shot through her before the rest of his words sank in. "You have a twin?"

"I do."

"Identical?"

He took a drink and inclined his head. "Enough to confuse people whenever we like. Although he and I tried that once on our mother. I think we were ten at the time. She gave us quite the hiding afterward, I'll tell you."

She contemplated that small revelation. "I bet you were a pair of hellions."

"Worse." He grinned. "Leo and I cut quite a swath in our day."

"And now?"

"Now he's married and leads a respectable life—or respectable for him at least. Nevertheless, he still claims that between the two of us, I'm the dull one."

"You? Dull? That's ridiculous."

"Well, I suppose he is right up to a point. I do take far more enjoyment from the pursuit of dry, intellectual discourse and erudite legal inquiry than he ever will. And Lord knows I have no interest in penning lurid tales of mayhem and murder."

"What do you mean? Does he write novels?"

Lawrence grimaced, looking like a small boy who'd just been caught out. "Oh no. I wasn't supposed to let that slip. He's trying to keep it private, don't you know?" He gave a guilty little laugh, then grew serious again. "But you won't tell, will you, Ross?"

"No, I won't tell. You can trust me."

"I can see that." An odd, strangely enigmatic light shone in Lawrence's eyes as he gazed deeply into her own. "You're the sort who's good at keeping secrets, aren't you? The kind who can conceal things that others wouldn't even dare to attempt."

Without warning, her pulse began to race, alarm suddenly prickling across her skin. "What do you mean?"

How had the conversation taken such an unusual turn? *Surely he couldn't . . . doesn't suspect me?*

Long seconds ticked past, their gazes locked. She tamped down her nerves, refusing to look away first.

Abruptly he lowered his eyes, idly swirling the liquor in his glass. "Why, only that you're a barrister, of course. It's our duty to keep the confidences of our clients. Whatever else did you imagine I meant?"

Her pulse began to slow again, her concern fading. "Nothing. What else could you mean but that?"

He swirled the whiskey in his glass again, then swallowed what remained. He set the glass aside. "Are you hungry? It's a bit early yet for dinner, but I suspect the kitchen can manage something if we let them know we're ready."

"Yes. That sounds most agreeable."

"Good." He rubbed his hands together, then sprang out of his chair.

She relaxed back into her own as he went to ring for a servant, relieved that her fears had all been for naught.

I really am a devil toying with her like this, Lawrence thought nearly two hours later as one of the footmen cleared away the last of their dinner. Yet, cruel as it might seem, there was a kind of sweet satisfaction to the game as he watched her put on her act. Truthfully she could have trod the boards at Drury Lane. The role of Portia would have been a natural one for her, considering how adept she was at pretending to be not only a man but a lawyer as well. And as he'd acknowledged more than once, she was an excellent litigator, her mind as sharp and nimble as any man's.

Yet despite the red herring he'd used to lure her here tonight, he hadn't actually intended to debate the law with her. When she'd brought up the subject over dinner, though, he decided to play along and tossed out a legal conundrum that he really had been contemplating in the course of his work.

Her insights shouldn't have surprised him, yet somehow they did, her clever maneuvering and rich understanding of the law making for a lively round of intellectual sparring that had proven more interesting and entertaining than any he'd enjoyed in recent memory.

Or perhaps ever, come to that.

Yet admire her brain though he might, he could not admire her deceit. She was a fraud, a charlatan who'd plied her tricks on him and others. She'd made him question himself. Worse, she'd made him question the very nature of his own sexual desires, and for that alone, he could not—would not—excuse her.

The time of reckoning had arrived.

With the servant gone and the study door closed, Lawrence picked up the decanter of after-dinner port. He leaned forward and moved to fill her glass.

She shook her head and held out a hand to stop

him. "No, thank you, I've had more than enough already."

"Surely you can tolerate a few sips of this. It's sixty-year-old tawny from Portugal. Believe me, you won't find better."

He'd been careful throughout the meal to serve her just enough wine to leave her mellow but not drunk— a fine art, considering her limited tolerance for spirits as well as her general unwillingness to imbibe.

"Have a little," he coaxed. "I promise my coachman will drive you home, so you've no need to worry on that score."

"Nevertheless—" She frowned.

"Go on. You can nurse it slowly." He filled his glass, then her own. After setting down the decanter, he raised his glass, silently encouraging a toast.

Despite her obvious reluctance, she lifted her glass. "To what are we drinking?"

"Hmm, let's see," he mused aloud. "To friendship, shall we say?" He locked his eyes with hers. "And honesty."

She blinked but didn't look away. "To friendship and honesty."

He clinked his glass with hers, and together they drank.

After refilling their glasses again despite her audible demur, he got to his feet and crossed to one of the bookshelves. From it, he retrieved an ornately carved rosewood box that he carried back to the table. He unlatched one side and laid it open to reveal a clever, multipurpose gaming board. "What shall we play? Chess, checkers or backgammon?"

"What an exceptional piece." She stroked her fingers against the wood admiringly. "Where did you get it?"

"It was a gift from my brother Cade. He acquired it during some of his travels years ago when I was still a stripling. It's portable, so I took it to school with me. By some miracle, I've managed not to lose any of the pieces—not yet anyway."

"I should hope not. It's much too fine to ruin."

"So? Which game? Any particular favorite?" He waited.

"I like them all. Backgammon maybe, since I need my wits sharper than they are tonight for chess."

"Backgammon it is, although it is not without the necessity of skill as well."

With easy movements, he laid out the board and dice. Once done, he shrugged out of his coat, then reached up to tug loose his neck cloth. Unwinding the linen strip from around his throat, he tossed it aside atop his jacket. He looked back to find her eyes on him.

"What are you doing?" she said.

He hid a smile. "Just getting comfortable. It's a warm evening, do you not agree? Far too warm to stay trussed up in layers of clothing. It's only us two men tonight, so why stand on formality when shirtsleeves will do? Join me. Otherwise I'll feel underdressed."

To her credit, she managed to maintain her composure. "I'm comfortable as I am." She made no effort to remove her coat.

He arched a brow and pressed a little harder. "Now, that, my fine friend, is clearly a lie. I can see the sheen of perspiration along your hairline. Don't tell me you're still shy? I thought you'd gotten over that during our billiards game."

"I'm not shy," she declared.

"Well, then?"

She paused, clearly wrestling with her decision. On a near-silent huff, she eased out of her jacket and, after another moment of hesitation, reached up to boldly untie her cravat and yank it free.

He studied the contours of her chest beneath her waistcoat and the exposed line of her throat but couldn't find any overt evidence of her femininity. Either she was extremely small-breasted or she kept her breasts bound. His hand clenched against his thigh as he thought about that—and the delicious idea of unwrapping them. As for her throat, it was long and smooth and pale. He imagined pressing his mouth to the spot at its base where her skin disappeared beneath her shirt. He wondered how sweet she would taste and smell as he nuzzled the cloth aside with his nose.

"Lawrence?"

He looked up and realized he'd been caught daydreaming. Regrouping quickly, he picked up the die, shook it noisily inside a dice cup, then let it spill out onto the board.

She followed suit with her own die, winning the opening turn. She bent her head to consider her move.

They played for a few minutes, back and forth in an easy rhythm while both of them paused occasionally to sip from their respective glasses of port—he twice as often as her.

"Cheroot?" he asked after taking the first point.

"What?"

"Do you care for a cheroot?"

Without waiting for her answer, he got up and retrieved a narrow box containing the cigars along with a flint and tinder, and a small dish for the ashes.

He knew he really oughtn't spin things out too much longer, but an impish streak tempted him to see exactly how far he could push her. Would she rise to the challenge or break under its pressure?

Silently he held the open box out to her, displaying the fragrant, tightly rolled cigars. "These came all the way from the West Indies. You do smoke, I presume?"

"Oh, of course. On occasion."

Another lie.

He watched as she reached out and gingerly selected one of the blunt-tipped cheroots, holding it between her fingertips as if expecting it to ignite right then and there.

Or explode, perhaps.

Hiding another smile as he turned away, he chose his own, then closed the box with an audible snap.

Visibly, she startled.

This time he couldn't keep from grinning.

He returned to his chair, then reached for the flint and tinder. After conjuring a flame, he held it up to the cheroot and drew in a few quick, deep puffs in a way that made the end flare red. Tipping back his head, he blew a stream of smoke into the air.

Across from him, her nose wrinkled with clear distaste at the pungent scent.

"Your turn." He held out the still-burning tinder and waited to see whether she would balk.

For a moment, he thought she was going to do exactly that, but with a bravado he could only admire, she stuck the cheroot in her mouth and leaned forward. He touched the hot tip to the end of her cigar and waited, nearly warning her to go easy as she took a trio of fast, deep puffs in an exact imitation of himself.

The cheroot caught, the tip briefly flaring red as she pulled in one more hearty inhalation. Smoke curled out of her mouth and nostrils, and her eyes popped wide. She yanked the cheroot free of her mouth as she began to gasp and sputter. A series of racking coughs burst from her lungs, the sound penetrating as a cannon shot.

Hurriedly he snuffed out the tinder flame, then crushed his cheroot tip-first into the china dish before coming around to her side. While she continued coughing with the agony of a consumptive, he took the cigar from her hand, squashed it out in the dish next to his, then reached out to pull her to her feet.

With his arm around her waist, he half dragged, half carried her to the nearest window. She continued her fitful coughing as he flung up the sash to let in drafts of warm night air. He moved so that she stood in front of him, his hands clasped supportively around her upper arms as she fought to regain her breath.

She leaned back against him, little shivers of distress running through her as her coughing finally began to subside. He rubbed her arms, up and down in slow, soothing strokes. She coughed once, twice, then fell still, only the quiet sounds of nocturnal insects and the distant clop-clop of horses' hooves intruding into the silence.

"Better?" he asked, hands continuing their up and down slide.

She nodded, the soft hair at the top of her head brushing against his jaw. He leaned closer and took a moment to breathe her in. Then he slid his arms around her.

He felt the instant her body turned stiff against his. "Lawrence?"

"Hmm?" He rubbed his chin against her temple.

"What are you doing?" Her usually deep voice ended on a high note.

"What do you think I'm doing?"

She swallowed. "Whatever it is, it is most irregular. You can release me."

"I know I can." He traced his fingers along the buttons of her waistcoat. "I know something else as well." He put his mouth next to her ear. "Want me to tell you what it is?"

"No. Now, enough of whatever this is you're playing at." She tried to pull away, but he tightened his hold instead.

"Not until I tell you about the secret." He slipped one of her waistcoat buttons free, then a second.

"What secret?"

"Why, yours, of course."

He slid his hand beneath her waistcoat and laid it flat against the thin material of her shirt right where her left breast would be. A warm rush of satisfaction went through him when he discovered a thick, incriminating banding of cloth underneath. "Or do you finally want to share?"

"Share what?" she blustered, unable to suppress the shudder that moved through her. "I have no idea what you're talking about."

"Oh, don't you, now?" Abruptly he spun her around and looked into her eyes, finding her pupils so dilated they all but obscured the gray. "Remember earlier how we toasted to honesty? Why don't you be honest for a change and tell me the truth?"

"About what?" She lifted her chin, even now refusing to admit defeat.

"Stubborn to the end, I see." He caught her chin between his fingers. "Aren't you, *Miss* Carrow?"

Chapter 13

Rosamund wrenched herself away from him, her heart thundering frantically in her ears.

He knows. God help me, he knows!

But how? And why this elaborate charade? She realized in a sudden rush that he must have been toying with her the entire evening like a cat with a mouse.

And now what? What was she to do? Come right out and admit her deception or try to bluff one last time and hope by some miracle he believed her?

But she could see from the fierce gleam in his gold-green eyes that it was too late for tricks.

"It's not what you think," she said, holding out a hand as if to ward him off.

"Isn't it, now, you impudent bit of baggage? Passing yourself off as a man. Not to mention pretending to be a barrister. Whose idea was it anyway? Yours or Carrow's?"

She didn't answer, instead darting a glance toward her discarded coat and neck cloth. Maybe if she ran fast enough, she could grab them and somehow manage to escape the house before he caught up.

"Don't even think about it," he said, clearly aware of her desperate intentions. Before she even had a chance to react, he went to the door and twisted the key in the lock. Turning back with a menacing smile, he slipped the key into his pocket. "Now, where were we? I believe I asked you a question."

She looked toward the open window and wondered fleetingly what her chances would be trying to escape through it. But she discarded the idea before it had even fully formed, knowing Lawrence would be on her the second she moved. And considering her rubbish luck tonight, she'd probably just end up breaking something—like her ankle.

Or her neck.

Crossing her arms, she took up a defiant stance. "I am afraid you'll have to refresh my memory, Counselor. I don't recall what it is you wanted to know."

He stared at her, then barked out a laugh. "You really are bold as brass. I'll give you that. Then again, if you weren't, we wouldn't be standing here tonight, would we? Very well, I will ask you again. Exactly whose idea was—this?" He moved his hand in a way that encompassed the whole of her. "Before you tell me, though, why don't we start with a few basics, such as your name? Somehow I don't think it's Ross."

Briefly she considered refusing to tell him. But what was the point? He knew the worst, so what did the rest matter now?

"Rosamund," she admitted, abruptly reverting to her natural speaking voice.

He stared for a moment as he absorbed the change but recovered just as quickly. "Rosamund, is it?" He rolled her name on his tongue as if savoring a sweet-meat. "Far more lyrical than Ross, I must say. It suits you. And your surname? Is that something else as well?"

She frowned. "No, it's Carrow."

"So you really are Carrow's cousin, then? You're not . . ."

"Not what?"

"Something more?"

"More? Well, I suppose you could put it that way."

His eyes darkened. "So the two of you are lovers. You're not married to him, are you?"

"Married! Good God, no."

"Well, that provides some reassurance at least. It's one thing to steal another man's lover, quite another to take his wife. Though in your case, I might have made an exception."

Her arms dropped to her sides, air squeezing from her chest. "What?" she said, sputtering. "How could you think that he . . . that I . . . that we—" She shuddered. "*Ugh!* For heaven's sake, Bertram is my brother."

Lawrence was the one to look shocked this time. "Your brother?"

"Yes. My younger brother. Why would you think . . . well, whatever it is you were thinking?"

"Because you live together, for one. And though you both share similar coloring and perhaps a faint resemblance around the eyes, that doesn't necessarily mean you're related. As for your being cousins, cousins marry, sometimes even first cousins, though I personally find that rather too close a relationship for comfort. So the idea that you and he might be cousins didn't preclude the two of you being . . . more. I have to say, though, that I'm happy he's your brother. It'll make everything so much simpler."

Her scowl deepened. "Make what simpler?"

What was he talking about? And what exactly had he meant about being willing to make an exception and steal her away? She thought about how he'd held her a few minutes ago. The way he'd caressed her temple and whispered into her ear. But surely he'd just been taunting her, aware she was a woman when she'd still thought that he thought she was a man. Which reminded her . . .

"How long have you known?" she said.

"About you?"

She gave a sharp nod.

"A while. A little over a week."

"A week? But if you've known, why didn't you say something? Why go to all this trouble tonight rather than simply confronting me? Or else reporting me to the Inn and the court."

"Believe me, I thought about doing both. I was furious when I first realized and wanted nothing more than to throw you to the wolves." He dragged his fingers through his hair, leaving it disheveled in the most attractive way. "But it seemed far too easy and curiously unsatisfying, considering all the unanswered questions I have. Then too, I guess I wanted the pleasure of unmasking you. Though technically I have yet to see absolute proof of your femininity." His gaze lowered to her chest where her waistcoat still hung partially open.

"I presume you do have a pair of breasts concealed under that binding around your chest? You could always remove it and let me see. Just so I can make certain."

Warmth burst like fire into her cheeks, turning them what she was sure must be the color of ripe cherries. She reached for the buttons on her vest and with shaking fingers quickly fastened them.

Lawrence laughed. "I'll take that as confirmation of the existence of said breasts. I reserve the right, however, to see physical proof of them at a later time."

"And I reserve the right to refuse any such requests."

He flashed her a wicked grin, the look in his eyes sending tingles radiating over her skin. "You can always try."

"If I'd had my wits about me," she said, "I would have told you my chest is bound because I cracked a rib. Is that why you've been plying me with liquor all evening? So I wouldn't have time to think up a reasonable excuse?"

"That and the fact that it's rather amusing watching you get tipsy on a thimbleful of alcohol."

"I'm not tipsy tonight. Just relaxed. Or rather I *was* relaxed before you started this whole inquisition."

"It's not much of an inquisition yet." He motioned for her to take a seat again. "You've barely told me any of it, such as why the hell you decided to play pretend barrister."

Suddenly realizing just how shaky her legs were, she went to the chair and sank down. "It's a long story."

"I have time." He settled into the chair across from her. "Pray, enlighten me."

*   *   *

Lawrence listened, letting her tell her story with far more directness than he had any right to expect. He watched her as she spoke, allowing her gestures and unstudied way of expressing herself speak for her every bit as much as her words. Her eyes shone with bright forthrightness and quiet determination, yet beneath it all he glimpsed the haunted shadows of guilt and regret.

She didn't plead or attempt to cajole; she just explained, concise and straightforward, laying everything out as she would one of her legal cases. It was that, more than anything, that gave him the most pause.

When she finished, a shroud of silence fell over the room.

Lawrence studied her where she sat, her eyes cast down and shoulders set as she awaited her sentence, whatever he might deem it to be.

He didn't know why, but he found himself believing her, though he certainly had no reason to. Yet in spite of her former pretense and the intricate web of lies she'd woven, he thought he understood why she'd done what she'd done. Now all that remained was how he was going to respond.

She sighed. "I suppose the only ethical thing for you to do is to expose my deceit to everyone. I am prepared to accept the consequences."

"Are you?" he asked without inflection.

She drew in a breath, then nodded. "Yes, only . . ."

"Only what?"

"Would you be willing to wait a few days?" She raised her eyes to his. "I wouldn't ask for myself. But my brother, I'd like to give him a short while to get his affairs in order."

"A chance to leave the city, you mean."

Her face turned blank—a sure tell that she was prevaricating, he now realized. "No, I didn't say that."

"You didn't need to." He waited as his meaning sank in. "We both know if I give you away, I give him away as well. After all, he's the one who vouched for you at Lincoln's Inn and saw to the certification of your credentials with the court, not to mention serving as your cocounsel at trial. No, the pair of you are inextricably bound together in this whether you wish it or not."

"Please, don't do this to him." She leaned forward in her chair, pleading for the first time since she'd begun her confession. "Bertram is a good man and doesn't deserve to have his entire life ruined. He was in a state of grief over our father's death and wasn't thinking clearly at the time. Really this is all my fault. I should be the one to pay, not him."

"You were grieving too," he said, his voice rising sharply. "And why not him when, if I understood you correctly, it was his idea from the start?"

She wrung her hands. "Yes, but I am the one who agreed to do it. I should have refused and let the worst he faced be a loss to his pride. But he just needed a chance, the time to transition into work more suited to his nature. He's a smart man, a capable lawyer. It is only that our father could never see how much Bertram hated litigation, how being a barrister tormented him because of his speech difficulties. Difficulties he barely has except when he is under stress or scrutiny."

"Have you always mothered him?"

She scowled. "It's not a question of that. I just look after him as any caring sister would."

He arched a knowing brow but decided not to press further. "So, for your brother's sake, you would let him flee and leave you to take the brunt of whatever might come?"

"Of course. Assuming he would go, that is. I rather doubt he will agree, but I'll try to persuade him nevertheless."

"If he is any kind of man at all, I would hope that he wouldn't turn tail and abandon you. Luckily in this instance, we won't have to find out."

"What do you mean?"

He steepled his fingers together. "I mean that I've decided not to say anything. I am going to keep your secret."

Her lips parted on an astonished gasp. "But why?"

"I'm not entirely sure. Let me just say that I don't like the idea of your falling on your sword to save the person responsible for getting you into this fix, even if he is your little brother. Which reminds me, just how old are you really? Given the fact that you've admitted to being the elder sibling, I rather doubt you're four and twenty."

Her lips pursed together briefly. "I am twenty-eight."

He lowered his hands. "Really? Then we're of an age. I am twenty-eight as well, though not for long, since I've a birthday next month." His eyes met and held hers again. "Any more fibs you need to reveal? If I'm to keep your confidences, then I want no further secrets between us. Is that understood?"

"Completely. And there's nothing else, not that I can think of at present."

The corners of his mouth turned up. "I trust you'll tell me if anything comes to mind."

She nodded. "I will. My lord . . . Lawrence, I don't know how to thank you. It is beyond generous of you not to reveal what you've learned, especially considering the ethical implications involved. I certainly wouldn't wish any of this to cause you difficulty."

"I don't see how it could." He gave a dismissive shrug. "All I need say is that I had no more idea of your deceit than any of my fellows. Plausible deniability and all that. Besides, you're not planning to carry on with this charade indefinitely, or at least that's what you led me to believe earlier when you were explaining things."

"That's right. Once I close the last of my father's cases and Bertram is satisfactorily established in his new practice, *Ross Carrow* will go back north and I shall resume my old life. After all, it's not as if I can live the rest of my life as a man."

"No, that would be pushing your luck rather too far. Still, it seems a shame."

"What does?"

"You. Not being allowed to use that exceptional mind of yours. It's a sad waste of talent."

A shy little smile crept over her lips. "Do you think I've an exceptional mind?"

"How could I not? I've watched you work and have debated legal precedent and theory with you on more than one occasion, including tonight. Your father taught you well."

"Yes, he did."

"Besides, you defeated me in court. What would that say about me if I didn't think you to be exceptional?"

She laughed, her face lighting with a pleasure that did odd things to his system, both above and below his waist.

"Well, it's kind of you nonetheless." Her eyes sparkled like polished silver. "Most men would not be so broad-minded or enlightened in their opinions about a woman's intellectual capabilities."

"That's because most men are idiots, or haven't you figured that out yet?"

Another laugh rippled from her throat, the rich, yet unabashedly feminine sound of it vibrating through his blood. *Lord above, she is pretty when she laughs.* He would have to be sure to make her do so again and often.

They each fell silent as the humor slowly faded away.

"Lawrence, I truly am most grateful for your willingness to keep my secret," she said, meeting his eyes again. "I have no right to expect such forbearance, or forgiveness, most especially since I've lied so shamelessly to you. If there is anything I can do, anything at all, you've only to say. And once I tell Bertram about tonight, I am sure he will wish—"

"You will tell your brother nothing," he interrupted.

"What? But—"

"Rosamund." *Christ*, he liked the sound of her name. "Rosamund, my knowledge of your true nature is a secret, one I expect to be kept between you and me and no one else, not even your dear brother."

She frowned, plainly puzzled. "But I don't see what it matters if Bertram knows."

"It matters because I wish to keep seeing you and somehow I suspect your brother won't give you nearly the same latitude to spend time in my company if he knows I've twigged on to the fact that you're a woman."

"Oh. Well, no, I suppose he wouldn't." She worried the tip of one fingernail between her teeth for a moment. "Actually I already have to sneak out of the house to see you. He doesn't approve even now. He says . . ."

Lawrence crossed his arms and leaned back in his chair. "Yes, what does he say?"

"That you've a dreadful reputation when it comes to women and that I oughtn't be alone with you, not even if you believe—or rather believed—that I'm a man."

"Your brother is right. And far more intelligent than I've given him credit for. I see that I shall have to reassess my opinion of his capabilities in future."

"What do you mean he's right?"

"Exactly that."

"I'm sorry. I'm afraid I don't understand."

"Do you not?" he drawled, his tone gentle. "I suspect you understand far more than you think you do."

Her eyes widened. "But we're friends. Or at least we were until I told you I've been lying."

"Oh, we still are. Friends, that is."

"Then what are you saying?"

He got to his feet, then reached out and pulled her to her own, securing her against him with an arm around her waist. He looked down into her eyes. "I'm saying that I want to be more than just your friend."

"But . . . but . . . ," she sputtered. "This doesn't make sense. Until a week ago, you thought I was a man."

"Yes, and it proved damned confusing and uncomfortable, I can tell you that. I've never had such inappropriate thoughts about one of my chums in my life."

She drew in a sharp breath. "Then you—"

"Want you?" He laid a palm against her cheek. "Yes, Rosamund, I do. Quite badly, as it happens."

"But . . . is that why you've decided not to betray my confidence? So you can—"

"Blackmail you?" He smiled slowly. "No, my dear. Whatever you and I decide to do in private has no bearing on my promise. Whether you say yes or no, I'll keep your secret. You have my word."

He felt her relax slightly against him.

"Then again, I believe I have reason to be offended," he said. "I assure you I've never in my life had to force a woman into my bed."

"No, I don't suppose you have," she murmured, so softly he almost didn't hear her.

He nearly laughed. Instead he reached out and tugged free the cord that held her queue in place, letting her short, straight dark hair fall around her face. It softened her features, making her look like the woman she was.

"So, what shall it be?" he asked. "You did tell me you'd do anything to express your gratitude. Surely a kiss wouldn't be too much to ask."

"I—I suppose not," she whispered.

And before she had a chance to change her mind, he pressed his lips to hers.

Chapter 14

Fire shot through her veins the instant Lawrence's mouth touched hers, her entire body tingling from scalp to toes. For years she'd thought she knew what it was like to be kissed, but in a few quick seconds her entire perspective shattered around her. The memory of those long-ago kisses had been tender and sweet, rife with the promise of innocent hope and young love.

But there was nothing innocent about this kiss as Lawrence claimed her with a sophisticated passion that muddled her mind and stole her breath. He tasted of wine and smelled like warm, clean man, the grain of his whiskers slightly rough against her smooth cheeks. But she found she didn't mind. In fact, she was excited by the sensation rather than repulsed. Her heart hammered out an erratic beat as he plundered her mouth with a thoroughness that left her reeling.

She blinked dizzily up at him, her spectacles tilted at an awkward angle when he let her briefly come up for air. To her surprise, she found her fingers twisted in the material of his shirt as if she'd been trying to anchor herself to him. She tried to make herself let go but only ended up petting his chest instead.

Lawrence stared down at her, his eyelids heavy with a look that sent fresh quivers chasing over her skin. "Hmm, not too bad for a first kiss," he murmured. "Shall we see what we can do with a second?"

Considering that he'd nearly made her head explode, she didn't see how it could possibly get better. But if he thought so . . .

She supposed she must have nodded, or else made some faint noise of agreement, since he paused for only a few seconds more before tunneling the fingers of one hand into her hair to cradle the back of her skull. Gently he angled her head, tipped his own to one side and began to kiss her again.

Although she'd assumed it would be impossible to top his first effort, this second kiss was indeed even better. What began as a slow, sultry dance of passionate warmth and tactile sensation soon turned incendiary, her limbs becoming liquid as she trembled in his embrace.

But she needn't have worried—his strong arms were there to support her as he arched her body even closer against his. Catching her lower lip between his teeth, he played upon her tender flesh, nibbling gently until her mouth opened on a shaky breath. Without hesitating, he slid his tongue in deep to trace every silken inch. Her mind spun, overwhelmed, as he led her places she'd never even thought to go.

Without quite realizing, she began to kiss him back, following his lead with an eagerness that ought to have shocked her but only left her wanting more. She tangled her tongue with his, meeting his demands with an instinctive need that transcended any doubt or shame. She'd been drunk before on alcohol, but she hadn't realized that she could get drunk on a man's touch, each new caress more intoxicating than the last.

Dimly she felt his hand reach down and tug the tail of her shirt free of her trousers before delving beneath the material. She shuddered as his fingers moved in a hot slide across her bare skin, over her back and around to her stomach. She sucked her belly in on a gasp, shifting her thighs against the sudden, inexplicable ache that lodged itself between them.

Kissing her all the while, he worked to untie the cloth that bound her breasts. But it was too well secured for an easy release and too tight for him to slip his fingers underneath. He stroked her there anyway, over the cloth, her ribs straining uncomfortably as she fought for air.

Then he gave up.

Or at least she thought he had until his hand turned and went in the opposite direction.

"Oh!" She jumped, her eyes flying open as he slid his palm over the curve of her buttocks. He cupped her there, massaging her flesh through the fabric of her trousers before giving a gentle squeeze. Her hips arched involuntarily, pressing her closer.

But he wasn't through. Using the hand on her bottom to guide her, he pressed a muscular leg between her own so that without her quite knowing how he managed it, she suddenly found herself straddling his thigh. He rocked her there against his leg, kneading her buttocks as he urged her to ride him. The intimacy of the act both shocked and enthralled her, leaving her dizzy with a need she couldn't fully comprehend.

He continued kissing her with ardent intensity before breaking off to bury his mouth against her neck. He teased her there with the tip of his tongue before scattering kisses along the length of her throat. Onward he roved, over her chin and cheek, temple and ear. He caught the lobe between his teeth, then suckled for several heart-stopping moments before blowing warm breath across her damp skin.

Hot chills burst like gooseflesh all over her skin, her eyelids falling shut on a wave of uncontrollable delight.

"I never realized before how advantageous a pair of trousers could be on a woman," he murmured darkly. "Gives a man all sorts of unanticipated access."

His hand slid lower, then lower still. He took her mouth again in a series of raw, openmouthed kisses as he insinuated his fingers between her legs, nudging them even farther apart. He rubbed her through the cloth, eliciting sounds she barely recognized as her own. Hazily she became aware of a growing dampness where he was stroking her, each touch more sinful than the last.

"That's right," he said, bouncing her lightly against his thigh as he continued rubbing her with his fingers. "Just let it happen."

Let what happen? she wondered, too lost in the sensations to protest anything he did. Not that she wanted to, the ragged ache lodged deep in her core too insistent to be denied. She felt as if she were poised on the precipice of something extraordinary, though what she didn't know.

He rocked her again, turning his hand over so she was rubbing against his knuckles now, while behind, he stroked and squeezed her buttocks.

Suddenly, with no warning at all, a staggering pleasure erupted inside her, spreading hot throughout her body. She sagged in his arms, grateful for his strength. Otherwise, she knew she would have fallen in a heap to the floor.

He held her secure, supporting her weight as if it were nothing, then crushed his lips to hers. He kissed her long and hard, demanding her participation. She reciprocated as best she could, moaning as she let him drink his fill of her.

His breathing was coming in quick drafts by the time he raised his head. "God, you make me wild. I could lay you down on the floor and take you right here, right now."

He made her wild too. Why else would she be here with him like this? If he wanted her now, would she have the strength to deny him? Would she even wish to?

"It's getting late, though," he continued, his voice strained with clearly suppressed longing. "Our first time together shouldn't be some hurried coupling here in my study. When I take you to my bed, I want there to be no rush, no interruptions."

He brushed his lips over hers, once, twice, in slow, plucking touches. "I plan to be quite thorough with you, Rosamund Carrow. Any woman as passionate as yourself deserves to be satisfied to the fullest extent possible. What days do you have free this week?"

"What?" She blinked, confused by the question.

"Your schedule. Which days can you slip off by yourself for several uninterrupted hours? If I recall correctly, I've this Wednesday open."

"I—I don't know." She frowned, trying desperately to think, but he seemed to have driven all the sense out of her.

He laughed softly at her befuddled expression. "Don't fret. We'll figure it out later. For now, I suspect we need to get you home before your brother realizes you're not in the house."

It took a moment before the words sank in. Once they did, she stiffened in his arms. "What time is it?"

He angled his head to look at a small clock that sat on one of the shelves. "A few minutes shy of eleven."

"Eleven! Oh, dear Lord, I've got to go. He's rarely out past midnight and he'll be sure to hear the door if I get back after he does."

She pressed her hands against Lawrence's chest to extricate herself, lurching away as she looked wildly around for her discarded clothes. Off balance, she stumbled and might have fallen had he not reached out and caught her in time.

"Whoa there," he said, steadying her, hands on her shoulders. "It won't do to have you break a limb. Talk about spoiling all the fun." He smiled at her with amused reassurance. "Now take a deep breath, Counselor. Everything is going to be fine."

Her eyes were wide as they met his. "Will it?"

"Yes," he said with quiet authority. "We've ample time yet to see you safely across town."

She frowned. "Not if I have trouble finding a hack."

"You aren't taking a hack. I shall escort you home."

"But, Lawrence—"

"No arguments. I may be amenable to letting you continue your charade, but I won't have you traipsing around London alone at night."

"You're as bad as Bertram. As I keep reminding him, everyone who sees me thinks I am a man."

"Perhaps so, but even men are set upon by thieves and miscreants on occasion. I am accompanying you home." Gently he reached up and adjusted her spectacles so they sat straight on her nose. "Now, tuck your shirt in. Then I'll assist you with your neck cloth and coat."

"You need to put yours on as well." She eyed the open collar of his shirt, noticing the hint of golden chest hair that peeked over the lower edge.

"Indeed." He skimmed a fingertip across her flushed cheek. "But ladies first, even ladies who dress as gentlemen."

In under ten minutes, Lawrence had them both neatly attired once again. He'd even smoothed her hair and tied it back into its usual tidy queue.

With an efficiency she could only admire, he ordered his coach and in a few scant minutes more, the two of them were on their way. She leaned back against the plush upholstery, studying him through the darkness as an occasional streetlamp illuminated the interior.

From the seat opposite, he watched her as well.

"You're not going to be able to look at me like that when we're in company, you know," she murmured softly.

"And how am I looking at you?"

She hesitated before whispering, "Like you want to ravish me."

"That's because I do." A wicked smile spread over his face before he sobered again. "But I'll be careful. I promise. At least when we are not alone."

A small silence fell, the rhythmic rumble of the coach wheels rising to fill the void.

She ran nervous fingers over her trouser leg. "Lawrence, maybe this isn't such a good idea."

"What isn't?"

"You and me. What happened between us tonight. I think you may have the wrong impression of me."

"Really? What impression is that?"

She drew a shaky breath, wondering if she should go on. But she was the one who'd started this, so she couldn't very well refuse to answer now. "That I'm a bit of an adventuress, I suppose. Someone who is brave and bold and unafraid of the consequences, no matter how scandalous they might be. But I'm not. Neither am I the kind of woman who is in the habit of taking lovers."

"I know that."

"You do?" She couldn't help the sound of surprise in her voice.

He chuckled softly. "Unquestionably. I realized that the moment I kissed you. You're delightfully . . . untried."

"Then why?"

"Why do I want you?"

She nodded.

"That's simple enough," he answered. "You are without qualification the most fascinating individual of either sex I've met in a long time, perhaps ever come to that. Plus, you're remarkably beautiful."

"I'm not."

"Oh, but you are. Inside and out."

He shifted seats so that he was suddenly next to her. Leaning close, he took her chin between his fingers. "I know I probably oughtn't press you, shouldn't try to lure you into my bed where I can corrupt you in the most shameless of ways. But, you see, I just can't seem to help myself. You bring out the very devil in me, my dear Rosamund."

Her heart pounded, her breasts straining against their binding as if longing for his touch. As for the place between her legs, it was aching again, her flesh remembering.

His lips met hers in the dark for a soft, slow kiss that shook her to her core. It was only when he drew away that she realized the coach was no longer moving.

They had arrived.

He lowered his hand and drew back a couple of inches. "I shall await word from you, to let me know when we can meet."

"And if I change my mind? If I don't contact you?"

"Then I will be more disappointed than you can imagine. But regardless of your decision, your secret is safe, exactly as promised. Now, you'd best go inside before your brother returns from his evening out. I don't want you rousing his suspicions before we even have a chance to begin the next chapter of our association."

She stood, her legs wobbly beneath her. Somehow

she managed to climb safely down to the pavement before turning back.

"Good night, my lord," she said quietly.

"Good night."

She turned and made her way up the steps. As silently as possible, she inserted the key into the lock and opened the door. Behind her the coach was still waiting. Only after she was inside did she finally hear it drive off.

She leaned back against the door and released a shaky exhalation. Around her, the house was shadowed and silent, the servants all abed. She waited, half expecting to hear Bertram's familiar footfalls coming down the hallway.

But the house stayed quiet. He must still be out with his friends.

Knowing she had better not push her luck any further, she headed for the stairs and hurried up them. It was only after she was inside her bedroom with the door securely shut, her men's clothes stripped off and her nightgown pulled over her head, that she let her feelings give way.

Sinking down on the bed, she wondered what she was going to do. And whether she had the strength to resist both her heart and the siren call of her body.

Chapter 15

Lawrence escorted Phoebe Templestone off the dance floor, her small hand resting lightly on his sleeve. Other partygoers thronged around them, the air filled with a steady hum of conversation and the occasional clink of a glass now that the music for the last set had ended.

"What jolly good fun that was," she declared, a tiny pair of dimples appearing in her fair cheeks as she turned to smile up at him. As he knew, her dimples were much admired this Season, having inspired more than one ode from several foolish, lovelorn swains who were all vying for her affection.

"I adore dancing, especially the quadrille," she continued, her carefully coiffed blond curls bobbing attractively around her face. Her blue eyes were brilliant as a cloudless summer's day, her bow-shaped mouth sweetly pink. No one could deny, most certainly not himself, that she was beautiful—the epitome of the perfect English rose.

So why was it that he found himself dwelling on a

pair of serious, bespectacled gray eyes instead and a mouth that thinned with concentration, even as it begged to be kissed?

"Nothing is quite as delightful as the waltz, though," Phoebe said, intruding into his thoughts. "Papa says it's fast, but as I've remarked to him on more than one occasion, the patronesses at Almacks wouldn't allow young ladies to indulge in the practice were it not completely proper. Do you not agree, Lord Lawrence?"

He conjured a smile. "Indeed, I do. The patronesses are all that is wise when it comes to determining how a lady ought to conduct herself in polite society. That is why I have already secured the supper dance with you, which as you may recall just happens to be a waltz."

She gave a girlish giggle and fluttered her fan before her face.

The memory of a warm, full, throaty laugh played in his thoughts, teasing his senses in a way that warmed his blood. His mind drifted off again, delivering him inside his study and into a pair of lithe feminine arms, her lips moving against his with honest, unfettered need.

". . . think you might be there?"

He stared at Phoebe, aware that he had absolutely no idea what it was she'd just been saying. Quickly he cast about for an excuse, but none came easily to mind. "Your pardon, Miss Templestone. I beg your forgiveness, but might you repeat the question? I am afraid I heard only a portion of it."

A little frown creased the space between her pale eyebrows, and for a moment he wondered if she was going to take offense. But then she must have thought better of it, the smile returning to her mouth. "I was remarking on all the entertainments coming up soon and Lady Monkton's afternoon garden party this Wednesday. I wondered if you plan to attend."

Wednesday, the day of his and Rosamund's intended tryst. Not that anything was definite as of yet. It had been three days since he dropped her off at her town house and two since he sent word to her confirming that he would be at home all that day and would she grant him the very great pleasure of joining him there at half past eleven?

So far she had not written back.

He was beginning to wonder if she would and whether it had been a miscalculation to leave the decision entirely in her hands.

"Wednesday, you say?" he repeated. "Alas no, I am afraid I have a prior commitment that day."

She gave a small sigh. "Of course. Your work, no doubt."

He made no effort to correct her assumption.

"Despite your being a gentleman," she went on, "I know better than most the demands of a barrister's life. Papa is forever occupied with his legal duties and obligations in serving the court. I ought to have known you would not be able to put everything aside for a pleasure-filled day out."

No, but for a pleasure-filled day *in* with a certain someone, he found he could cheerfully spare the time.

Still, Phoebe looked so downcast he found he couldn't simply leave it at that. "You must allow me to make it up to you, Miss Templestone. A drive in the park on Saturday perhaps? The courts are closed that day, if you will recall."

She brightened instantly, her dimples popping out again. "A drive sounds lovely, Lord Lawrence. I shall be most happy to accept."

Just then a young man, who couldn't have been a day over twenty, appeared at their sides. He hovered anxiously, then bowed before darting a nervous look at Phoebe. "Pardon me, my lord. Miss Templestone, I believe the next dance is mine."

"And so it is," she agreed. "Lord Lawrence, if you will excuse me?"

Lawrence inclined his head. "Your servant, Miss Templestone."

She strolled away on the arm of her eager puppy of a dance partner.

He watched her for but a moment more before his thoughts turned back to Rosamund and their upcoming assignation. When he'd told her he would be seriously disappointed if she turned him down, she didn't know the half of it. He supposed he ought to feel like the worst sort of blackguard for offering her an affair. Yet he couldn't seem to help himself.

He wanted her that badly.

Besides, it wasn't as if she were some ingénue in her first blush of youth. She was a woman grown who presumably knew her own heart and mind. All he could do at this point, though, was trust she would give in to her own natural instincts and desires and come to him.

And if she doesn't?

Scowling darkly, he turned in the direction of the

room where his host's liquor cabinet was kept. Quite abruptly he found himself in need of a drink.

Rosamund focused on the legal brief in front of her, the office quiet where she and Bertram were working.

She'd been reading now for the past half hour and was no further along in her analysis of the facts than she had been when she sat down. The only thing she seemed to be able to focus on was tomorrow and whether to accept Lawrence's invitation.

Assuming one could call an indecent proposal an invitation.

An invitation to sin.

An invitation to revel in the most exquisite of corporeal pleasures.

She shifted on her chair, willing the intimate areas of her body to quit aching.

Good God, what has he done to me?

One time in Lawrence Byron's arms and he'd turned her wanton. And he hadn't even had to take off her clothes to do it! His kiss and touch alone had been enough to set her senses ablaze.

Yet bad as the days were, the nights were even worse, lying there in her bed thinking about him. As for her dreams, they were the worst of all, the Lawrence of her imagination doing the most wicked things to her body—or at least as wicked as she was capable of imagining.

Stop it, she chastised herself. *Concentrate on your work.*

But try though she might, the work was going undone and she couldn't seem to turn off her lurid thoughts. Not even the mortifying knowledge that her brother sat less than ten feet away seemed to have any effect on stemming the tide of her carnal fantasies.

Lord Lawrence Byron, she decided quite abruptly, was sin incarnate. A seducer so skilled she was sure he could tempt a nun to break every one of her vows and be glad of it afterward.

Yet Rosamund was no nun, even if she had spent most of her life living like one. She was a twenty-eight-year-old woman. A highly intelligent, exceedingly well-educated bluestocking who hadn't been courted by a man since her youth. Facts were facts—she was an old maid and would almost surely live out the rest of her days unmarried and childless. The most she would ever be able to hope for in that regard was assuming the role of doting aunt should Bertram decide to marry and have a family of his own.

Still, by some curious twist of fate, she had suddenly found herself the focus of a man's attentions again—and not just any man but a rich, handsome, debonair aristocrat who clearly had his pick of the most beautiful, interesting women in the city, if not the entirety of England itself.

True, he was a rakehell of the worst stamp, but somehow that only made him more intriguing. Yet was the near-certain pleasure she would discover in his arms worth the loss of her chastity and reputation?

Of course, chances were slim that anyone would ever find out about their affair, especially if they took care to be discreet. Lawrence was the son of a duke, while she was nothing more than the daughter of a middle-class lawyer. Except for the occasions when their paths crossed as barristers, the two of them moved in entirely separate realms—his world so distant from her own he might as well live on another planet. In that regard, she would likely be safe.

But there was also the matter of giving herself to him without benefit of marriage. She couldn't fault him for his honesty—he wanted her and he took no pains to hide it. As for behaving honorably . . . well, it had probably never even occurred to him to offer her anything more than an affair.

Not that she wanted him to. It wasn't as if she were any more in love with him than he was with her.

Still, were she a highborn woman of good family, she was sure he would never dream of making her such an indecent proposal. He would have either asked for her hand in marriage or simply let her go.

But she wasn't an aristocrat and he clearly did not feel bound to resist the temptation to bed her. Nonetheless, he had left the choice up to her. Had he wanted, he could have taken her the other night, there on the floor of his study. It was no secret that she wouldn't have stopped him.

Yet he hadn't.

He was waiting for her to decide.

She closed her eyes and swallowed against the desire still pulsing through her body. Remembering his kisses and the glimpses of heaven she'd known at his touch.

Could she deny him?

Could she bear to deny herself?

Should she even bother trying?

A minute ticked by, then two and three.

Suddenly, without giving herself any more time to consider, she reached for a blank sheet of stationery, quill and ink. Bending her head, she scrawled a few words, folded up the sheet, then sealed it with a glob of hot red wax.

She stood. "I'm going out for a few minutes."

Bertram looked up from his work. "To where?"

"I've a letter to post, and the boy has already come by today."

"I can put it with mine." He extended a hand. "I have a stack of correspondence myself that needs posting."

She shook her head. "Give me yours instead. I could do with a walk."

He studied her for a moment, then shrugged and leaned over to collect the bunch of letters on his desk. A small surge of relief went through her as she took them in hand, slipping the one to Lawrence onto the bottom where Bertram wouldn't have a chance to see it.

She gave him a quick smile, then made for the door.

"The post, my lord."

Lawrence looked up from his breakfast plate and newspaper the following morning to find Griggs, his butler, waiting, a silver salver with a quartet of letters resting on top. Lawrence acknowledged the man with a nod, took the mail in hand, then set it aside to return to his toast and eggs.

He picked the correspondence up again ten minutes later, riffling idly through as he sipped his coffee. Two were bills, one was an invitation to a ball he had no intention of attending and the last one was a complete mystery.

Setting his cup aside, he broke open the seal and read the few brief words inside. A broad grin spread slowly across his lips.

Rosamund had agreed and would join him here at his town house tomorrow, thirty minutes before noon.

Desire hummed through his body, anticipation turning him instantly hard. He gave himself over to the sensations for a minute, his mind filled with images of her lying flushed and naked in his bed.

He groaned low in his throat, knowing the day—and night—to come were going to be long ones.

Still, his mood had lifted, secure in the knowledge that she would soon be his.

In the meanwhile, however, he was going to have to get himself under control, particularly since he was due in court an hour from now. And if he couldn't manage, well, at least he had the consolation of knowing that he would be wearing robes.

Chapter 16

Rosamund had to force herself to step out of the cab the next day, her fingers half-frozen with nerves despite the sunny, late-morning warmth. She'd nearly changed her mind about coming, barely able to sleep last night for all her vivid, fitful dreams. Nor had she managed to choke down more than a single bite of breakfast and was too anxious even for tea. Yet here she was and right on time, Lawrence's town house looming large before her.

At least she hadn't had to deal with Bertram when she left. Her brother had had an early appointment with a client who lived just outside the city and he'd told her he didn't expect to return before evening. Really, matters could not have gone better if she'd arranged everything herself.

Even so, she might have turned coward now and retreated had the hack not driven away less than a minute after she arrived. Which meant there was no going back.

Not that she truly wished to call things off. Her

desire for Lord Lawrence was as strong as ever—her dreams last night were testament to that. No, she supposed her reluctance all boiled down to a fear of the unknown and the knowledge that after today, nothing would ever be entirely the same again.

Turning, she looked up at the front door with its glossy black paint. As she did, it opened, revealing not the butler as expected, but Lawrence himself.

He smiled invitingly, his gold-green eyes bold and possessive even from a distance. She pulled in a breath, excitement pushing aside a measure of her nerves.

Zounds, could he be any handsomer?

She moved up the steps and inside, an answering smile on her face. He shut the door behind her and closed out the world. To her surprise, he took her into his arms despite the fact that she was dressed as a man.

"You're here," he said huskily.

"I am. But where are your servants?" Glancing around, she tried to pull free, but he held her in place.

"Don't worry. I've given the staff the afternoon off," he said. "Except for a kitchen maid who apparently drew the short straw on the dinner preparation and a hall boy who I was informed is confined to his bed with head cold. Otherwise we've got the place to ourselves."

He leaned in for a kiss, but she stopped him with a hand to his chest. "Even so, perhaps we should wait until we're alone."

For a moment, she thought he was going to argue the point. Instead he lowered his arms to his sides. "Perhaps you're right. Given the way you're dressed,

I suppose we cannot be too careful. Come along, then."

He turned toward the stairs and started up. With her heart knocking loudly in her chest, she followed.

At the top of the landing, he turned left and led her along a corridor that was every bit as quietly sophisticated as the rest of the house. About halfway down stood a polished wooden door.

He opened it to reveal a spacious, decidedly masculine sitting room done in shades of royal blue, rich green and chestnut brown. There were a pair of comfortable, sturdy-looking chairs, side tables, a bookcase, a liquor cabinet and a sofa that was wide enough for a grown man to sleep on. Oil paintings hung from the walls, warm Turkey carpets lay across the wooden floor, while a pair of tall blue-and-white Chinese urns flanked a massive, central fireplace. Logs had been laid for a fire, but it was unlit at present; no coal fires for His Lordship apparently.

Golden midday sunlight streamed in through a number of large windows, sheer draperies pulled across to block the view of any curious neighbors. Beyond, through a connected door that stood half-open, she caught a glimpse of another generously sized room done in more of the same masculine colors and style.

Lord Lawrence's bedchamber, she presumed.

Without her conscious awareness, her hands fisted at her sides, her fingers still cold as a winter's day. Behind her, Lawrence closed the sitting room door, the hardware giving a faint, well-oiled click as the mechanism settled into place. A different click followed and she turned in time to see him rotate a key in the lock.

"So there's no chance of us being disturbed," he said by way of explanation.

She nodded, her breath shallow in her lungs as her earlier anxiety returned full force.

"Would you care for a bite to eat?" He gestured toward a few cloth-covered plates set on a sideboard that she hadn't noticed before. "I had the kitchen make us something before the staff left for the day. Sandwiches and fruit and a pitcher of lemonade. Somehow I didn't think beer or wine would be a good idea, considering how spirits affect you."

"No." Her voice sounded thin even to her own ears. "Nothing, thank you. I'm . . . not hungry."

"Maybe later, then. Afterward." He stepped closer. "What's wrong? You look quite pale." He reached for her hands. "God, your fingers are like ice. Here, let me warm them."

And he did, chafing them gently, one at a time, between his big, capable and very warm hands. She shivered, not from cold this time, but from his touch, which was every bit as lovely as she remembered.

"There's no need to be nervous," he said, his voice as warm as his hands. "It's only me."

She gave a faint laugh that burst out without conscious thought.

"Why is that funny?"

"It isn't. It's only that, I think that may be part of the difficulty."

He arched an eyebrow. "Oh? How so?"

She looked into his eyes, losing herself for an instant

in the glorious depths with their translucent rings and flecks of gold and brilliant green. "You're experienced," she murmured, "far more than I. You know what to expect. Despite what happened between us the other evening, I worry that I may prove a great disappointment to someone of your obvious sophistication."

His eyes widened with clear surprise, his head tipping to one side. "I assure you, my dear Rosamund, that is utterly impossible."

"But—"

"No buts. If anything, it is I who should worry about disappointing you."

"Why?"

"Because it's your first time. Or am I mistaken?"

A fresh shiver ran through her and she shook her head. "No, you are not mistaken."

Reaching up, he traced the tips of his fingers over her cheek and along her jaw. "Now it's my turn to ask you why. Are all the men you've known really so blind? You're a beautiful woman. I fail to see how one of them didn't scoop you up long ago."

She looked away, her lashes sweeping down. "There was someone once. He died. The war, you know, and we never . . . well, I was very young. So was he, come to that."

"And there's been no one since?"

She glanced up again. "I haven't wanted anyone since. At least not until . . . you."

His eyes darkened with a look of passion she was coming to recognize. He skimmed a thumb over the fullest part of her lower lip in a way that caused her to draw a quick, shaky inhalation.

"I suppose I'm an unprincipled rogue, tempting you to give me your innocence," he said. "Loath though I am to say this, it's not too late to change your mind. If you want, I can walk you back downstairs and put you in a coach. No harm done. But I confess that I would rather not."

She trembled, one of her hands held inside his as he continued to caress her mouth and cheek with his other.

"So, what will it be, Rosamund?" he asked. "Last chance to say no before I strip you bare and take you to my bed."

A harsh shudder went through her, sudden need burning in her veins like liquid fire. "Kiss me, Lawrence. Just kiss me."

He smiled. "I can think of nothing I'd rather do more. But first, let's dispense with these." Reaching out, he gently plucked the spectacles off her nose and set them aside. Next, he unfastened the tie at her nape, allowing her hair to swing free.

He combed his fingers through the strands, then eased them around to cradle her head in his hands. "Just like silk." Bending, he pressed his mouth lightly to hers. "And your skin." He angled his head in the opposite direction and feathered another kiss against her lips. "So soft."

And another. "So sweet."

One more. "So delicious."

Then suddenly he was kissing her with increasing intensity, each touch deeper and more demanding, every moment more exhilarating than the last. Sweeping her up into his arms, he lifted her off her feet. She clung, wrapping her arms around his neck as she kissed him back, all her fears falling away beneath the force of their mutual desire.

She opened her mouth and sought out his tongue, circling hers around his the way he'd shown her the last time they'd kissed. He answered in turn, tracing every silken corner of her mouth—teeth, tongue and lips— before demonstrating a new, even more intimate kind of joining that left her dizzy and desperate for breath.

Without warning, she was on her feet again, his fingers lacing with hers, as he pulled her after him toward the open doorway that led to his bedchamber.

Inside, he spun her around to face him, his fingers already busy with her neck cloth. He yanked it loose with a few deft tugs. After tossing it aside, he went to work on her jacket and waistcoat, freeing the buttons with a haste that left her faintly astonished.

Soon he dispensed with those as well.

And all the while, he kissed her—lips and cheeks, forehead and chin, nose, eyelids, temples and neck, scattering caresses over her skin with a seductive skill that made her toes curl inside her shoes and her pulse beat madly.

"Raise your arms," he commanded, his mouth brushing against her own as he spoke.

With her nerve endings sizzling, she obeyed, lost to him as he eased her shirt over her head. She lowered her arms again and stood, half-naked except for the bandeau of cloth bound tightly over her breasts.

He glided his hands across her collarbone and bare shoulders, then down her arms to her wrists, which he encircled between his thumbs and forefingers.

Taking a step back, he looked at her. "Why, you're as exciting as a present waiting to be unwrapped. Who knew I was going to get an early birthday gift this year?" A naughty, almost boyish grin lit his face, his eyes gleaming with prurient delight. "Hmm, shall we see what's inside?"

She made no effort to stop him, watching through half-slitted eyelids as he found and freed the small knot that held the cloth in place. Slowly he started to unwind it—around and around and around again. The process seemed to take forever, yet likely took no time at all, before he reached the end.

Then she stood exposed, faintly embarrassed when the tips of her breasts drew into tight peaks.

She closed her eyes, afraid to see his reaction. She'd never been one of those bosomy women who filled out a bodice to maximum effect. Not that she was flat-chested either, but what if he wanted more? What if she didn't live up to his expectations?

But she needn't have worried, she realized, when he cupped one of her breasts, cradling it tenderly in his palm as he rubbed a thumb back and forth over the aching peak. A throaty little gasp caught in the back of her throat, sensation spiraling outward in all directions. Her jaw slackened, tiny tremors running just beneath her skin.

"Like that, do you?" he asked, his voice silky with knowing.

Dazed, she could only nod.

"Good, since it only gets better from here."

He pinched her nipple and she cried out, a mixture of fear and excitement washing through her, along with the daunting knowledge that he just might be right.

Before she knew what he was doing, he stripped off his jacket, flung it aside, then dropped to his knees. Locking an arm around her waist, he pulled her to him and closed his mouth over the breast he'd just been fondling.

Her body flushed with heat and surprise, the sweet suction of his lips and tongue enough to turn her legs to jelly. Reaching up with his free hand, he began to play with her other breast, cupping and kneading it gently while circling the straining tip with his thumb in ways that drove her wild.

Without conscious thought, she buried her fingers in his hair and arched her back to press him closer. He responded, deepening his draws on her before flicking her nipple with his tongue.

He stunned her when he caught the throbbing peak between his teeth, simultaneously finding her other nipple with his fingers and pinching so she experienced both sensations together.

She quaked, making sounds she didn't even recognize as her own. With her fingers still lodged in his hair, caressing his scalp and neck, he switched breasts and began to repeat the same delicious torment he'd performed before.

Her mind whirled, growing muzzy, thoughts so indistinct she could scarcely remember her own name.

Then he was on his feet again, his mouth ravishing hers with frenzied ardor as he backed her toward the bed, then down.

She toed off her shoes and lay back against the

counterpane, captivated by the sight of him as he undressed, his fingers tearing at the silver buttons on his waistcoat with such haste that he popped one loose. He kicked off his own shoes next, then peeled his shirt from over his head to reveal a set of wide, powerful shoulders, long sinewy arms and a taut stomach that made her own clench with longing.

Her gaze wandered from the pelt of golden curls on his broad, muscled chest down to the slender arrow of hair that vanished beneath his trousers. She couldn't help but notice how it seemed to point directly toward the heavy bulge that strained impatiently against his falls. Clearly that part of him wanted to be set free.

She caught her lower lip between her teeth, breathless and on edge as she waited to see if he was going to accede to its demands.

Instead he came down on one knee beside her and stretched his long body out next to hers. "I don't want to get ahead of myself," he murmured, as if he knew exactly what she'd been thinking. "You're far too much of a temptation and I can't risk losing control."

She realized in that moment just how much larger and stronger he was. If he wanted, he could hurt her easily. But she had no fear, her trust in him absolute.

Unassailable.

As was her desire.

Heat rippled through her, burnishing her skin a translucent pink in the afternoon light that concealed nothing as he went back to palming her breasts and teasing her nipples.

Taking her jaw in one hand, he fell to kissing her again, pulling her under with long, slow, openmouthed drafts that sent her reeling. He drew her deep, then deeper still, down to a place where nothing and no one existed except the two of them.

Without realizing, she began to touch him, her hands moving over his hard muscles and sleek flesh as if trying to memorize each and every inch.

He shuddered and kissed her harder, thrusting his tongue in and out of her mouth. She moaned, writhing beneath him as she threaded her fingers into his hair again and responded with everything she had.

She didn't even know he'd unfastened her trousers until she felt his fingers glide over her naked belly, caressing her there for a moment, before they stole beneath the thin cotton of her men's drawers. Boldly he parted her legs and cupped her mound, eliciting a cry from her, then another as he parted her folds and eased a finger into a place where she'd never before been touched.

"God, you're tight and wet," he said, his breath warm against her ear. He scattered kisses along her cheek and throat, pausing to run the tip of his tongue along her nape. Below, he slid his finger deeper, up past his knuckle until his long digit was well lodged inside. "Let's see if we can get you even wetter. I want you good and slick by the time I take you."

Her inner muscles contracted around him as if in agreement, leaving her mortified yet amazed by the instinctual reaction of her body. Worse, she found she had no control, helplessly enslaved as he began to stroke her, sliding his finger in and out in a devastating rhythm that soon had her clutching handfuls of the counterpane beneath her. Her head rolled, her breath coming in gasps as blistering need surged through her, each beat more overwhelming than the last.

He eased out suddenly, only to return seconds later with two fingers. Her eyes went wide as he pushed in, his combined girth stretching her open in a way that was just short of pain. She gasped, but he smothered the sound as he covered her mouth with his. Soothing her with kisses, he coaxed her to accept his more forceful touch, giving her just enough time to adjust before he pushed her further. She moaned, quivering and arching into his hand.

She grew slicker; even she could tell the difference as her body relaxed to ease his way. Increasing his pace, he bent his head to suckle her breasts, laving each one before catching a puckered tip with his teeth.

Between her legs, he did something unexpected with his thumb, pressing a spot that shot a jolt of pleasure through her so strong it was as if she'd been struck by lightning. She shook and convulsed around him, a keening cry echoing through the room.

Her eyelids drifted closed, her body delirious with sensation.

But he wasn't done, she realized as he leaned up and moved her just enough to yank back the covers and lay her against the soft, faintly cool sheets. Then he stood and began stripping off what remained of her clothing, exactly as he'd promised he would.

She opened her eyes again in time to watch his pupils dilate, the black warring with the gold and green as he looked his fill of her naked body. She made no effort to hide herself, his earlier ministrations having apparently robbed her of the last of her inhibitions.

Arching sinuously, she stretched her arms over her head, pleased by the admiration she saw on his face.

His eyes flashed again and he smiled with a grin worthy of the devil himself. "I knew you'd be passionate. But you'd better be careful, my girl, or I may never let you out of this bed again."

"I may never want to leave, not after the things you just did to me," she said. Lowering one arm, she reached out a hand to him. "Come to me, Lawrence, I want you to show me the rest. I want you to teach me everything."

He made a sound like a growl, low in his throat, his eyelids heavy with lust as he unbuttoned his falls with quick, practiced movements and stepped out of the trousers, drawers and stockings.

Her breath caught at the sight of him, dazzled by his sheer masculine beauty. She guessed one wasn't supposed to describe a man as being beautiful, but he was, his lower half as impressive as the top. His flat, firm stomach tapered down to a set of narrow hips, long, finely proportioned legs and a pair of rather elegantly shaped feet—quite apropos for an aristocrat. His thighs were taut and heavily muscled—from riding horses, she presumed. As well as other things, she thought, with an unexpectedly naughty turn of mind. As for his buttocks, she couldn't catch much more than a glimpse, but they looked tight and undeniably tempting.

And then there was the expressly male part of him that jutted out from his body, providing her with the answer to her earlier question as to what lay at the base of that intriguing arrow of hair that started just beneath his stomach.

He showed not an iota of modesty as he stood before her, his shaft appearing to swell even more when he glanced up and caught her looking.

She swallowed, a little nervous despite her newfound confidence. She'd never seen a naked man before, and it was quite an enlightening experience. He was a large man and that part of him was as well. Fleetingly she wondered if all men were similarly endowed but rather doubted it, considering that Lawrence tended to outshine his peers in nearly every regard.

Then he was back in the bed, braced above her as he boldly fit a hair-roughened thigh between her own, his erection pressed hard and hot against her side. He ran a hand over one of her shoulders before trailing his fingers in a lazy slide down the center of her body—between her breasts and across her stomach before finding their way to the dark triangle of curls at the apex of her thighs.

She quivered and gazed up at him, her pulse hammering raggedly in her throat.

Angling forward, he lightly touched his lips to hers. "Don't turn coward on me now, dear Rosamund. We'll go at whatever pace you require . . . even if it ends up killing me."

"Mighten it?"

A quick laugh burst from his chest. "No. I'm only teasing you, sweet."

"Oh." He must have seen the renewed glint of the fear in her eyes, she realized, and sought to ease the tension.

She managed a smile, then reached up and laid her hand against his cheek to caress his smoothly shaven skin. His eyes closed and he turned his face into her palm and kissed her there. Opening his mouth, he drew a small wet circle in the center of her palm with the tip of his tongue.

She let out a ragged gasp as sizzling heat burst across her skin. Her arm and breasts seemed to catch fire too before the sensation made an impossible leap from the spot on her hand straight down to the place where his fingers were threaded in her distant curls.

Gently he began to stroke her there, remaining just on the surface without delving inside. As he did, he kissed and tongued her palm, using darting little licks and caresses that made her hand tremble against his mouth.

Yet she didn't pull away. She couldn't; it was simply too good to stop.

Her legs shifted against the thigh he'd settled between hers, sliding wider apart in order to give his fingers greater access. But to her frustration, he didn't take the bait, seemingly content to brush the tips of his fingers up and down in a leisurely glide rather than moving inside to satisfy the heavy inner ache that was building quickly within her again.

She whimpered and arched her hips, silently trying to communicate what she wanted, but he eluded her and went on with his infuriatingly teasing touch.

And he was teasing her, she suddenly realized. Playing with her in a game of sensual torment whose rules she barely understood.

"Quit it," she said, pulling her hand from his face.

"Quit what?" His eyes twinkled with false innocence.

"You know what."

He rubbed his fingers over her just then with a diabolical purpose that made her squirm.

"Ah gods, you're driving me mad." She involuntarily arched her hips, her body shimmying downward seemingly of its own accord to press herself more fully against his hand and thigh.

He eased back just far enough to deny her.

"Do you mean this?" He brushed her with his fingers again, dipping one briefly into the wetness gathered there before moving out again.

"Yes, you devil."

He chuckled. "And so I am. But then, you knew that before we began. Tell me what you want."

"You know what I want."

"Tell me something else."

Her breasts chose that moment to throb, the tips drawn up hard and red as berries. Still, the words stuck in her throat.

He tickled her down below again, rubbing his thigh tantalizingly between hers.

She moaned. "Kiss me."

Leaning low, he obliged, plundering her mouth with a slow yet blatant intimacy that spoke of far more than mere kisses. He made it last, taking her lips thoroughly, so that by the end she felt even needier than before.

"Anything more?" he said when he finally let her come up for air.

"M-my . . . You know . . . like you did before," she confessed shyly.

"You'll have to say the words. There are several 'you knows,' I'm afraid. It could be any one of them."

She wanted to curse him. "My breasts," she whispered.

"What about them?"

"Ooh, just wait. As soon as I'm able, I'm going to pay you back for this."

He grinned. "I look forward to it. Now, you were telling me about your breasts."

"Kiss them."

"Of course." Lowering his head, he gave her a few rather chaste little pecks that were lovely yet somehow managed to avoid the most sensitive parts.

"Not like that."

"Like what, then?"

"You know what. Take them in your . . . mouth. Suckle me the way you did before."

"With pleasure." Smiling, he bent his head and did as she bade, opening his mouth to feast on her with obvious relish.

The world spun away, his movements both dark and delicious. Her yearning doubled, her body ripe with unsatisfied hunger.

"More," she moaned, tangling her fingers in his thick, springy hair so that she could press herself more fully against him.

He obeyed, drawing on her with a quick, fierce suction that left her delirious.

Adrift, she ran her other hand up and down the length of his body, exploring the shape and texture of whatever she could reach—arm, shoulder and back. He was blazingly warm and hard and silky all at the same time, as was the male part of him that pressed insistently against her side.

Yet while he pleasured her above, he continued to torment her below, careful to let her inch closer to what she craved before drawing away again. Every so often, he would dip in a finger to brush across the ultrasensitive nub of flesh between her folds but lightly enough and only long enough to heighten her agony without appeasing it.

Racked with an almost violent longing, she bent one knee to the side and slid it upward against the sheets, opening her legs wider to give him more access. Her femininity throbbed, yearning with an emptiness that insisted on being appeased. She was wet too, so slick her inner thighs were damp from the excess moisture weeping from her core.

"Please," she begged, barely even aware she'd said the word.

He raised his head, his eyes heavy and dark, jaw clenched with barely controlled desire. "Please what? Tell me and I'll give it to you."

She met his gaze, realizing in that moment that he wanted her complete and unconditional surrender, as well as her unqualified participation in this ultimate act of possession.

"Take me, Lawrence," she said. "Please, just take me."

He stared into her eyes for a few seconds longer, then crushed her mouth beneath his with a kind of deep, quiet exhalation.

Kissing her still, he levered his body over hers, using his knees to nudge her legs even wider. Careful to keep a portion of his weight off her, he settled himself between her thighs, then guided himself firmly yet slowly inside.

It was good at first, so good she didn't know why she'd ever had any hesitation at all. She threw her arms around his shoulders and kissed him back, tangling their tongues together as she gave herself over to the pleasure.

He drew back, then pushed again, this time gaining twice the distance as before. She squirmed, aware of a sudden measure of discomfort, a feeling of being stretched a bit too much.

He hushed her with whispered words, letting her adjust before repeating the process again. Out and then in, then out and in again, thrusting deeper and more forcefully so he was lodged a bit more each time.

It was only then, though, that she became aware just how much farther he had to go, that he was actually barely inside her despite the continued sensation of being overstretched.

He kissed her slowly, tenderly, then moved his hands down to take hold of her hips, his fingers cradled around the pliant flesh of her buttocks. "I think there's only one good way to do this. Trust me?"

"Yes," she panted, not entirely sure what he meant.

"This is likely going to smart and I'm sorry for that. But it's your first time and you're just too tight for half measures. I promise it'll be good afterward, though. I'll make sure it's good."

In silent demand, he angled her hips so she was even more exposed to him. "Wrap your legs around me."

Doing as he asked, she hooked one leg around his hips and the other across his lower back, the new position forcing him a bit deeper.

Yet still it was not enough.

He claimed her mouth again, kissing her in long, sultry drafts that quickly swept her away, leaving her as spellbound with pleasure as she had been earlier. Sighing, she rubbed her breasts against his chest as he moved to nuzzle her neck, her nipples tight and tingling from the contact. A little hum of delight rose in her throat as she mindlessly glided her hands up and down the length of his back.

Then suddenly, with no real warning, he shifted his hips and pulled nearly all the way out, his hands tightening on her bottom to hold her in place. Gathering himself, he thrust into her using a single determined stroke that drove his shaft deep.

Pain burst through her and she gasped, her nails digging reflexively into his shoulders. She bucked her hips as her body instinctively fought against his intrusion, yet the movement had the contrary effect of seating him even more deeply within her. She panted and moaned, feeling impossibly and thoroughly impaled.

"Shh," he hushed, dusting kisses over her lips and cheeks and temples, then along her neck and ear. "It'll be better soon. Just be still."

As if I could even consider moving with him in me like this, she thought, squeezing her eyes closed against the discomfort.

He continued kissing her, gently, lightly, communicating with each touch his remorse at having caused her pain. It was only then that she noticed the way he was trembling, how his muscles were rigid with the effort to hold himself quiet.

"It's all right," she murmured, running a hand over

the back of his neck and into his perspiration damp-ened hair. "Go on. Do what you need to do."

He met her gaze, his eyes brilliant in the hazy sun-light that filtered past the curtains. "Not without you."

"I don't know if I can."

"Oh, you can," he said with complete confidence. "You will. I told you I would make certain of it."

She shivered and kissed him, forcing aside her doubts.

And that was when he began to move, slowly to start, as he did nothing more than rock their hips together. "All right?" he asked.

She nodded, surprised to discover it was true. The pain was still there but less intense, having faded to little more than a dull ache.

Sliding a hand between them, he sought out her breasts and began caressing them in all the ways she most liked, rolling and plucking at the already sensi-tized tips with a consummate skill that soon had her whimpering.

"Good?" he questioned.

"Yes." She nodded, her breath picking up speed at the same moment his hips began to move a little faster.

She shuddered, but with a different sort of discom-fort this time as he established an easy, shallow rhythm. Nascent tendrils of renewed need curled through her and he captured her mouth for a long, steamy, tempestuous kiss. She kissed him back, wel-coming the warm, wet thrust of his tongue in her mouth while she accepted the thick, heavy pressure of his shaft plunging in and out of her feminine core.

She tightened her hold and ran her hands over his shoulders and back before delving lower across the base of his spine to find the shifting muscles of his buttocks.

He arched and groaned, increasing his rhythm as he thrust even faster, his kiss turning wild.

And all she could do was hold on, pleasure and pain blurring into an indistinguishable line from which there was no return.

He reached down and shifted her hips again, angling her higher so she was forced to take more of him.

And she did, astonished that she even could, her body craving his now like a drug. She felt him everywhere, utterly engulfed and grateful for it.

She breathed in, the air thick with their mingled scents. Gasping out his name, she pressed her heels against his back as he drove her higher, then higher still. Her mind spun, senses dulling until there was nothing but the two of them left in the world.

His hands moved over her again, seemingly everywhere all at once before he trailed one across her breasts down to her stomach. He paused to dip a forefinger into her belly button, wiggling it in a way that made her jolt and cry out, pumping her hips hard into his.

She took him, more of him than she'd ever imagined her untried body could handle, yet still it wasn't quite enough.

Bliss lay just beyond her reach and she wanted it.

Wanted him.

"Lawrence, please," she moaned, need pouring through her hot as an inferno. Rolling her head and her hips, she whimpered, urging him on in a kind of delirium.

He reached lower to the place where they were joined, finding her there even while he continued to thrust fiercely in and out.

A high keening wail that had to be hers filled the air, her body shaking hard as intoxicating bliss crashed through her with the force of a riptide. Caught in the storm, she had no choice but to give herself over to it, letting the savage pleasure roar and swirl around her with a power as unstoppable as a hurricane.

She clung to Lawrence, adrift save for him, as he thrust inside her even faster, his shaft seeming, quite improbably, to thicken more. A heavy shudder went through him, his jaw tight, as he strained to claim his own pleasure.

Abruptly he gave a hoarse shout and pulled out of her, pumping his hips once, then twice more before his seed spurted from his shaft in warm, wet arcs. A few droplets landed on her stomach, the rest across the sheets.

With a groan, Lawrence collapsed beside her. He lay unmoving for a brief interval as they each fought to reclaim their breaths. Reaching out, he drew her close, curving an arm over her shoulder and leaving a hand draped across one breast.

Delirious and deliciously exhausted, Rosamund smiled and closed her eyes.

Chapter 17

She was still floating a short while later as glorious after-echoes continued to ripple through her system. Occasionally one of her muscles would give a tiny twitch while blood continued to pump inside her arteries and veins with the force of a rushing river.

Gradually awareness began to return, along with a renewed sense of where she was, as well as the knowledge of everything she and Lawrence had just done.

She ought to have been shocked—and there was no denying that a good portion of her was. Yet she couldn't deny the thrill of it all or the curious sense of freedom she'd found in their intimacy. For despite her shyness and inexperience, there had been moments when she barely recognized herself, the woman in his arms turning out to be just as daring and passionate as he'd declared her to be.

Still, she didn't know how she was ever going to be able to look at him without blushing. Or manage to conceal the desire she knew must show in her eyes.

For even as unquestionably satisfied as she was at present, a part of her was already wondering how soon they could do it again.

Assuming he wanted to be with her again.

They hadn't talked about anything past today. Maybe this one time was enough for him.

Then there was the way he'd withdrawn at the end, spilling himself on the sheets rather than inside her body.

She didn't think he'd been disappointed; he was holding her close now. But maybe he simply felt guilty for having taken her virginity. Perhaps, in the end, her inexperience had turned out to be more of a bother than he'd anticipated and not worth the trouble in retrospect.

She frowned.

She must have made some sort of sound as well, since he turned his head to look at her. "Are you all right?" he asked.

She nodded, refusing to meet his eyes.

She could sense him watching her, studying her. Slowly, gently, he eased away and slid out of the bed.

She closed her eyes again, wondering where she was going to find the strength to get up, locate her clothes and dress. Would he want her to leave right away? Or would he at least give her some time to put herself back together again before he ushered her out of the door?

She heard the sound of water being poured.

Was he washing? Bathing away the traces of her?

But then he was there again, standing beside the bed. She opened her eyes to find him holding a towel and a basin, the latter of which he set down on a nearby bedside table.

"You must think me a brute," he murmured, remorse clear on his face.

"Why would you say that?"

His gaze moved down her body, stopping when it reached her pelvis and legs.

It was only in that moment that she saw the blood, crimson smears of it staining the sheets with more on the inside of her thighs. There was blood on him as well, his own thighs and shaft tinged a peculiar red.

"Oh!" she said with abrupt understanding.

"Exactly." Carefully he sat down next to her, the mattress dipping as it took his weight. "How badly have I hurt you?"

"You haven't. I didn't even notice . . . this . . . until you pointed it out." She reached out, wanting to reassure him. "I'm fine. Truly. It's only to be expected, being that it was my first time and all."

A panoply of emotions chased across his features as he considered her words. "I suppose you're right. It is to be expected, especially given how narrow you were."

Her inner muscles flexed at the reminder, her body recalling the brief pain, then the exquisite pleasure, of his possession.

He met her eyes. "I confess I haven't much experience initiating virgins. You're only my second and I was a green boy with the first. It was all a great deal of hasty fumbling as I remember and not terribly satisfactory for either one of us. Since then, I've confined myself to women who know the game." He took hold of her offered hand and bent to kiss her palm. "It would seem you are the exception to the rule."

"And was I—" she began, wishing as soon as she began that maybe he hadn't heard her.

But of course he had. "Were you what?"

Her heart hammered and she forced herself to speak. "Satisfactory? Seeing as I'm not what you usually prefer."

"Is that what you've been lying here puzzling over?"

She flushed, not only her cheeks turning pink. She started to turn away, but he caught her and held her still, a hand on her chin so she couldn't avoid his look.

"Did you not listen earlier when I told you what an absolute impossibility that was?" he said. "Believe me, you were much more than satisfactory, Rosamund. You were stellar. This day with you is one I shall never forget, not even if I live to be as old as Methuselah."

Her flush changed from one of shame to pleasure. "Really?"

"Yes, really." He laughed. "You know, for someone of your keen intellect and cunning legal mind, you can be remarkably silly sometimes."

"I am not silly."

He grinned, then winked. "You keep telling yourself that, my dear. Now lie back again and let me clean you up."

"Oh, I can do that." She started to lean forward, but he gently pushed her back down again.

"No." He gave her a possessive look that permitted no disagreement. "I shall do it. Though, if you like, you can do me afterward."

Her eyes turned round, her body getting hotter—
and pinker.

He laughed again, the carefree sound filling the room.
Chuckling still, he dipped the towel in the basin.

She fought the urge to be embarrassed as he
cleaned her, which, she admitted, did seem rather silly
considering everything they'd done together in his
bed. He was infinitely tender, taking care to cause her
no further discomfort, the cool water soothing against
her most delicate parts. He even washed her stomach
where the evidence of his satisfaction still lay.

"May I ask you something?" she whispered.

He glanced up. "Of course."

"Why did you . . . at the last . . . you—" She broke
off, shaking her head as her daring disappeared.

"Why did I what?" He dropped the cloth in the
bowl, the water now tinged pink, then turned back.
"Tell me. We're lovers now, which means there is nothing too intimate to ask." He stroked a hand across her
damp thigh. "Or to want."

She drew a breath, then plunged ahead. "Why did
you pull out of me before you . . . ."

"Climaxed?" he offered helpfully.

She nodded.

He looked at her for a moment as if the answer
should be obvious. "I'm trying to keep you from getting with child," he said softly.

"Oh."

Well, of course, she thought, feeling like a complete
dolt. She ought to have thought of that rather important consideration long ago, she realized. Yet some-

how, despite all her agonizing over whether to give herself to him today, it hadn't really occurred to her that she ran the very real risk of getting pregnant.

"You must think I'm the stupidest woman alive," she said.

"We both know that's not true."

"The most naive, then."

He stretched out beside her and leaned in to kiss her. "The sweetest." He touched his lips to hers again. "You're sweet. And very trusting."

"A ninnyhammer. Yes, I agree."

"Don't be hard on yourself. It's my job to look after you and see to such matters. After all, I am the one with the experience, as you so rightly pointed out. Which is why I've already taken the liberty of obtaining some herbs from a chemist I know. You should begin taking them immediately. The compound won't absolutely prevent conception, but if we're careful, it should do the job."

"So we're going to continue . . . seeing each other, that is."

He stilled. "Well, of course we are." A scowl creased his forehead. "Unless you don't want to."

She ran a hand over the length of his arm. "Yes, I want to. I just didn't know if you would."

A peculiar glint shone in his eyes. "So you thought I'd lured you here today to steal your maidenhead, then callously send you on your way?"

"No . . . well, I wouldn't put it like that exactly. I just wasn't sure how long you'd . . . if you'd want to continue seeing me past today."

He rolled his eyes skyward and shook his head with

a rueful laugh. "Remind me to always be brutally honest with you so there are no misunderstandings."

Claiming her mouth again, he left her in no doubt of his continued passion. "Believe me, Rosamund, I plan to fuck you well and thoroughly every chance I get. You must be sure to send me your schedule and I'll send you mine so we can make the necessary arrangements."

She quivered at his blunt talk, knowing she ought to be scandalized. Instead reawakened desire curled inside her like tendrils of hot smoke.

"Oh, look," he said, "it would seem I'm ready again right now."

She glanced down at his heavy erection. "You haven't even finished washing."

"I haven't, no."

She hesitated for only a moment. "Lie back. I'll do it."

Smiling, he did as she instructed, folding his arms beneath his head.

She sat up and reached for the cloth. After wringing it out, she turned back.

"You know, if you're sore," he said conversationally, "there are other things we can do."

"Really?"

He chuckled at her obvious enthusiasm. "Definitely." Reaching for her hand, he guided her fingers and the wet cloth around his shaft. "Let me show you."

The remainder of the afternoon passed in a curious blending of fast and slow—or at least that was how it appeared to Lawrence—with some moments so intensely gratifying they seemed to move in a kind of delirious, syrupy haze while others flashed by, quick as lightning. Yet far sooner than he would have wished, he and Rosamund were dressed again and he was kissing her good-bye.

She'd refused to let him accompany her home in his coach, insisting on taking a hack in case her brother had arrived back earlier than planned. He'd wanted to argue but had given in, knowing her caution was well advised.

Afterward, he'd gone to his study, intending to work. But he'd soon realized it was no use, his mind drifting back to Rosamund again and again.

All told, it had been a day unlike any he'd ever known, filled with passion, pleasure and discovery. In some peculiar respects, it had almost felt like a wedding night—or wedding *afternoon*, he thought with a bemused smirk.

After another highly satisfying bout of lovemaking, during which he'd taught Rosamund a couple of new tricks that had left them both limp with blissful exhaustion, they had roused themselves long enough to slip into robes—she'd borrowed one of his—and adjourn to his private sitting room.

There, they'd feasted on the cold meal awaiting them, eating every last crumb with great gusto. While they'd dined, they talked, conversation flowing easily from one topic to another with nothing too abstruse or out of bounds to mention, the natural rapport between them stronger than ever.

In the past, he'd never had much inclination to converse overly long with his mistresses, since their idea of good conversation tended to focus almost exclusively on the latest fashions, how he thought they might look wearing them and the juiciest social gossip. Not that those couldn't be amusing subjects at times, but as a steady diet, he preferred weightier topics. No, his mistresses provided him with energetic, mutually satisfying sex, while he provided them with clothing, housing and gifts—jewelry being a particular favorite.

Yet somehow he didn't think Rosamund would take kindly to him giving her a diamond necklace. She'd just as likely throw it at his head, followed by a burst of her finest invective. No, she most definitely was not his typical mistress, assuming he could call her his mistress at all. He supposed "lovers" was the best way to describe this new relationship of theirs, their affair entirely unique, exactly like Rosamund herself.

When he told her he'd previously confined himself to sexually experienced women, he hadn't been lying. Yet as he thought about the afternoon just past, he couldn't deny the deep, almost visceral pleasure he felt in knowing he'd been her first. She belonged to him now in a way she never would to any other man.

The knowledge alone was enough to turn him hard as a pikestaff again; he wished she hadn't needed to leave. Then again, maybe it was for the best, since she needed time to rest after her enthusiastic initiation today. Had she been closer at hand, he wasn't sure he could have resisted the temptation to take her again no matter how sore she might be at present.

A part of him wished he could set her up in a house here in London. Somewhere nice—Half Moon Street perhaps—where he could come and go as he pleased and make love to her as often as both of them desired.

But she wasn't that sort of woman, and to offer her such an arrangement—even if she weren't currently disguising herself as a man and practicing law as a barrister—would debase the very essence of what and who she was.

Instead he would have to confine himself to clandestine rendezvous and stolen moments when and wherever they could manage them. Considered in those terms, he supposed, the uncertain nature and delayed sexual gratification of the arrangement would only serve to heighten the pleasure when they did manage to meet.

He only hoped he could stand to wait out the times in between.

Before she'd left, she'd promised to meet him again soon, but they hadn't agreed on the particulars. She would contact him, she'd said, since that way they ran less risk of alerting her brother to their affair. Lawrence had wanted to pin her down then and there but realized he would have to leave the ball in her court, so to speak.

Deceiving her brother bothered her, though, he knew. He'd glimpsed the guilt in her eyes whenever his name was mentioned. But keeping this from Bertram Carrow was essential, since Lawrence knew the other man wouldn't take kindly to his dallying with his sister, no matter whether she was past the age of consent or not.

And so Lawrence would be patient.

He only hoped he didn't need to be patient for long.

Chapter 18

"Feeling better?" Bertram asked her the next morning from across the breakfast table. "I missed you at dinner last night. Mrs. Banks said you came home with a headache and took supper in your room. You're not coming down with a c-cold or anything like that, are you?"

"No." Rosamund busied herself spreading butter on a piece of toast. "It was only a headache, but I'm much recovered now."

She kept her eyes lowered as she reached for the strawberry jam, pushing aside the guilt she felt for lying to him.

"That's good." Bertram ate a forkful of sausage and eggs. "Summer colds are the very devil."

"They are, yes." She bit into her toast and concentrated on composing her features. "So, did your business go well yesterday?"

She sipped from her cup of hot tea and continued eating her toast while he launched into a lively recounting of his journey and the day's events. Idly she listened, nodding at appropriate intervals as her thoughts spun backward to the hours she'd spent with Lawrence.

Somehow, in the bright light of day, it all seemed rather fantastical, as if she'd dreamed the whole thing.

Only she knew she hadn't.

For one, she could never have imagined half of the shocking, intimate details that kept playing in her memory: the glorious slide of his hands roaming everywhere over her body; the dark, forbidden bliss of his mouth and tongue as he kissed her; and most convincingly of all, the stunning fulfillment of having him lodged heavily inside her as he brought her the most exquisite pleasure she'd ever known.

Still, if that weren't proof enough, there was the lingering soreness between her legs that not even a hot soak in a slipper bath had been able to completely relieve—the undeniable physical proof that she was no longer an untouched maiden.

Yet shameful as she supposed some might deem her behavior, there was nothing she would change about yesterday. Lying in Lawrence's arms had been beautiful, one of the most wonderful experiences of her life and one she could not wait to repeat.

Her only regret, if she had one, was the necessity of having to keep it all secret from Bertram. She hated deceiving him, since they had always been honest with each other. But he wouldn't understand or approve, and she wasn't about to break things off with Lawrence, not now, when everything was so new, so good.

Later, at some point, she and Lawrence would have

to part. It was inevitable and not even she was naive enough to think otherwise. But for now she planned to enjoy herself to the fullest, revel in the thrill and sheer, unbridled intensity of the passion she knew she would discover in his arms.

At least he'd already proven himself to be a conscientious and considerate lover. Even now she felt like an utter cloth head for not thinking of something as obvious as the possibility that she could find herself with child. She was usually so practical, so rational. But apparently Lawrence drove all such considerations straight out of her mind.

She was grateful for the herbs he'd pressed into her hands before she left his town house yesterday. It was one less thing over which she would need to worry.

She'd taken the first dose last night, brewed into a tea per the instructions. She would take a cup every night from now on for however long she and Lawrence remained lovers. Luckily she was already in the habit of taking tea in her room each evening, so no one would think anything of her new herbal concoction.

As for her and Lawrence's next tryst, she had yet to figure out a good day and time. He'd mentioned exchanging schedules. She would take a few minutes to copy hers out; then she would need only to figure out how to get it into his hands.

"—don't you agree? Roz?"

"Yes?" She looked up with a start. "What?"

Bertram cocked his head. "I asked what you think about my taking Talbert on more permanently. Were you not attending?"

She sent him an apologetic smile. "Sorry, I'm afraid I wasn't."

He frowned. "You're sure you're not coming down with something? If you need to spend the day abed—"

"I'm well, honestly. Mayhap just a little residual tiredness, that's all. Again, I apologize. Please tell me what you were saying about Mr. Talbert and I promise to listen with all attentiveness this time."

Bertram studied her quizzically as though he weren't entirely convinced by her explanation. Then, just as abruptly, his expression cleared.

She breathed a quiet sigh of relief as he began repeating the salient points of everything she'd missed. This additional layer in her new life of deception was going to prove challenging, she realized, particularly here at home.

But she would manage.

Somehow.

Lawrence thumbed to the reference page he needed, then compared it to a point of law in a brief he'd recently agreed to take on.

The four rooms that made up the law library at Lincoln's Inn were quiet for a Friday afternoon with only a handful of other attorneys scattered about. It wasn't surprising, since most of the courts had let out for the day, which meant his compatriots had either gone home or else nipped off for drinks and a round of convivial conversation with their friends.

Lawrence could have done so as well, but he'd decided to take advantage of the lull to get ahead on some of his cases, given that he was promised at a number of entertainments over the next couple of days. There was also his agreement to take Miss Templestone driving in the park—a commitment he'd nearly forgotten about until he saw the notation scrawled in his engagement diary.

He'd noticed it yesterday when he sat down to write out a schedule of his free time. He'd considered sending it to Rosamund but had erred on the side of caution and tucked it into his work folio instead. He had it with him now, in fact, though he didn't see when he'd ever have a chance to pass it along to her—not if she didn't contact him.

But he supposed he was being unduly impatient. Only two days had passed since she'd spent the afternoon in his bed.

Letting him sheath himself in her body.

Giving him her innocence, her absolute trust.

Scowling, he tapped the edge of his pencil against his notes, wondering where she was and what she was doing.

Has she been thinking about me? God knows I've been thinking about her.

Far too much, as it would happen. Far more than he could remember thinking about any woman for a very long time—perhaps ever, come to that.

Looking down at the brief, he forced himself to concentrate on the task at hand.

He'd been at it for perhaps five minutes when he sensed someone standing behind him. He startled as the person leaned close and blew lightly in his ear.

"Good afternoon, my lord."

"Rosamund." He whipped his head around.

"*Ross,*" she admonished in a whisper. "We're in public, remember?"

Lawrence scanned the room, which contained only three other lawyers now, all of whom were seated at tables some distance away. "Don't worry. They can't possibly have heard me."

"Maybe not." She dropped onto the chair next to his. "But it won't do to let down our guard."

He gazed into her silvery eyes. "Right."

She gave him a slow smile.

"That won't do either, you know," he said, his tone warm with amusement.

"What?"

"The way you're looking at me. Like you wish I was inside you this very moment."

Her cheeks turned pink. Then she surprised him. "Maybe I do."

He turned instantly hard, his fingers tightening dangerously around the pencil in his hand. "So, are you here to do research or did you come just to torture me?"

"Actually I came in hopes of arranging our next meeting." She shifted in her seat and reached for the leather binder that he only then noticed she'd laid on the table. "I asked in your chambers and they told me you were here, so I thought I'd take a chance and see if you might remember your schedule well enough to decide on something."

"I can do one better." Thumbing through his folio, he brought out a page covered in his own strong, dark handwriting. "All the dates and times I have free for the next three weeks."

She slid a page out of her binder and placed it beside his. "This is mine."

They both bent their heads and began to compare.

"You're frightfully busy." She sighed.

"You are as well. I thought the last of your father's old cases were going to be resolved in the near future."

"They're supposed to be, but the few that remain are rather involved. You know how these matters can drag on for far longer than anticipated."

"Indeed."

They resumed their analyses.

"Thursday afternoon seems most likely," Lawrence said a brief while later.

"Yes, I don't see anything sooner. Shall I come round at half past one that day?"

"Why not make it one? Unless you think you'll have trouble slipping away sooner. No point wasting half an hour. There's any number of pleasurable things we can get up to in half an hour's time."

Heightened spots of color dusted her cheekbones, her rosy lips parting on a silent inhalation.

"God, you've no idea how much I want to kiss you right now," he whispered.

"You've no idea how much I want you to."

He glanced around, then got to his feet. "Delay a minute, then follow me."

"What?"

"Just do it."

Without giving her a further chance to react, he strode away.

"Lawrence," she hissed quietly after him.

Rather than looking back, he kept walking, then

disappeared into an adjoining room lined floor to ceiling with books. He was pleased to find it empty, even if it wasn't his ultimate destination. As soon as Rosamund appeared in the doorway, he moved on, leading her through the room, past a portrait of a scantily clad woman holding a bleeding heart pierced through with a dart, then out into a hallway that led to the benchers' rooms.

He stopped several doors down on the right, then turned the handle. Waiting only long enough for Rosamund to slip in after him, he closed the door and shut the two of them inside. As soon as he did, he cradled her face between his palms and crushed his lips to hers, pressing her back against the door as he kissed her with impassioned zeal. She responded instantly, matching his ardent embrace, touch for touch, kiss for kiss, as she wove her arms around his back to draw him closer.

He drank her in, intoxicated by the honeyed taste of her mouth, the clean scent of her skin that was as pure and bright as spring sunshine. His senses reeled, desire burning inside him, hot and unpredictable.

He ran his hands over her body, seeking her breasts, only to find them hidden beneath their cloth binding. Frustrated, he moved on to fondle the lush curves of her bottom. Flexing his fingers, he lifted her up, high enough to fit the rigid length of his arousal against her soft mound. He swallowed her ragged moans of longing with his mouth as he rocked himself against her.

She quivered and kissed him harder, her tongue mating with his in a sleek, seductive dance that proved just how quick a learner she really was. His pulse beat in a crazy staccato, hunger pushing aside any sense of logic or caution. He reached for the buttons on her trousers and slid his hands inside, preparing to push them down.

Just then men's voices sounded outside in the hallway, growing louder as their footfalls came near.

He and Rosamund froze, their lips growing slack, breathing ragged as they waited in a paroxysm of suspense. Yet as quickly as the men had arrived, they passed by, their voices fading as they moved out of earshot.

"That was close," Lawrence whispered, his heart rate slowing but only slightly, given her continued intimate proximity—that and the fact that his hands were still inside her trousers, palms pressed over her hipbones.

She nodded and expelled a silent breath.

He fanned his thumbs across her satiny skin and dusted a kiss over her mouth. "So? Where were we?"

She pulled back as far as she could, considering he had her wedged between himself and the door. "Surely you can't mean to go on? Not after that," she said.

"They're gone. We're safe."

"But what if they come back?" She shook her head. "We could get caught."

"We won't. This room belongs to old Hopkins. That's why I chose it in the first place. He leaves every afternoon at three, so there's no danger of anyone finding us in here." He began kissing her again, dappling her chin and cheeks and forehead with softly scattered pecks.

"Even so, what if someone hears us? We had no difficulty hearing them just now."

Catching her earlobe between his teeth, he sucked on it for a moment before giving it a quick nip. She whimpered and arched her pelvis against his.

"Almost everyone is gone for the day." He traced the outline of her ear with his tongue. "We'll just have to be extra quiet."

"I don't know, Lawrence."

Controlling her hips, he circled her on his straining erection. "Don't you want me?"

She shuddered. "Of course I do. But we can't. Not here. There's not even a bed."

"We don't need a bed. Although we might wreck Hopkins's desk, since he's not the tidiest broom in the closet."

Almost in unison, he and Rosamund glanced toward the piece of furniture under discussion. He noticed the overflowing mounds of paper and books stacked on its surface, as well as around the room in general.

Inwardly he groaned, realizing she might have a point. He could always take her against the door— which he was randy enough to accomplish at the moment—but if he did that, there would most definitely be noise.

He closed his eyes briefly. "Christ, Rosamund, I can't bear to wait until Thursday. Can you?"

"No," she admitted. "But I don't see that we have much choice."

He concentrated, running options through his head

until he suddenly hit on something. "What time do you have to be home?"

"Today?"

"Yes, today."

"Five thirty. Six at the latest. Bertram's rarely much later than that."

He glanced at the clock that ticked quietly in one cluttered corner. "That gives us nearly an hour and a half. Not enough time to go to my town house and back, but this should work nonetheless."

"What should work? Where are you taking me?"

"You'll see." Quickly, so as not to squander their time, he moved away enough to fasten the buttons on her trousers that he'd so recently undone, then reached up to smooth her hair. If only he could as easily do something about the obvious bulge in his own trousers, but he was a grown man, so it was hardly the first time he'd found himself with an inconvenient stiffy in public.

"You go back out and gather up your things, then wait for me near the entrance. I'll follow after as soon as it seems prudent."

Tiny lines creased her brow. "Are you certain about this? We won't get caught wherever it is you're taking me?"

He kissed her. "We won't. Promise."

Cracking open the door, he listened for a few seconds, then waved her into the hall. He waited, listening to her own quiet footsteps recede. Once they did, he counted down one minute, then two before listening again at the door. With everything silent, he let himself out.

Chapter 19

Rosamund loitered as inconspicuously as possible just inside the entrance to Number 2 Stone Buildings, wondering how much longer Lawrence was going to be and whether she wouldn't be better off simply going home on her own rather than embarking on this crazy impromptu assignation.

Only she couldn't quite make herself go, the thought of deserting him—and worse, not being able to see him again for nearly a week—nearly unendurable.

Besides, she wanted him.

Badly.

Heavens, what dark magic has he worked upon me that I've turned so wanton?

And so she waited, grateful there were so few barristers in the library building this afternoon.

Suddenly Lawrence was there, his face devoid of expression except for his eyes, which brimmed with a mixture of devilment and desire.

What is it exactly that he has planned?

But then she had no further opportunity to specu-
late as he stepped out onto the pavement and gestured
for her to follow. They walked to the next street and
turned a corner, where a private coach waited—his
coach, apparently.

Lawrence motioned for the driver to retain his seat
on the box while Rosamund opened the door and
climbed inside. Lawrence spoke briefly to the coachman, though she couldn't hear what was said before
he got inside, shut the door and took a seat beside her.

"Where are we going?" she asked as the coach set off.

He looked at her. "To your house ultimately. For
the time being, he's going to drive around. I told him
we had business to discuss."

"Do we have business to discuss?" she asked uncertainly.

"We definitely have business." He reached out and
drew the curtains firmly closed over both windows
before turning back to her. "As for the discussion, I
suspect it will prove rather minimal."

He pulled her into his arms and found her lips.

"Here?" she gasped between kisses, a ripple of
astonishment running through her as the truth dawned.

"I told you there isn't time to go to my town house,
you vetoed old Hopkins's room and obviously your
house won't do, so this seemed a good solution." Locating the buttons on her waistcoat, he began to free them.

"But a coach? Where will we—" She glanced around
at the finely upholstered, admittedly well-sprung seats
that were generously sized but not enough for both of
them to lie down flat—not comfortably at least.

"We'll manage—you'll see." He tugged her shirt

free of her trousers, his lips traveling seductively along her jaw, then onward to find a spot behind her ear that never failed to drive her mad. It didn't fail this time either, her nails digging reflexively into his arms as tingles chased over her skin.

"Won't the coachman hear us?" she murmured.

He found her mouth again, sucking on her lower lip for a moment before giving it a nip. "The city sounds should drown everything out so long as we don't make too much noise." His fingers slipped under her shirt and got to work untying the binding around her chest. "Though if you feel the urge to scream, I recommend using your cravat or mine to muffle the sound. The knot can make an excellent gag."

Her eyes popped wide at the lurid suggestion, but then she forgot all about it as he crushed his mouth to hers and brazenly began to plunder.

Moaning, she kissed him back, weaving her fingers into his hair to draw him closer. He eagerly complied, ravishing her mouth with deep, silken strokes of his tongue that demonstrated in no uncertain terms what he planned to do to her body.

She shifted on the seat—restless yearning unfurling low in her belly and between her legs, demanding to be appeased.

Suddenly the binding around her chest loosened slightly. But rather than unwrapping her as he had done the last time, he reached up and hastily shoved it down so her breasts popped free. One hand covered her, fondling her breast with a practiced ease that made her realize yet again just how inexperienced she still was and how much she had yet to learn.

Shoving up her shirt, he bent to take her into his mouth, suckling gently at first and then harder as he pressed her hardened tip between his teeth and tongue. He lavished attention on one breast, then the other in a sizzling rhythm that made her senses whirl.

Abruptly he broke off. "We haven't time for over-indulgence." His voice was husky with undisguised longing. "Let's move on to the second course."

Before she could imagine what he meant, he sat up and plucked her off the seat to stand her before him, careful to make certain she was in no danger of falling as the coach swayed along its path.

"Shoes off," he said, his hands at her waist.

"What?"

"Kick your shoes off."

Silently she did as he told her.

"Now put your hands on my shoulders."

"Why?" she asked, even as she leaned forward to comply.

"So I can do this." In a flash, he undid her trouser buttons, then shoved her trousers and drawers down so they puddled at her ankles.

"Step out," he ordered.

"But, Lawrence," she whispered, feeling extraordinarily exposed of a sudden.

He gave her a lascivious grin. "I've seen everything before, you know."

"Yes, but not inside your coach."

A rumbling laugh shook his chest as he lifted her stockinged feet free of the cloth one by one. Picking up the garments, he tossed them haphazardly onto the seat opposite, then turned his attention back to her.

He brought his palms up to cup her naked buttocks, then slid them along the backs of her thighs, making whorls of heat burst over her flesh.

The coach swayed, rocking them both from side to side. She tightened her grip on his shoulders as he nudged her feet apart. He kept touching her, sliding his hands up and down and around but never where she most longed to be touched. Moisture collected between her legs, bedewing the dark curls that grew there.

Finally he slipped a finger into her, inserting it slowly, then circling it around. "Any tenderness?"

"No." She panted, her thighs trembling.

He eased out, then pushed in two fingers, slowly again but deeper this time. "How about now?"

"N-no."

"And now?" He scissored his fingers open, drawing a rough cry from her throat.

She shook her head, unable to speak.

"Good. You've healed quickly."

Rather than continue to pleasure her, though, he eased his hand free. She whimpered with frustration.

But he wasn't done surprising her as he took hold of her hips and sat her down on the seat, pausing for a moment to spread a handkerchief beneath her.

"Brace your hands and wiggle forward a little," he said.

Too awash with need to question him, she complied. Even so, she gasped when he dropped to his knees, settled himself between her legs and lifted one so her calf was hooked over his shoulder.

Then he buried his head where she least expected

it, his hands gripping her hips to hold her exactly where he wanted.

And he began to feast—she could think of no other way to describe it as he licked and kissed and suckled her most delicate flesh as if she were a rare delicacy of which he could not get enough.

She began to moan, softly at first, then louder, as each progressive wave of pleasure built higher, then higher still. Squirming against the overwhelming need, she tried to shift away, but he wouldn't let her, holding her steady as he forced her to accept this most intimate touch.

Her cries grew louder, and she was unable to maintain even the least semblance of caution.

Abruptly he broke off, his eyes ablaze as he gazed upward at her. Reaching out, he yanked her cravat loose, just enough to gather up a wad of cloth. "Open your mouth."

The moment she did, he stuffed the linen inside so it lay heavy against her tongue without smothering her. "Now you can be as loud as you want."

He returned to his wicked ministrations, building her hunger back to where it had been, then driving her beyond that point. She squirmed again, only this time it was in an effort to press closer, needing him in a way she had never known she could need before.

But he held her, controlling her with his hands and mouth and tongue so that she claimed her release only when he allowed it. She shouted out her bliss, the sound mercifully silenced by the cloth in her mouth.

He gave her no time to recover, lifting her up, then rearranging the two of them so that he sat with her straddled across his lap, one hand caressing her naked buttocks.

"Open my falls," he told her before he tugged the cravat end from her mouth, wrapped his other hand around the back of her head and brought her forward to accept his fervid, penetrating kiss.

Dazed and dizzy, she responded, having the curious experience of tasting herself on his tongue, even as she sought out the buttons that strained to contain his powerful erection.

The instant she freed them, his shaft sprang forth, heavy and hard. "Touch me," he urged, his clever fingers gliding over the trembling flesh of her bottom in the most distracting of ways. As he did, he reached under her shirt to tease her breasts, pausing every now and again to flick and pinch her ultrasensitive nipples so that she shuddered inside his hold.

Obedient to his demands, she wrapped her hand around his thick shaft to caress its warm, sleek length. His flesh throbbed and twitched beneath her touch, almost as if it had a life of its own.

With a groan, he pumped himself inside her grip, silently showing her what he craved. She tightened her hold and stroked him harder, back and forth, pausing briefly to explore the sacs drawn up at the base before gliding back toward the tip. She rubbed her thumb over the bead of moisture that collected there, the movement seeming to drive him mad.

He kissed her harder, with a savage intensity that she did her utmost to match. A dark river of heat and pleasure washed through her veins, one that threatened to engulf her completely. He reached around from behind and pushed a pair of fingers inside her, stretching her anew so that she cried out against the combination of pressure and agonizing need.

But no pain. All that existed was pleasure.

With breath panting from his lips, he broke their kiss. "Are you taking the herbs I gave you?"

"What?" she mumbled, feeling glassy-eyed and drunk on a surfeit of passion.

"The herbs. Are you taking them?" His voice was hard.

"Y-yes," she answered, as some still-lucid section of her brain managed to produce an answer. "Every evening."

"Excellent." Moving to take hold of her hips, he lifted her up so she was balanced on her knees above him. "Put me inside you."

The coach swayed around them, bouncing slightly as she guided him into her. As soon as she did, he pulled back again, then brought her down harder, thrusting deep so that she was thoroughly impaled.

He established a rhythm, pumping in and out, the coach aiding him ironically when it hit a hole in the street that bounced her up, then down again at exactly the right moment. He groaned along with her as they both became viscerally aware just how far inside her he was lodged.

Wrapping her arms around him, she held on as he scooted forward a couple of inches on the seat and began pumping harder, lifting her up and down as he showed her how to use her own leverage to meet him halfway.

He worked her without mercy, penetrating her with heavy, powerful strokes that made her shake, enslaving her body as her mind spun away. She closed her eyes, the world fading so that nothing remained but they two as he enflamed her senses to the breaking point.

She shook harder, on the brink, as he thrust once, twice, then once more before ecstasy exploded inside her, showering her with a pleasure as bright and brilliant as fireworks lighting up a night sky.

Clasping a hand to the back of her head, he pressed her mouth against his just in time to quiet her scream of release. He smothered his own shout of completion seconds later, his warmth flooding her womb in a way that gave her another level of satisfaction.

She collapsed against him, cradled in his arms, wishing she never had to move again.

"What time is it?" she mumbled a short while later, her cheek resting on his shoulder.

He shifted beneath her, their bodies still joined, and drew out his pocket watch. She watched from the corner of her eye as he opened the gold face and gazed at the dial.

He groaned. "Time to get you dressed, that's what time it is."

He lifted her gently off his lap so she was seated beside him, then reached up and rapped his knuckles twice on the ceiling. The coach turned at the next corner in response to an apparently prearranged signal.

"What time is it actually?" she asked as she bent down to collect her drawers and trousers.

"About five fifteen."

Her head whipped around. "Five fifteen! Oh dear Lord, how far away from my town house are we? What if we don't make it there before Bertram?"

"Don't take on so. Everything will be fine." Lawrence met her gaze, his eyes calm as he tucked his shirttail into his trousers, then fastened the buttons. "I told my coachman to travel in your general direction, so I expect we aren't more than ten minutes away."

"Well, that's some relief. Still, we're cutting it rather fine." She put her feet and ankles inside her drawers and pulled them up, arching her hips off the seat to shimmy them into place. She reached next for her trousers.

He leaned back in the corner and crossed his arms, clearly enjoying the show. "A miss is as good as a span, or so they say."

"I hope it's a miss. I'd rather not have to make up excuses." She tugged up her trousers but didn't button them, reaching under her shirt instead to rewrap the cloth she used to bind her chest. She wrestled with it unsuccessfully before yanking the shirt up and securing it under her armpits so she could try again.

"A little help would be appreciated." She glanced up to find his eyes riveted to her breasts, which jiggled a bit with the motion of the vehicle.

"Of course. Beg pardon." Leaning forward, Lawrence took hold of the cloth and unwound it. "Pull your shirt higher please."

She wiggled it up, holding her arms over her head, exposing herself even further. "Stop that. We've no time for ogling."

Caught, he grinned. "Now, that's a phrase no man ever likes to hear. But you're right, we do need to get you dressed even if it does seem a pity to cover up such beauty."

Still, he made sure that his fingers not only brushed

across the plump undersides of her breasts but grazed her peaked nipples as he wrapped the binding around her and secured it.

As soon as he was through, she pulled down her shirt and stuffed it into her trousers, then fastened them. He assisted her with her waistcoat buttons, and more important, her cravat, which she would never have managed half so well in so short a time. Her coat came next and shoes.

Then all that remained was her hair.

He finger combed the strands so they were as neat as could be managed, setting her scalp a-tingle as he retied her queue.

"How do I look?" she asked.

"Absolutely breathtaking."

"I'm not supposed to be breathtaking," she corrected, despite the glow she felt at his words. "I'm supposed to look like a man."

"Yes, but I know what's under those clothes, don't I? And it's all woman." Reaching out, he pulled her into his arms and crushed her mouth against his for a quick, yet amazingly thorough kiss. "I wish it didn't, but I guess that will have to hold us until next week."

"I suppose it must." She fought to slow her frantically beating heart.

He tugged the window curtains back just moments before the coach began to slow, and then they arrived, pulling up before her town house.

She frowned as she looked out.

"If he's home," Lawrence said, "tell him our paths crossed at the library and I gave you a lift. It's nothing but the truth, after all."

Yes, but everything else that had happened in between . . . She only hoped she could keep from blushing if her brother was already inside, waiting.

"I would assist you down," he said, "but I guess that would look odd, given that men don't generally assist other men down from coaches."

"Not unless they're foxed and in danger of falling flat on their face," she said, reminding him of the time they'd returned from the boxing match and he'd helped her down despite his confusion and suspicions.

"You had me in a tumult even then." He gave her a crooked smile that sent her heart racing faster. "Well, until Thursday."

"Until Thursday." She wanted to kiss him again but couldn't, not here where anyone might see.

She turned the door handle.

"Wait. Don't forget this." He was holding her leather folio.

Gratefully she accepted, then climbed out of the coach.

She jogged up the front steps and opened the door, then glanced back, expecting to find him gone. But he was still there.

Is he home? Lawrence mouthed.

She listened for a moment but was met with silence. "I don't think so," she called softly.

He smiled again and lifted a hand in farewell. Only then did he give the signal for the driver to move on.

Humming quietly under her breath, she went inside and up the stairs to her room.

Chapter 20

The next three weeks flew by in a heady rush, her days consumed with either work or Lawrence.

When she was with him, it was nothing short of heaven, each sweet, stolen hour better than the one that had come before. She'd already realized that he was an inventive, demanding, yet imminently considerate lover, who always took care to make certain she was thoroughly and astonishingly well satisfied. What she hadn't known was the sense of confidence he would evoke within her, the freedom to be wholly, unabashedly herself with no boundaries or restrictions. As he'd told her more than once, there was no intimacy they could not share and no desire too deep. He fulfilled her every need and taught her to crave ones she hadn't even realized she might have.

In bed, they were totally honest, completely themselves. Outside, well, she wasn't always sure what they were.

Friends, yes.

Lovers, most definitely.

But anything more . . . well, anything more was impossible, wasn't it?

Not that she wanted more. She didn't. They were having fun, that was all, their fling a kind of temporary insanity that would pass soon enough. Yet each time she kissed him farewell, her mind was already skipping ahead to their next interlude, her emotions tangled with an inescapable wish that they not be parted at all. When she wasn't with him, she did her best to put him from her thoughts, burying herself in work that needed to be done, particularly given the hours she was carving out of her schedule in order to be with Lawrence.

Luckily Bertram was busy with his own clients, most of them new with often complex issues that required his full time and attention. To her relief, he didn't seem to take note of her unusual, sometimes erratic schedule or her tendency to drift off into her own world on occasion.

But neither her affair nor her work as a barrister would last forever, since both were destined to end whether she liked it or not. Even so, she had a little time yet remaining, time she planned to use to the fullest extent.

Regardless, it came as a cruel surprise as she sat in the courtroom on that warm July day and listened to the judge render his decision.

"After weighing the evidence and testimony presented on both sides and having given the matter all due deliberation, this court finds on behalf of the claimant."

Quiet exclamations rang out, followed by handshakes of congratulations and a single, bitter curse of disappointment.

Rosamund stared blindly down at her notes for a moment, the fingers of her right hand curling into a fist against her robes. She tossed a glance over her shoulder and saw the dark-eyed glower of her client, who looked none too happy at having just lost. Rosamund wasn't terribly happy either, especially since she now had the less than pleasant duty of dealing with the aftermath.

Pulling in a breath, she turned and approached him. "Mr. Parum, I know it's not the result we were hoping for, but as you are aware, this was a difficult case that we always knew could go either way."

Parum turned his glower on her, the wool merchant's lower lip protruding at a pugnacious slant. "Alwa's knew, did we, now? Well, it's not yer blunt wot just got chucked in the piss pot, now, id it?"

Actually Rosamund had put in a great many extra hours of work on the case for which she would never be fully recompensed, so Parum was mistaken when he said he was the only one who had just suffered a financial loss. But considering the choleric hue of her client's skin, she decided now wasn't the best moment to bring up that particular point.

Without warning, he jabbed a thick finger her way, coming within an inch of striking her chest.

She took a prudent step backward.

"Knowing you lawyers," Parum continued, "I'm sure certain you'll still be sending a final reckoning my way, wanting ter be paid even though it's you wot cost me. I ne'er should ha' stayed on after old Elias

Carrow turned up 'is toes. Ought to 'ave taken me business elsewhere. If he'd been on the case, I'd be sittin' in catbird seat now rather than having that so-called gentleman farmer preening over his victory."

She forced herself not to flinch, his words comparing her unfavorably to her father striking home as no others could possibly have done.

She might have argued in her own defense. Could have told him that she'd tried every available means of winning the suit and that it was doubtful even her esteemed father would have prevailed. She might also have explained that they'd had a bad draw when it came to the presiding judge and that His Honor had been set against the defense's side from the outset.

But what was the point in even trying when Parum was so angry? When he was clearly already beyond listening to explanations, however reasonable they might be?

"I understand you are disappointed with the outcome," she said in as calm a voice as she could manage. "I am disappointed as well. Unfortunately the law is often less than perfect no matter how we might strive for it to be otherwise. Should you wish to discuss matters further, please send word to my chambers."

He glared at her for several blistering seconds, his mouth opening and closing rather like that of a fish that had been plucked out of a stream, before he spun on his heel and stalked out of the courtroom. It was only after he'd gone that she allowed the tension to give way, her hands shaking ever so slightly as she reached out to gather her belongings.

"What was all that about?" asked a smooth, reassuringly familiar voice from just over her shoulder. "Are you all right?"

Despite a part of her brain having already identified him, she startled anyway. "Lawrence!"

"Sorry." He sent her a rueful smile, his white barrister's wig and black robes casting his features into sharp relief so that he looked even handsomer than usual. "I didn't mean to give you a fright."

"It's nothing. I just wasn't expecting you to turn up out of the blue." Reaching out, she slipped her notes inside her leather folio, then gathered up a pair of pencils. "What are you doing here? I thought you had an appearance before Judge Typps today."

"I did, but it finished early." He turned around and leaned back against the table, hands braced so that he faced her, his shoulder near her own. "I thought I'd come down here to see how you were faring."

He grinned, his gold-green eyes twinkling with intimate warmth. She had a sudden urge to kiss him, but resisted, wishing they were alone rather than inside an open courtroom. Based on his look, she guessed he was thinking the same.

After a moment, his expression changed. "You never did tell me what was going on when I came in. I didn't much care for the way that fellow was behaving. It's a good thing he left when he did. Otherwise, I might very well have given his arm a good twist to move him along."

Her eyes widened. "Well, I'm glad you didn't. He's angry enough as it is without adding a charge of assault and battery to the equation."

"Justified assault and battery, since he was clearly

harassing you, an officer of the court. Who was he, by the by?"

She sighed. "My client. Or rather my former client. He's not at all happy that his lawsuit didn't prevail today."

"You lost?" He arched a brow in clear surprise.

"Yes, I lost. And you needn't look so smug about it."

"I'm not," he denied, wiping the hint of a smile from his lips. "Well, maybe a wee bit, since you never lose."

"You don't either."

"Only on very rare occasion. Although I do recall receiving a rather stinging defeat at your hands."

A faint smile played over her lips this time. "Hmm, I seem to recall that myself."

"Be careful," he murmured, keeping his voice low despite the fact that they were now the only two people left inside the courtroom. "I just might demand recompense."

She met his gaze, one hand coming to rest on the side of the table next to his. "I've already given you recompense for that, remember?"

"Ah, but that was before I took you to my bed."

"Don't," she hushed. "This isn't the place."

"No." He inched his hand over so the side of his palm touched the side of hers. "I wish it was, though, so I could strip you bare and take you on this table."

Her blood heated. "Shh, you're going to get us into trouble."

"I can think of all sorts of places I'd like to get into when it comes to you."

Her breathing quickened and she looked away.

"You know," he said huskily, "I'm finished for the day and if I'm not mistaken, you are as well. Why don't we repair to my town house? After all, it is your first time losing in court and I'd like to offer you an appropriate measure of consolation. Or should I say *inappropriate* consolation?"

She met his eyes again, her eyelids heavy with barely banked passion. "You are a wicked, wicked man, Lawrence Byron."

He hooked his pinky finger around hers so they were entwined. "Yes, and you love it."

He was right; she did.

Suddenly she found herself wondering what else about him she might love.

She frowned, then tugged her hand away. "Sorry, but I can't. I promised Bertram I would meet him this afternoon to review one of his cases."

He scowled. "Can't you send him a note and postpone?"

"And give what as a reason? I'm already making up half a dozen excuses a week to explain why I'm away so often."

"Very well." His eyebrows drew down with a displeasure that made her want to lean up and kiss it better. "What about Friday?"

"Don't you have a hearing most of the day?"

"Blazes, you're right. Saturday, then? I know we don't usually meet that day, but surely you're allowed to go shopping or some such."

"I do, of course, but this Saturday is difficult."

"Difficult how?"

"It's my father's birthday, or at least it would have

been his birthday." A wave of sadness overtook her. "I'm going to the cemetery to lay flowers on his grave."

"I see. Your brother will be with you." He said it as a statement.

"No. Bertram and Father . . . their relationship was complicated at the best of times, so he is not coming."

"In that case, I shall." He laid his hand over hers.

"But—" Her eyes met his.

"Unless you don't want me there."

Suddenly she realized that was exactly what she wanted, quite badly, in fact. She flipped her hand over and laced her fingers with his. "I do. Want you, that is."

In far too many ways to mention. In ways she had no right to expect.

"Then it will be my privilege to escort you."

Quickly they decided on a time and place to meet, since he insisted on taking her in his carriage. As for any plans afterward, he made no mention and neither did she.

Aware how it would look if someone walked in, he let go of her hand; the loss left her oddly bereft.

"I wish I could kiss you," he whispered, gazing deeply into her eyes.

"I wish you could too."

"I suppose we'll have to rely on dreams until Saturday."

"Yes," she said. "See you in my dreams until then."

And as he walked away, she realized how easy her last promise would be to keep, since he was the only thing she ever dreamed of these days.

Chapter 21

Lawrence stood within the burial grounds of Bunhill Fields in Islington that Saturday, waiting silent and respectful as Rosamund bent over the final resting places of not only her father but her mother as well.

He watched as she tidied the graves, carefully plucking weeds and leaves from the thick grass before she arranged bouquets of fresh white lilies and purple lilacs, whose perfume drifted sweetly in the warm summer air.

She'd given him a bit of a shock earlier when he drove up in his curricle to find her waiting at their prearranged meeting spot, wearing a black walking dress, an unadorned straw bonnet on her head and her arms filled with flowers.

For a first few seconds, he hadn't recognized her, scanning the crowd until she'd approached and spoken his name. He knew he'd stared, wondering now if he'd looked a fool, as he'd found it nearly impossible to look away from her.

He'd always considered her a beautiful woman, but

seeing her in a dress for the first time, looking indescribably soft and feminine, had produced a strange effect inside him. It was almost as if he didn't know her, and yet he did—quite intimately, in fact.

He'd helped her up into the curricle, vitally aware that he could do so now without anyone so much as glancing in their direction. Then, before he'd given himself a chance to think, he'd leaned over from his side of the seat and kissed her, nearly crushing the flowers between them as he claimed her mouth in a way he'd never openly been able to do before.

She'd laughed when he let her up for air, her cheeks burnished, her silvery eyes aglow. And that was when she'd become his Rosamund again, the two images of her merging inside his head to form a single, unique whole.

So now he waited while she knelt at her parents' graves, witnessing yet another side of the interesting, intelligent, complex woman he knew her to be.

With her eyes closed, she whispered a few words so quietly he could not hear; then she sniffed and got to her feet. Reaching into her pocket, she withdrew a handkerchief and wiped her eyes and nose. Only then did she look up at him.

He opened his arms and after only a second's hesitation, she moved into them, burrowing close as if they had been doing it forever. He held her, once again enjoying the freedom to embrace her openly, as they stood together here beneath the trees with the summer sun shining down upon them.

"He could be a hard man sometimes, but I miss him," she murmured.

"Curious how that works, isn't it?" Lawrence mused. "No matter how stern or disapproving they may have been, there's still that connection, parent to child. He was your father. That's all that needs to be said."

She tipped back her head. "And your father? Was he stern and disapproving?"

"He died when I was only a boy, so I have few actual memories of him, but I suppose to me he often was a stern figure. My strongest recollection of him was the way he would catch Leo and me, and sometimes our sister, Mallory, playing where we weren't supposed to be. He'd scowl reprovingly and tell us not to run in the corridors and staterooms at Braebourne. He was always sure we'd break something."

"And did you?"

He gave her an impish grin. "A time or two. When Leo and I were six, we escaped our nanny and set off to play chase with one of the dogs. While we were in full pursuit, we bumped into a table and sent a marble bust toppling to the floor. It broke the fellow's nose off in the most alarming way."

"Oh no, you must have been in dreadful trouble."

"I thought we were done for, but Mama reminded Papa how little fondness he'd ever had for that particular relation and hadn't we done him a very great favor by giving him a reason to toss out his likeness? Of course, we were still punished. Restricted to the nursery for the next two weeks with no pudding and set to the task of composing formal apologies, which we were marched down to the drawing room to recite aloud. But all told, it could have been much worse."

"A great deal, I would say. Your mother sounds lovely."

"Oh, she is. You'd like her. You'd like all my family, I think."

A tiny frown developed between her brows. "Yes, I'm sure I should, though I rather doubt my path and theirs shall ever have the opportunity to cross." Glancing away, she gently stepped out of the protective circle of his arms.

That was when he realized what he'd said and the sad reality that she was right. The Byrons and the Carrows moved in very different social circles. What was more, Rosamund was his lover, and a gentleman did not introduce his mistress to his family. So why did some part of him wish he could?

"How soon must you be back?" he asked, reaching out to take hold of her hand.

"Not for a while," she said. "Bertram has plans with some friends. He told me not to count on him for dinner, so I suspect he'll be late."

"Then what say you to our taking a meal together? I know a rather pleasant inn not too far distant that serves a marvelous chicken pie. Shall we sample a plate?"

He caught her look of surprise. Obviously she'd expected him to suggest they steal away somewhere for a heated tryst. But that could wait for now. She needed food and emotional comfort. Anything beyond that would be up to her.

"That sounds nice," she murmured.

"Good." Bending, he dusted a soft kiss over her lips.

"Lawrence," she said, her eyes luminous. "Thank you."

"For what?"

"For coming here with me today. I'm glad I didn't have to do it alone."

"Nor would I have wished you to." He kissed her again, then took her arm and threaded it through his own. "Now, shall we be on our way? I, for one, am famished."

She laughed. "Then by all means, let us not delay, my lord."

With an answering grin, he steered her in the direction of his curricle.

Rosamund sipped her glass of lemonade and watched as Lawrence polished off his third helping of chicken pie, which really had been as delicious as promised. He'd eaten with the enthusiasm and appetite of a boy, all the while regaling her with one entertaining story after another.

She knew he was trying to cheer her up and he'd succeeded, making her laugh and smile and not dwell on the earlier sadness of the day.

As the meal proceeded, she'd found herself simply watching him, relishing his gestures, both large and small, and the well-rounded tones of his baritone voice as he spoke. He had an endearing habit of tipping his head slightly to one side, a lock of his golden brown hair falling forward as he listened to whatever she was saying. Yet even more appealing was the way he focused his attention on her, as if she were the single most important thing in the world.

And as the minutes slid past, as they chatted and relaxed and partook of the meal like a pair of intimate old friends, she found herself wishing for more. Wished they could sit just so each day and share the small, insignificant details of their lives alongside the big, grand happenings—trials and triumphs both. Wished they had the luxury of time—weeks and months and years—without the need to ever be apart, day or night.

She nearly choked on her lemonade when the truth stole through her, gentle as a whisper. It was so simple and easy, as if it had been waiting there for her to discover all along.

I love him, she thought, hastily lowering her eyes in case he could see the knowledge shining in their depths. *I love him, this man who will brighten my life for a brief while and then disappear again like a star come the dawn.*

Carefully she set down her lemonade and prayed he didn't take note of her sudden silence. But she ought to have known better; Lawrence was nothing if not observant.

"Sad again about your father?" He laid his fork and knife neatly across his plate and gave her an understanding smile.

Guilt assailed her. Until that moment, she'd forgotten all about her father and the purpose for today's outing. "A bit," she prevaricated. "It's been an emotional day."

"Maybe I should take you home."

Her eyes flew to his. "No, not yet. We still have some time. Besides, you haven't had pudding yet."

"Nor shall I." He patted his waistcoat and the lean stomach underneath. "But you should enjoy something sweet. I suspect they have a treat good enough to tempt your palate."

"I'm sure they do, but I couldn't eat anything more."

"Tea, then?"

"No, I . . . I'd rather just be with you." She laid a hand on the table and reached toward him.

Something shifted in his gaze and he leaned forward to weave his fingers through hers. "We don't have to be intimate today, not with so many other things on your mind."

"Maybe that's exactly why we should be, so I won't have to think at all, except about you." She moved her thumb in a slow circle against his palm. "Unless you don't want me."

Naked desire flashed in his eyes. "I always want you. Surely you know that by now."

"Then I'm yours for the taking. Shall we go to your town house or get a room here?"

His fingers tightened around hers. "We'd have more time together if we stayed here. Unless you object."

"Not in the slightest."

He stood and bent to kiss her hand. "I'll be back straightaway."

"I'll be waiting."

Then he was gone, his footsteps echoing against the wooden floors as he went below to speak to the innkeeper.

He returned as quickly as promised, then took her hand to lead her down a hallway and up a flight of stairs to a room at the end. He fit the key in the lock and pushed open the door.

The bedroom was neat and clean with a large wardrobe that dominated one wall and an even bigger bed spread with a blue-and-yellow chintz coverlet. Clouds that promised rain were visible through a pair of windows that overlooked a small, quiet back garden. They'd been opened a few inches to let in a breeze, a pair of sheer white half curtains across the bottom panes billowing with the air currents.

Yet she and Lawrence paid little attention to their surroundings as he locked the door, then took her into his embrace. She looped her arms around his neck and stretched up on her toes to kiss him, softly at first, then more deeply until he eased her away and reached to unfasten her gown.

He undressed her slowly, as if they had all the time in the world instead of only a few short hours, pausing to scatter random kisses over her body as each new area of skin was exposed.

She returned the favor, searching out buttons and sliding fabric free to reveal his long, leanly muscled body whose beauty never failed to steal her breath and make her heart speed faster.

Then they were in bed, the covers pushed haphazardly to the foot as she and Lawrence twined their naked bodies together, each kiss, every caress more enthralling, more ardent than the one that had come before.

In those moments, Rosamund gave herself over to him completely, saying with her body what she could not allow herself to say in words, silently declaring her love in the only way she dared.

And when he sheathed himself inside her, she sighed from the sheer majesty of the sensation, her fingers tunneling deep into his thick, silky hair to draw him closer as she answered his demands with demands of her own. She slid one leg high over his back, urging him on, her hands gliding across his skin in long, lingering strokes that made his muscles ripple beneath her touch.

He took her mouth with a feverish zeal that drove her own need higher, her thoughts scattered, her heart and body open and utterly abandoned to him as he linked their fingers together above her head. She arched upward, dizzy and drunken, as she accepted him fully, taking more, taking everything, while he thrust faster and more fully inside her. Closing her eyes, she gave herself over, letting her love pour forth, heady and powerful.

She hardly recognized her own keening cries of pleasure as the air filled with sound, thunder crashing and lightning sparking match-bright to illuminate the room's now shadowy interior.

When he moved to pull out, she instinctively held him inside her, wrapping her legs tighter and mindlessly refusing to let him go. He thrust harder, faster, as lost to their mutual hunger as she, as he pushed her over the edge into a soul-shattering release.

And the clouds burst open, a deluge of rain pouring from the sky, while inside the safety of their room, he poured himself into her. The two of them shook, their mutual cries of completion muffled by the storm raging outside. But neither of them noticed, too caught up in their own storm to care.

*   *   *

Some while later, Rosamund lay with her head against Lawrence's shoulder, listening to the rain drumming outside. Earlier, he'd gotten out of bed and closed the windows to keep the wetness from blowing in before hurrying back to enfold her inside his arms again. They'd dozed briefly, then awakened to lie warm and comfortable beneath the sheets.

"I wish we could just stay here," Rosamund sighed, idly skimming her fingertips over his chest. "It's too wet to go back out."

"Hmm, that's a tempting thought. Though if you don't stop what you're doing with those fingers of yours, I may decide never to let you out of this bed again and damn the consequences."

"I like the sound of that." She tipped back her head and met his gold-green eyes. "We could just go on living here in this room and do nothing but sleep and eat and make love."

"I wouldn't object in the slightest, though I believe I'd reorder the list so that 'make love' comes first." He kissed her forehead and cheek before moving on to nuzzle a sensitive spot underneath her jaw and another behind her ear.

She shivered, her fingers gliding across his stomach. Before she could go any lower, he captured her hand and linked their fingers together as his mouth took hers in a leisurely joining she wished would never end.

When he raised his head again, she willed her heart to slow, pressing her cheek to his chest again before he saw more than she wanted him to see. She sighed.

"I suppose if we don't want to be found out, we need to dress and be on our way, rain or no rain."

"It will probably stop soon or at least slow to a drizzle. You said your brother won't be home until late, so we should have a little more time to wait it out."

"Yes, a little more."

But not enough. Forever would not be enough for me.

And suddenly, despite her wish to stay with him, she knew she needed to leave, needed a chance to be alone and find a way to get her emotions in check.

"Even so, I should go," she said, freeing herself from his arms and sitting up. "The servants will wonder what's become of me if I don't return soon."

He reached out and caught hold of her arm before she could leave the bed. "What's wrong?"

She shook her head, refusing to look at him. "Nothing."

"Clearly that is not the case. What is amiss? I haven't done something to upset you, have I?"

Her heart beat painfully in her chest, throat tight. "No, of course not. What could you have possibly done?"

He sat up beside her. "I don't know. Rosamund, what is it?" Taking her in his arms, he laid a hand against the side of her face and gently forced her to look at him.

To her horror, tears welled in her eyes. Furiously she tried to blink them away. But it was already too late.

"It's nothing, really," she told him in a hurried rush, searching for an excuse, any excuse rather than the truth. "It's just been an emotional day, that's all. Exactly as you said. Forgive me, I don't know what's come over me. I'm just being silly."

"It's not silly." He brushed a thumb over the dampness on her cheek. "Not silly at all." Then he pulled her close inside his arms and rocked her, letting her weep quietly against his chest.

She wrapped her arms around his back and held on, grieving for herself and her father and everything that had been lost. But mostly she grieved for Lawrence and for all the things she would never have with him.

He didn't love her, nor did she expect him to. Yet what a fool she'd been to think she could have an affair with him and come out unscathed. Because he was going to break her heart someday soon . . . and she was going to let him.

She had let him already.

Yet she was wasting their precious time, she realized, as she huddled against him, blubbering away like a ninny. He was here with her now, so why was she squandering this opportunity? Why be miserable today when she would have weeks and months and years in the future to miss him once he was gone?

Sniffing, she leaned back and wiped the back of one hand across her cheeks.

"Better?" he asked.

She nodded. "Sorry."

"Don't be. Everyone needs a good cry once in a while."

"Even you?" she asked with a watery smile.

He chuckled and winked. "You just might be surprised." Picking up the sheet, he used a corner to dry her eyes and nose.

"I must look awful," she said.

"No. You look beautiful, just as you always do."

She gazed into his eyes, tracing their bands of gold and green. Then, without giving herself time to think, she set her hands on his shoulders and pushed, but he barely budged. "Lie back."

"I thought you were worried about the time."

"Not anymore." She gave him another small shove; this time he complied, stretching out across the mattress. She followed, straddling his hips to find him already erect. Taking him in her hand, she slid his hard length deep inside her, then leaned forward to claim his mouth.

"No," she murmured, as she began to move against him. "I'm not worried anymore."

Chapter 22

A week later, Rosamund stepped out of the hackney
cab and onto the pavement in front of Lawrence's
town house on Cavendish Square. Disguised in her
masculine attire once again, she quickly paid the
driver, then jogged up the stairs, a smile on her face.
Lawrence wasn't expecting to see her today, but when
her meeting with a client concluded early, she'd
decided to surprise him. According to his schedule,
he was at home, working on a case this afternoon.

She greeted Griggs when he opened the door.

In the past month, she'd come to know a few of the
servants. They were always pleasant and respectful,
each one the epitome of what a proper servant ought
to be, helpful when needed and all but invisible the
rest of the time.

If any of them suspected the truth of her relationship with Lawrence, they didn't let on, not by so much
as the extra flicker of an eyelash. Yet occasionally she
wondered if a couple of them might have seen through
her disguise, the butler in particular. When she'd men-

tioned her suspicions to Lawrence once, he was unconcerned, assuring her that even if his servants had figured out her ruse, they were too discreet to say anything.

"Is His Lordship in the library?" she asked, handing Griggs her hat and gloves.

"He is."

"There's no need to announce me." She motioned for the servant to remain where he was. "I know the way."

"Yes, but—"

She didn't slow to listen further, already making her way along the corridor that led to the rear of the house. Since her coming here was an unexpected surprise, she hoped to surprise him even more.

Luck was on her side as she walked silently into the room to find Lawrence seated at a long table, his back to her, his dark golden head bent over a book. After closing the door soundlessly behind her, she crept up with the stealth of a cat and leaned forward to wrap her arms around him from behind. He startled as she nuzzled his neck, then caught his earlobe between her teeth for a playful nip.

"Surprise, it's me," she murmured huskily into his ear. "Where would you like to tup me first? Upstairs in your bedchamber? Or should we try out this table, since it's so big and long and hard like you?"

"Both sound equally intriguing," he said with an amused tone as he reached up to loosen her hold. "But I fear my wife might object to your saucy plan."

His wife?

It was only then that she became aware of something

different about him, something very un-Lawrence-like. She lowered her arms and stepped back, staring as he turned in his chair to face her. He looked like Lawrence, even sounded like him, and yet there was a peculiar discordance, as if she were observing a copy—albeit an exceptional one—rather than the original.

And his eyes. They were the usual mix of gold and green, only they weren't.

These eyes were greener.

Much greener.

Yet at the same time she was puzzling him out, he seemed to be doing the same with her, his eyes widening as one golden eyebrow arched high, in obvious disbelief as he stared at what must look to him to be a man.

Just then a footstep sounded from somewhere above them and she looked up to see Lawrence—another Lawrence—standing on a railed platform above, a thick book cradled in one hand. "Rosamund?" he called down.

The first Lawrence—who clearly wasn't Lawrence at all—glanced back and forth between her and the real one, then smiled. "*Rosamund*, is it? I must say that's a relief. I was worried for a moment he'd taken to batting for the other side."

Suddenly everything fell into place, mortified heat rushing into her cheeks, hot as a volcano. "Dear God, you're his twin!"

His eyes twinkled in a way that was disturbingly familiar, yet wasn't. "Lord Leopold Byron at your service." He executed a short bow. "Not to worry, you're far from the first to mistake me for Lawrence.

Even now some of our relations can't tell one of us from the other."

She could understand why; the resemblance really was uncanny.

"Been a while, though," he continued, "since I entertained such a tempting suggestion from anyone other than my wife. If it weren't for the fact that I'm hopelessly in love with her and unerringly faithful as a result, I'd be thinking up ways to steal you from my brother. Either that or share."

He winked, chuckling quietly as she opened and closed her mouth without so much as a sound coming out.

"That is quite enough from you," Lawrence reprimanded his brother in a hard voice, appearing suddenly at her side.

She glanced up at Lawrence and watched an unspoken message pass between him and his twin.

A flicker of surprise crossed Leopold's face, followed by a kind of introspective curiosity. Abruptly his flirtatious demeanor disappeared and he returned his gaze to her. "Your pardon, ma'am. It was not my intention to offend. I hope you can forgive me."

"Yes, of course, my lord," she said, wishing her cheeks would quit burning like a bonfire. "I can hardly blame you when I am every bit as much at fault for our misunderstanding."

"No," Leopold said slowly, as his gaze traveled briefly between his brother and her. "The blame is entirely mine. Perhaps we might begin anew. Lawrence, will you do the honors and make a proper introduction?"

"I'm not so sure I will," Lawrence grumbled. Then he relented. "Rosamund, my brother, Leopold, as I believe you already know. Leo, Miss Rosamund Carrow."

"A pleasure." Leopold made her another brief bow, his demeanor as refined and gentlemanly as if they were meeting in a ballroom. As for the fact that she was wearing male garb rather than a dress, he showed no signs of disapproval, not outwardly at least. "Carrow?" he mused. "Any relation to the barrister Ross Carrow whom my brother has mentioned a time or two?"

Now it was her and Lawrence's turn to exchange speaking glances.

"You might as well go ahead," she said with a shrug. "I'm the one who botched everything up by deciding to drop in on you unannounced. I just wanted to surprise you and look where it's landed me."

Lawrence smiled and took her hand. "Don't worry. He's irritating on occasion but amazingly trustworthy."

She smiled back before the enormity of the whole situation settled over her again. He squeezed her hand reassuringly.

"Trust me with what?" Leo looked between her and Lawrence.

"With the fact that Rosamund *is* Ross Carrow," Lawrence confided.

Leo frowned, looking so much like Lawrence it was unsettling. "What do you mean *she's* Ross Carrow? But that would mean that she . . . that she has . . . that— it's impossible."

"Improbable perhaps," Lawrence said, "but far from impossible. She fooled me for a good long while and she continues to fool everyone else."

"So she's actually practicing law? And appearing in court?"

"She is," Lawrence declared, voice brimming with pride. "And with splendid success. Bloody brilliant if I do say so myself. She's won every case save one, and that was a likely loser from the outset."

"Didn't he—I mean *she* beat you?" Leo continued. "You were dashed vexed about it, as I recall."

"I've since recovered."

Leo crossed his arms over his chest and looked between them again, a far-too-knowing expression in his eyes. "Yes, I can see that you have."

"Pardon me, gentlemen," Rosamund interjected, "but you do realize that I am standing right here. If Lord Leopold has questions, I would appreciate him asking them of me directly."

"Oh, she does have a good barrister's voice," Leo remarked. "Nice and authoritative."

"You ought to hear her in court."

Rosamund loudly cleared her throat.

The sound got through this time, the brothers turning their keen green and gold gazes her way. Having clearly been caught out, they sent her a pair of sheepish grins that were mirror images of each other.

"Sorry, my dear." Lawrence squeezed her hand in apology. "Leo and I tend to get carried away sometimes."

"Rather more than sometimes, as it happens," Leo added. "Drives our friends and family mad, especially when we don't bother to finish our sentences. Twin-speak. Learned in the cradle, perfected over the years." Leo showed her his white teeth, smiling with such good-natured yet unrepentant warmth that she couldn't find it within herself to stay angry—particularly since he looked just like Lawrence.

"But you are quite right, Miss Carrow," Leo said. "He and I are being unconscionably rude. I do beg pardon. Again."

"Accepted. Just see you don't make a habit of it, my lord."

Leo's smiled widened, his gaze meeting his brother's once more. "She's a firecracker."

"Isn't she just?"

"So, Miss Carrow, where did you train in the law, if I might be so bold? It's not the usual thing for a woman."

"No, it is not. I assisted my father and earned an education at his side."

"And your father is?"

"Elias Carrow. Bertram Carrow is my brother."

"I see," Leo said. "My condolences for your recent loss. Even I, who hold a barrister's credential in name only, was familiar with your late father's work and accolades."

"Thank you, my lord."

"Leo, please. Not much point standing on formality now; don't you agree?"

"I suppose so."

"So how did you ever come to take up a disguise and become a working member of the bar?"

"That," Lawrence said, breaking in to the conversation, "is an interesting story but far too long to tell right now. If you don't object, Rosamund, I'll fill him in on the details later."

She turned toward Lawrence. "Yes, of course. And I really am sorry to have dropped in on you today unannounced." Not to mention her lingering embarrassment over whispering lewd suggestions into his brother's ear believing it was him. "I ought to have realized that you might be otherwise occupied."

"I'm not sorry." Lawrence took her other hand in his, lowering his voice as Leo retreated to give them some semblance of privacy. "I'm delighted to see you. I only wish Leo had chosen another afternoon to surprise me with a visit as well."

"Did his wife come with him? Is she here? I should go. It wouldn't be appropriate for me to . . . well, I doubt she would be pleased to make my acquaintance."

"Of course she would. Thalia doesn't stand so high in the instep that she would refuse to know you. But no, she isn't here. She's back at their country home. Apparently they discovered a foundling. A newborn left in a basket under a tree on the edge of their estate. Leo and I are looking into the legalities of their keeping her."

He cast a glance over at his brother, who had resumed his seat at the table. "They're childless, you see. And although Leo is perfectly content with their family never being any bigger than the two of them, Thalia longs for a child. Now one has come into their lives. He wants to make sure if they adopt the baby, she can't ever be taken away again. He fears such a

loss, after a bond had been forged, would devastate
Thalia beyond repair."

"Of course it would," she said fiercely. "No woman
could come to love a child as her own only to see it
torn away from her later. If there is any way I can help,
just say the word. Bertram is acquainted with a couple
of solicitors who have dealt with such matters. I can
give you their names."

"That is very good of you. But then, you are good."
He sent her a warm smile. "At so very many things."

She looked into his eyes with their preponderance
of gold amid the green and knew him for the man she
loved. Never again would she have difficulty distin-
guishing him from his twin.

Yet when he leaned forward to kiss her, she shifted
away fractionally, all too aware that they were not
alone. Obviously intuiting the reason for her reluctance, he paused and sent his brother a quick glance
before turning to lead her to the door. He ushered her
out into the hall, where he dropped her hand and had
her follow him.

The moment they were inside his study with the door
closed, he pulled her into his arms and found her mouth.
She kissed him with a sweet, fiery passion as she lost
herself inside his ardent embrace. Far too quickly she
pulled away. "We can't. Not with your brother here."

"Believe me, he won't mind."

"Maybe not, but I will. He already thinks . . ." Her
words trailed off.

"Yes, what does he think?

"Nothing good."

He cocked an eyebrow, a teasing smile playing over his lips. "What did you say to him exactly?"

Her cheeks warmed again. "Please, don't make me repeat it. I thought he was *you*," she added with a hint of accusation.

"Oh, come, now. It cannot have been that bad. Whisper it in my ear."

"Lawrence—" she complained.

"Go on." He bent closer. "I won't be cross whatever it might be."

She wanted to resist, but lately it seemed she could refuse him nothing. Standing on tiptoe, she told him.

His eyes widened and he smirked. "No wonder he looked like he'd just been jabbed with a hot poker."

She swatted his shoulder. "It's not funny."

"It is a little." He chuckled.

"No, it isn't. I'm sure he thinks me a harlot."

All of Lawrence's humor vanished. "He most certainly does not!"

"But, Lawrence, how can he think anything else? Obviously he knows I'm your lover."

He took hold of her arms, waiting until she looked up and into his eyes. "Just because we're lovers doesn't make you a harlot. And I don't ever want you to say such a thing about yourself again. Do you understand?" When she didn't respond, he asked her again. "Do you understand?"

"Yes. I understand."

But it changed nothing, she realized. Whatever Lawrence might say, she was no more suitable for him than if she really were a harlot.

"I should go." She sighed, running a hand over the smooth silk of his waistcoat.

He frowned. "No, don't. Go upstairs and wait for me. I'll tell Leo to push off."

"You can't tell him to push off. From what you've said, this is his home too. Besides, he needs your help, he and his wife." She caught him around the neck with a hand and stretched up for a warm, passionate kiss. "I shall see you soon, when we can be alone. Until then, go be with your brother."

For a moment, he looked as though he wanted to argue. Then he nodded. "Damned waste of a good surprise if you ask me."

This time she did laugh—warmth, and something far richer and more precious, spiraling inside her.

They shared one final kiss, and then she preceded him out to the entry hall and went on her way.

"I like her," Leo said a while later. He and Lawrence were seated across from each other at the library table, books and notes scattered between them. "She's unique, your Rosamund."

Your Rosamund, Lawrence repeated in his head. *Yes, she is mine and no one else's.*

So why did he feel unsettled somehow, as if an imperceptible shift had occurred, a turning point from which there could be no return?

"She is exceptional. The most remarkable woman it's ever been my privilege to know." Lawrence did nothing to hide the pleasure and pride in his voice. "I am glad you had an opportunity to meet her even if the circumstances weren't ideal."

Leo gave him a look. "A shame Thalia wasn't able to accompany me today so she could have met her as well."

"It is, yes. Although Rosamund needs to keep her identity secret for a while more."

After Rosamund's departure, he'd told Leo the pertinent parts of her history and the reasons for her deception; how she'd done it for her brother and that once the last of her father's old cases were concluded, she would be hanging up her shingle as a barrister.

"And then what?" Leo asked. "When she goes back to being plain Miss Carrow?"

"I don't know." Lawrence rolled a pencil between his fingers. "We haven't really discussed it."

Until now he and Rosamund had been too caught up in the thrill of their affair to think much beyond the immediate future. But Leo was right. What was going to happen once she went back to being herself? Would she be content when she was no longer able to do the work at which she excelled and so obviously loved? Or would she be miserable? And where would that leave them when *Ross* Carrow couldn't drop by to visit him anymore?

He scowled, not liking the direction his thoughts were taking him.

"So?" Leo leaned back in his chair. "Still going to Baron Judge Templestone's for dinner this evening?"

Lawrence looked up. "Of course. I am promised to attend."

"I presume Phoebe Templestone will be there."

"And her mother and the judge."

"Anyone else?"

"I really couldn't say, since I wasn't asked to consult on the guest list."

Leo made a humming noise in his throat.

"What's that supposed to mean?"

"Nothing. Just that I'd beware. Any invitation where you're outnumbered by Templestones constitutes a family dinner."

"Well, this isn't one. His Honor and I have business to discuss, and the baroness was kind enough to invite me to share a meal with them."

"Are you sure they know that? Just don't come away engaged, not unless you mean to be. That's all I'm saying."

"Don't worry. I can handle myself, *Mama*. Now, shouldn't we be getting back to your issue?"

"Quite right." Leo shifted forward in his seat again. "Do be sure to give Miss Carrow my best when next you see her. I've always been a great admirer of clever, resourceful women. A man could spend a lifetime with one such as she and never grow bored. A shame she lacks breeding."

"There is nothing wrong with her breeding." His fingers tightened dangerously on his pencil.

"Oh, she has education and manners to be sure. I'm merely pointing out that she's not an aristocrat. Nor does she come with the sorts of familial connections that could be of benefit to furthering one's position or career. But then, I've never cared about such things."

"You married an earl's daughter."

"A disgraced, *divorced* earl's daughter who people still gossip about behind her back. But I love her and she loves me and that's all that matters."

"Rosamund and I are lovers; it doesn't mean we're in love."

"Of course not." Leo's eyes gleamed in a way that set Lawrence's teeth on edge.

"When did you turn into such a meddler?" Lawrence demanded. "I think that fiction writing of yours is going to your head, imagining things that don't exist."

Leo laughed and bent his head to concentrate on his reading.

It took Lawrence some while before he was able to do the same.

Chapter 23

"You simply must come visit us in the country at Templestone Manor this autumn, Lord Lawrence," declared Lady Templestone from where she sat at the end of the long formal dining table inside the Templestone House dining room. "We run a fine covey of birds on our land; do we not, Templestone?"

She cast a glance at her husband, who sat opposite her at the table's head, but didn't pause long enough to let him answer—assuming he was even inclined to do so. Lady Templestone was a master of never letting the conversation lag, no matter how mundane the topic.

"It's nothing to compare to what your brother, the duke, can provide, I am sure," she continued on, "but we've a decent collection of game nonetheless. I think you will find the shooting quite to your liking and you would be most welcome to join our party of friends next month. Would he not, Phoebe?"

Phoebe Templestone looked up from her place directly across the table from Lawrence. Daintily she swallowed the spoonful of crème caramel she'd just put in her mouth, then patted her lips with her napkin. "Yes, very welcome."

She fluttered her pale lashes and smiled.

Phoebe was looking particularly lovely this evening, her blond beauty enhanced by the pale pink of her stylish silk gown, her blue eyes startlingly brilliant in the candlelight. Yet for all her exquisiteness, he felt only an abstract kind of appreciation rather like a connoisseur who could see the value of a fine work of art without investing anything emotionally in the piece.

As for a certain darker beauty, she had no trouble evoking a strong emotional reaction. Straight, shoulder-length dark hair. Determined chin. And a pair of clever gray eyes that had a way of seeing through a problem or a person, perhaps to the very heart of a man's soul. Some might say she couldn't compare to the incomparable perfection of one such as Phoebe Templestone, but to his way of thinking hers was the beauty of real worth.

With a sharp inner jolt, he returned to the present and forced a pleasant smile. "My thanks for your generosity, ladies. It sounds a most excellent diversion. Regretfully, however, I am promised here in the city. Business matters, you understand."

Lady Templestone's mouth tightened; clearly she was not about to be done out of his agreeing to accept her invitation. He, however, had no illusions as to what such a visit would signal to the Ton. As Leo had warned him, this dinner tonight, with only the four of them present, was significant enough. A week spent at their country home would be as good as taking out an engagement notice in the *Morning Post*.

He ought to have listened to Leo and cried off tonight, he realized now. Yet it wasn't so long ago that he'd all but decided to offer for Phoebe Templestone, convinced she would make him an excellent wife, sure that an alliance with her and her family would offer him unparalleled opportunities to advance his legal career.

So why was he hesitating rather than sealing the deal? Why resist when he would clearly be welcomed into the Templestone fold with open arms?

There was only one answer.

Rosamund.

"Come, now, my lord," Lady Templestone pressed, drawing him back into the conversation. "If the judge can afford time away, I am sure you can do so as well. The law cannot always take precedence no matter how much you men try to convince me that it should. Even the most dedicated among us needs to indulge in a bit of fun every now and then."

He'd never been one to deny himself pleasure, no matter how demanding his work. He'd been especially committed to such indulgences since Rosamund came into his life and into his bed. He only wished he could have her there tonight—and every night—rather than for a few stolen hours in the afternoon whenever they could manage. He ought to have taken her this afternoon, kissed and caressed aside her reservations and locked her inside his bedchamber where they could have slaked their mutual passions at length.

In the past, with his other lovers, such carnal cravings would have been lessening by now, the initial rush of lust and longing starting to fade gradually until their affair came to its inevitable conclusion. Instead the more he had of Rosamund, the more he wanted. It was almost as though she were becoming an obsession, one he could not seem to shake.

One he wasn't even sure he wanted to shake.

But most worrying of all was how much he enjoyed simply being with her. He could talk to her for hours and hours on end and never once grow bored. He could probably spend the whole of his life doing nothing *but* talking to her and never have cause for complaint.

His gaze moved to Phoebe Templestone. Sweet and pretty and pliant with a brain that was, while not necessarily unintelligent, stuffed with a great deal of useless nonsense nevertheless. Just the memory of some of their conversations made him want to sigh.

Mentally he gave himself a poke and fought to recall what Lady Templestone had just been saying.

That's right. The invitation.

He smiled. "You are quite correct that no man can live solely for the law, dear ma'am," he said smoothly. "And although I cannot promise to join you next month, I shall endeavor to do my best."

Lady Templestone looked as though she wished to press him further, but unbent instead, an almost girlish smile on her lips. "You are too charming by half, Lord Lawrence. It's no wonder you are so successful in everything you do. Phoebe was telling me only the other day how expertly you drive a carriage, while Templestone says you command a courtroom by your mere presence alone. I predict great things in your future. Very great things."

"That remains to be seen," Lawrence said. "But you are all that is kind."

With a wave of his hand, Lord Templestone indicated that the servants could clear the dessert course. A look passed between him and his wife, and then she laid her napkin gracefully aside.

"If you and Templestone will excuse us," she said, "Phoebe and I shall retire so you gentlemen can enjoy a libation at your leisure."

Lawrence and the judge stood while Phoebe and her mother made their way to the door. At the very last instant, Phoebe turned back and gave Lawrence a shy little smile.

A hopeful little smile.

It sent a frisson of unease over his skin.

"Port?" Templestone asked, once the women had gone.

"Yes, please."

Lawrence waited while the butler poured, accepting one of the glasses proffered on a silver tray. The servant withdrew, leaving them alone.

"I crossed paths with Stifton a couple of days ago," Lawrence began, "and he was telling me about a rather intriguing argument he used recently. It seems he—"

"Yes, yes, you'll have to tell me all about it, as well as that other bit of business we needed to discuss," Templestone interrupted. "But first there's another matter I would like to address."

"Oh yes, of course."

"The Season, as I'm sure you are well aware, has all but come to an end. Aristocratic families are returning to their country estates by the day with only a few balls and parties yet to be held for those of us staunch London sorts."

Rather than comment, Lawrence downed a mouthful of liquor, not sure he liked the direction he suspected the conversation was heading.

"My Phoebe has taken well and has had a marvelous time of it these past few weeks from everything I've observed." Templestone drummed his fingers against the table. "Cost me a damned great stack of blunt too, I'll tell you, what with all the dresses and bonnets and feminine folderol the ladies insist they require. But I don't mind, not really, since she's my girl. My one and only child who deserves the best of everything and whatever it is her heart desires."

Templestone pinned him with a pair of blue eyes that were the exact shade of his daughter's but infinitely shrewder and not nearly so sweet.

"Here's the thing, Byron." The judge's jaw tightened in the same implacable way it did when he was about to render a verdict. "You've been squiring my girl about all Season long, dancing attendance on her and giving her the impression that your intentions went a great deal deeper than a simple flirtation. So I'm going to ask you straight out, what are your intentions? And before you answer, there are a couple additional points on which you ought to be briefed."

"And those are?"

Lawrence kept his voice and expression even, refusing to reveal his sudden inner turmoil. Leo had warned him that his hosts were hoping to pin him to the wall tonight, and apparently he'd been right.

Bollocks.

Templestone steepled his fingers against his trim stomach, his white-blond eyebrows drawn into sharp lines. "First, I know you've got a reputation with women, and to some that would make you a less than ideal matrimonial candidate. But I don't hold that against you. A man's entitled to his pleasures—only means he's a man. Frankly I'd think less of you if you hadn't been with your fair share of whores and fancy women by your age. Once you marry, you'll be ready to settle down, all those wild oats well sown and ready to be left in the past.

"My wife, as you saw tonight, finds you charming and your pedigree all the more so. You may not be titled, but you're brother to one of the most powerful peers in the country, so an alliance between our families would prove highly beneficial to the Templestone line."

The judge ran a finger along the base of his glass. "As for your own aspirations in the law, you're a damned fine barrister with a keen head on your shoulders. There's no telling how far you could rise given the right assistance and connections. With my own wise hand to guide you, I have no doubt you will soon find yourself on the bench in a position of immense authority. Who knows, you might even rise to the high court so rapidly you'll find yourself serving at my side."

Rather than respond to such overt blandishments and temptations, Lawrence sipped his port and waited to hear the rest, whatever it might be.

"And so we come to the crux of the matter," Templestone said. "She might not want me telling you this, but my Phoebe's got her heart set on you. She received three perfectly respectable offers of marriage this Season and turned them all down, including one from Viscount Fallows. Eight thousand a year and a winter home in Italy, he's got, and she tossed them away along with a chance to be a viscountess. So long as he's suitable, I promised to leave the choice of husband up to her because I want her to be happy."

The judge locked eyes on him again; Lawrence forced himself not to look away. "So, then, Byron, I ask you again, what are your intentions toward my Phoebe? And keep in mind that my assistance with your career can launch you into the most elevated circles imaginable. On the other hand, if you disappoint my girl, the opposite effect may well occur. A shame if your brilliant legal ascent were to take an unfortunate downward turn. Solicitors are a fickle lot and often change their minds about the capability of certain members of counsel. Steering their clients in the direction of other barristers happens all the time, if you catch my meaning."

Yes, Lawrence thought grimly. *Meaning more than caught.*

The judge smiled, showing his teeth with foxlike cunning. "What do you think, then, Lord Lawrence? Will our families soon have good news to celebrate?"

Lawrence forced down the churning bile in his gut. Whatever he'd been expecting tonight, it hadn't included being blackmailed by a respected high court judge. What he wanted to do was to tell Templestone to take his threats and go bugger himself. Instead he fought for control, wishing again he'd listened to his twin.

Not that it would have made much difference in the grand scheme of things. Templestone had obviously been working up to this for a while, no doubt hoping Lawrence would voluntarily ask for Phoebe's hand so he wouldn't have to resort to threats. But Templestone had obviously grown tired of waiting and decided to have it out with him.

So now what?

Clearly an alliance between him and Phoebe would be beneficial for them both. He'd once thought in such calculating terms, willing to marry her as a stepping-stone to greater things.

Then he'd met Rosamund.

"I'll need a short while to consider," he said, pushing his glass of port aside. "And while we're being so plainspoken, I have to tell you that I am not the sort of man who responds well to threats. I may say no solely to make that point clear and let us see which one of us prevails."

Templestone opened his mouth, but it was Lawrence who forestalled him this time. "Let us say no more on the subject tonight. I'll let you know my decision soon."

Chapter 24

Rosamund sat at the breakfast table two days later, clear July sunshine pouring through the windows of the dining room. She breathed in a fragrant tendril of steam from her cup of morning Assam before taking a long, satisfying sip.

Across from her Bertram sat reading the newspaper while he applied himself to his plate of eggs, ham and toast. She'd just taken a bite of buttered crumpet spread with her favorite blackberry jam when he folded the paper into neat quarters and slid it into her line of sight. He said nothing, just tapped a fingertip atop a story, then returned to his meal.

She looked, curious to see what it was he wanted her to read.

> *Only the other evening, a certain extremely eligible gentleman bachelor was spotted visiting the Kew home of none other than His Honor Baron Judge T and his esteemed wife. The legally inclined Lord LB, who*

curiously enough serves as a barrister despite his ducal connections, was apparently the one and only guest invited to dine en famille with the Ts. During much of this past Season, he's been observed innumerable times in the company of Baron and Lady T's Incomparable daughter, Miss PT, dancing with her at balls, escorting her to fetes and taking her for fashionable drives in Hyde Park. So what are we to make of this intriguing evening out? And can an announcement of a much closer sort be too far behind?

Rosamund's jaw slowed as her eyes moved across the page, the crumpet turning to paste in her mouth. Somehow she managed to swallow, struggling as she forced the lump past her throat.

She set the no-longer-appealing crumpet on its plate and reached for her tea, taking a long swallow as she worked to compose her shaken nerves. Without looking up, she pushed the newspaper toward Bertram, careful not to let the teacup rattle when she placed it back on its saucer.

"When did you take to reading the Society column?" she asked in as casual a tone as she could muster. "I wouldn't have thought such foolishness would interest you."

"Ordinarily it w-wouldn't." He laid his fork on his plate. "But in this instance the names caught my eye."

"The initials, you mean. Hard to tell who they're

even talking about." Even to her own ears, her voice sounded brittle.

"Oh, I wouldn't say that. I think y-you and I know exactly to whom they refer. Let us stop dissembling, Roz. I believe we've been doing that f-far long enough."

Finally she looked up and into Bertram's eyes that were filled with a combination of sympathy, anger and hurt. "How long have you known?" she said.

"About the affair you're having with Lawrence Byron?"

At his blunt confirmation, she felt her heart drop into her stomach. She nodded.

"Almost from the beginning, or at least what I presume was the beginning. I may s-stutter, but I'm not blind or s-stupid. All those trips to court and hours spent at the l-law library. Not even you can do that much research."

She hung her head, ashamed. "I'm sorry I lied to you. I hated doing it, but I thought . . ."

"Yes? What did you think?"

"That you'd try to stop me from seeing him," she said on a near whisper. "Why didn't you, by the way? And why tell me now when you've had so many chances to before?"

He stuck his teaspoon into his cup and stirred, then set it aside. "Because you're an intelligent, adult woman who's capable of looking at all sides of an issue and making up your own mind. I'd already c-cautioned you against Byron. You knew my thoughts regarding his character—which hasn't improved, by the way—yet you continued to put yourself into his orbit. Once you'd decided in his favor, I doubt there's little I could have done or said to have p-prevented you, short of physically locking you in the house, and I wasn't going to do that. I spent my entire life being d-dictated to by our father. I didn't want to do that to you. You've a right to live your life, even if I might have urged you to choose a different path."

"So you think I was wrong? That it's sinful for me to be with him?"

He met her gaze. "Not sinful, no. Only human. It's just that . . ."

"What?"

He sighed. "I worry you're going to be d-dreadfully hurt when it ends. And it *is* going to end, Rosamund."

"I know that," she said in a quiet voice.

"Do you? Do you really? You asked me why now?" He nodded toward the newspaper with its damning bit of gossip. "He's never going to marry you. He's a b-bloody nob and he's going to marry another b-bloody nob like Templestone's daughter or one exactly like her, and when he does, where will that leave you?"

She skimmed a fingertip across the tablecloth. "I never supposed he would marry me, so you needn't entertain any fears on that score. I've always known my relationship with him would be of a short duration."

"And did you also know you'd fall in love with him?"

Her eyes flew to his, then quickly away. "What makes you think I'm in love?"

"Rosamund," he said knowingly. "I thought we were done with the lies. You've been positively floating these past few weeks, so happy even Cook has noticed and she hardly ever even leaves the kitchen. It pains me to spoil it."

"Then why have you?" she demanded, voice catching on a near sob.

He flinched. "Because I've seen your work and know that your final case is about to conclude. When it does, you'll have to go back to being yourself, your real self. Without the disguise, it won't be so simple to see him anymore."

He reached for the teapot and refreshed both of their cups.

She picked hers up and used the porcelain to warm her fingers, which had grown frigid despite the summer heat.

"I blame myself," Bertram said. "I should never have coerced you into this b-blasted deception in the first place. It was wrong and cowardly of m-me and I must b-beg your pardon. If I'd just t-taken Father's cases on myself, none of this would have happened."

"No, don't berate yourself." She reached out and laid a hand over his. "I knew the risks and agreed to the plan. I did it of my own free will and have had not so much as an instant of regret. These past weeks have been the most exciting, fulfilling time of my life. It's been beyond brilliant and I would never wish it away, not for anything."

She drew her hand back, then turned her head to stare out the window. "But you are right. It is time for it to end, all of it. I've been living in a fantasy and I need to come back to the real world."

"So you'll break it off with Byron?"

Panic rose in her chest, squeezing painfully beneath her ribs as she considered his question. She wasn't ready to break it off, not yet. She could stretch out her work awhile longer despite what Bertram said. A few more weeks. A couple of months, even three, four . . .

She suddenly stopped herself, realizing, as she had done not so long ago, that no amount of time with Lawrence would be enough; even forever would be too soon.

"Yes," she said hollowly. "I will break it off."

Bertram nodded. "I really am sorry, Rosamund, but it's the right thing to do."

Perhaps so, she thought. *But if it is, then why does it still feel so wrong?*

Lawrence paced the floor of his study, his thoughts filled with uncertainty and indecision. Nearly a week had passed and he still hadn't made up his mind whether to offer for Phoebe Templestone. On the surface, it seemed a simple enough matter, the only logical choice really, particularly in light of her father's edict.

So why was he still hesitating?

He didn't love Phoebe, but then, love had never factored into his calculations concerning a potential match between them. Theirs would be a marriage of convenience and suitability, a union that would provide benefits to them both. She would gain social entrée as his wife that she did not enjoy now, while he would be in line to achieve even his loftiest career goals. As Templestone had pointed out, with the judge's assistance there was no door within the law that would remain closed to him, including the high court. Conversely those dreams would be all but dead should he refuse.

But he didn't want to think any more about it right now. Rosamund was due to arrive any minute and he longed to forget everything but her for a while and lose himself in her silken embrace.

He went to the liquor cabinet and had just poured himself a glass of Madeira when his butler appeared at the door.

"Your pardon, my lord, but a caller has arrived. I told her you were not receiving this afternoon, but she insists on seeing you."

"*She?* Are you certain this person isn't looking for Lady Leopold?" He took a drink of his wine.

"Quite certain, since she asked for you most specifically."

"And her name?"

Griggs's face took on an expression of quiet disapproval. "She prefers to remain anonymous. Shall I show her out?"

Rosamund—or rather Ross—would be here shortly, but he was intrigued now. Whatever this woman wanted, he was sure it wouldn't take long. "No, show her into the drawing room."

Once his butler withdrew, Lawrence quaffed more wine, then set the glass aside.

He was already in the drawing room when the mystery woman was shown inside, her identity rendered even more mysterious by the wide bonnet and heavy veil that obscured her face. She was dressed all in black, including her gloves and shoes. Given the way she was clothed, she could have been almost anyone.

"I am afraid you have the advantage of me, madam," he said, waiting to speak until after Griggs departed. "Perhaps you would be good enough to reveal yourself so we might converse more comfortably."

Rather than answer, she stepped closer. As she did, a sense of familiarity came over him.

She reached for her veil. "I should think you would know me by now, my lord, considering the intimate nature of our relationship."

"Rosamund?"

Her lovely face came into view as she folded back the veil, her silvery gray eyes entrancing as a moonlit sea.

He stared for a few long seconds, then took her hand and pulled her after him into the study. He shut the door, closing them inside. "What are you doing here dressed like that?"

"Surprising you again or so it would seem. Although considering your reaction, I think it safe to assume Griggs didn't recognize me either."

"And a good thing too. So why the gown? I thought you were visiting me this afternoon as Ross."

Moving to the side table where he'd left his glass of Madeira, she picked it up. "Yours?" At his nod, she drained the half that remained.

"Should you be doing that?" he asked, well aware of her low tolerance for alcohol.

She set down the glass with a quiet clink, then reached up and took off her hat and gloves. "I'm not worried, seeing that I have all night with you." She moved to stand in front of him and laid her hands against his chest. "Assuming you want me to stay the night. Or are you otherwise engaged?"

"I'm not, and even if I were, I'd send my apologies."
He wrapped his hands around her upper arms. "But
what has happened? Why can you suddenly stay? Has
your brother gone out of town?"

She shook her head and stretched up to feather her
lips across his jaw. "No, he's at home." She repeated
her sensual foray along the other side of his jaw.
"What's changed is that he knows."

"Knows? Knows what? About us, do you mean?"

"Exactly." She located a spot just beneath his ear
and swirled the tip of her tongue in a tiny circle.

He tightened his hold and pulled her back enough
that he could look into her face. "And he isn't furious?
He's not planning to storm in here to confront me and
demand we meet on the field of honor at dawn, pistols
drawn?"

"Of course not. He's a lawyer, remember? Dueling
is illegal."

"So is having one's sister pretend to be a man so
she can try cases as a barrister, but that didn't stop
him."

She gave a small sigh. "Apparently he's known
about us for some while. He doesn't approve, but says
I'm a grown woman and that it's up to me to make my
own decisions."

He arched a brow. "How surprisingly enlightened
of him. I'm not sure I would be so forbearing."

"Oh, don't mistake me. He still doesn't like you
and he's not happy about it. But he's decided not to
stand in our way, so why look for problems where
there aren't any?"

He frowned, something about her story not sitting

quite right with him. But then she went back to nuzzling his neck, and the thoughts grew indistinct in his mind, especially when her hand slid downward to find his already thickened shaft through his falls.

She stroked his eager flesh. "I want you, Lawrence. Take me upstairs to your bed."

He pulled her closer and found her lips, kissing her with a fiery intensity that left both of them shaking. "I'm not sure I can wait that long."

Her eyes grew lambent with desire as she kissed him back. "Then don't."

Lifting her off her feet, he carried her across the room to his desk. He shoved books and papers to the floor, uncaring where they fell as he set her on top, then parted her legs and stepped between.

Her mouth was lush and satiny, sweet with the flavor of the wine she'd drunk as he kissed her with ever-deepening intensity. She answered each sweeping foray of his tongue with an equally enthusiastic response, her own tongue swirling and darting and gliding against his in ways that drove his need higher. She tunneled her fingers into his hair and kissed him harder, kissed him as if she never wanted to stop.

He reached for the buttons on the back of her gown, unfastening enough of them that he could tug her bodice down. To his immense delight, he discovered that she wasn't wearing stays, only a thin cotton shift. A ribbon and a few buttons more and her naked breasts were exposed, her warm, creamy flesh trembling slightly as she awaited his touch.

He found her nipples first, fingering them in exactly the way she liked so that the tips drew up hard as berries. Taking hold of her arms, he set her hands flat on the desk behind her so that her back was arched, her breasts extended toward him like an offering. Bending low, he took her into his mouth, suckling hard, then pausing every so often to press one of her engorged nipples between his teeth and tongue.

She cried out, her head hung back as he feasted.

Straightening abruptly, he reached for the skirt of her dress and pushed it up over her legs to her waist. She was bare there as well, no pesky drawers to get around this time. Heat roared through him, his erection hard and pulsing. His nostrils flared at her delicious feminine scent, his gaze moving to the dark triangle of curls between her legs that was moist with obvious arousal. He stroked the satiny length of her legs, slowing to tease her inner thighs with a diabolical purpose that made her moan and tremble before he slid a pair of fingers into her wet, clinging core.

But she had devilish plans of her own, his thoughts turning dark and half-dazed as she unfastened his trousers and drawers and took him into her hand. He'd taught her well, perhaps too well, he realized, as she stroked him with a finesse that nearly brought him to his knees.

They began kissing in a frenzied mating of lips and tongues that presaged the mating they ultimately craved.

And suddenly he had to be inside her, had to make her totally and completely his own. Taking hold of her bare hips, he eased her back across the desk and thrust possessively into her, sheathing himself as far as he could go.

Yet somehow it wasn't far enough.

He needed more.

He needed everything.

Everything that she was.

Everything she could give until he had all of her, so no secrets remained, no truths hidden or questions that lay unanswered.

Hooking her legs over his arms, he inched her forward and opened her wider, holding her so that she was his to take, his to control. She didn't resist, her body absolutely enslaved. Her eyes opened, glassy with passion as they looked into his.

He looked back, not breaking contact, as he began to thrust heavily inside her, letting her know with each powerful stroke to whom it was that she belonged.

"Say my name," he demanded.

"Lawrence." She moaned, her breath coming in rapid pants between her parted lips.

"Tell me that you're mine."

"I'm yours."

"And only mine."

"Only yours."

"Will you ever want another?"

"No. Only you. God, Lawrence, only you. Always."

Thrusting faster, he plunged in and out, struggling not to claim his own satisfaction as he drove her onward toward hers.

Suddenly her velvety inner muscles began to convulse, milking his shaft with a power that left him helpless. And as her keening cries rang in his ears, he gave himself over to the bliss, spilling himself powerfully inside her with a hoarse shout.

Chapter 25

Rosamund awakened to early-morning darkness, momentarily startled to find herself in unfamiliar surroundings. Then, almost in the same breath, she became aware of the large, extremely comfortable mattress beneath her and even more so of the large male body curved along the length of her back.

Lawrence slept next to her, one deliciously heavy arm hooked around her waist, one of his calves nestled between hers. The sheets were a tangled mess around them—no surprise, considering all the times they'd made love since they'd come upstairs so many hours earlier.

After their first coupling in his study, he'd helped her dress, taking care to put her bonnet and veil back on so her identity would remain a secret should they encounter one of the servants. Once inside his bedchamber, they'd stripped each other bare, then tumbled onto his bed, where he'd taken her with a feverish hunger that even now had the power to make her heart skip a beat.

They'd slept for a while, then awakened to share an evening meal of ripe cheeses, cold meat, yeasty bread and succulent summer fruits. When she bit into a whole fresh peach and juice dribbled over her chin and down onto her naked breasts, he'd insisted on licking her clean. But he hadn't stopped there, kissing and laving his way over her entire body, paying especial attention to her most intimate parts.

He brought her to a peak so many times over the next few hours that she'd lost count, while she'd done her best to pleasure him in return, relishing the sounds of his fierce need and his even fiercer satisfaction.

Finally they'd slept, entangled in each other's arms. It was a night she knew she'd never forget—their first together and their last.

She lay still now, memorizing every detail, listening to the soft rhythm of his breath as he slept, his warm body spooned around her own. She found his hand and wove her fingers ever so gently between his, then pressed his arm tighter against her, wishing she could stay like this forever. Wishing somehow she never had to leave.

Behind her she felt him stir. She held her breath for a moment as he quieted again, then ever so softly shimmied back, unwilling to lose even a fraction of their closeness.

"You know if you keep doing that I won't be held responsible for my actions," he murmured groggily. "Go back to sleep."

She waited until he settled, then shimmied again.

This time when he stirred, a particular part of his anatomy did as well. He groaned. "Didn't I tire you out enough last night?"

"You did, but I'm awake again now." She moved his hand so it cradled one of her breasts.

With his thumb, he stroked an already sensitized tip. She moaned softly and arched her bottom against him. "Go back to sleep. I'll just lie here."

He grew harder. "Sleep? How could I possibly sleep now? You've turned into a siren, the sort who leads good men to their doom."

"Then isn't it lucky you're not a good man?" she teased in a breathless voice.

He chuckled and kissed her shoulder. "Hmm, yes, lucky for you."

She started to turn around to face him, but he kept her where she was, sliding his leg higher so his thigh was now wedged between hers.

"Lawrence?"

Rather than answer, he parted her thighs even more and thrust deeply inside her, penetrating her fully with a single stroke. She felt him everywhere, surrounded as he began rocking them together. He tightened their clasped hands, his rhythm slow and easy, as if they had all the time in the world. She bit her lip and gave herself completely to the moment, losing herself to him one final time.

And as the dawn light began to break over the horizon, he brought her to an exquisite climax, her cries drowning out the sorrow waiting like a shadow in her heart.

"It's still early yet," Lawrence said a while later as he stroked his fingers down her arm. "Why don't you stay? We'll have breakfast together." Catching her hand in his, he brought it to his mouth and caressed her palm. "You could even stay for lunch. I have work but nothing so pressing it can't wait."

Rosamund leaned up from where she lay beside him and pressed her mouth to his, lingering for several long bittersweet moments before she forced herself to roll away and sit up. "It's better if I leave now. I need to get home."

She stood and padded naked across the soft Aubusson carpet. Her shift lay in a messy heap on the floor, next to her petticoat and a solitary stocking. It took her several seconds to locate the other one dangling from atop his shaving stand. As for her garters, one was hooked around the doorknob, while the other had quite improbably landed on one of the fireplace irons. Luckily her dress had fared better and was draped with relative neatness over a nearby chair together with her hat and gloves.

She began with her undergarments first, bending to retrieve them from the floor, her back—and backside—turned toward him.

"You know," Lawrence drawled, "if you persist in doing things like that, I may just lock the door and never let you out again."

She turned her head and gave him a faint smile before straightening to slide her shift on over her head.

He sat up. "What's wrong?"

"Nothing," she said with casual denial. "Why would anything be wrong?" She reached for her petticoat. "Did I tell you that my last lawsuit is nearly finished? The clients have indicated a willingness to settle, so I won't even need to appear in court again. It should all be over in the next couple of days."

"Ah, I see." He left the bed, pausing to put on his trousers and fasten them.

She collected her stockings and garters from their various locations and moved toward a chair. Before she could sit down, he was there before her.

Gently he wrapped his hands around her upper arms. "I'm sorry, Rosamund. I know how much you love the law."

She shrugged, refusing to meet his eyes. "I always knew it was a temporary situation. And I certainly won't miss having to bind my breasts every day. I don't find my stays nearly as oppressive as I used to."

Rather than comment, he drew her into his arms.

She stood stiffly for a few seconds, then gave up and leaned into him, breathing in the warmth of his skin and the delicious, underlying scent that was pure Lawrence. She buried her nose against his chest and inhaled, wanting to memorize him so she would never forget.

He rubbed a slow hand along her back. "Are you sure you have to give it up now? I know what I said before about you stopping, but you're such a good barrister. Somehow it doesn't seem right to make you quit solely because you're a woman."

"And a fraud, since the legal world at large believes I'm a man." With a sigh, she straightened. "No, I've pushed my luck as far as I dare. It's time I went back to being plain, ordinary Rosamund Carrow."

He met her gaze. "There is nothing plain or ordinary about you."

When he bent to kiss her, she pulled away and retreated to the bed, where she took a seat and began to put on her stockings. He stared, brow creased, his fists on his hips. "And what of us? Once you go back to being yourself?"

A knot formed at the base of her throat, but she ignored it, forcing herself to do what she must. "What of us? We've had a great deal of fun, I'll admit, and I've adored our time together. It's been vastly educational." She flashed him a smile she hoped looked carefree when inside she was dying. "But we've always known this arrangement would be temporary. This seems as good a time as any to say our farewells."

He looked stunned; then his eyes turned stormy. "Did you come here yesterday planning this? What was last night? Some sort of energetic good-bye?"

"Last night was wonderful and this morning as well. I'll never forget it or any of our other times together. But our affair needs to end. I can't very well come over here wearing my hat and veil every time one of us has an itch to scratch. Doing it once was scandalous enough."

Crossing to the chair where her dress was draped, she picked it up and slipped into it. She turned her back to him. "Will you button me up, please?"

For a moment, she thought he was going to refuse, and then he moved behind her and reached for the fastenings. Silently he secured each one, but rather than releasing her when he was finished, he wrapped his hands around her shoulders and pulled her tightly against him.

"Maybe I'm not ready to end things," he murmured

as he brushed a kiss along her throat. "Maybe I don't want to let you go. Perhaps I need you with me both day and night."

Her pulse leapt, some nascent glimmer of hope flaring to life inside her. What did he mean? Surely he wasn't implying that he wanted something permanent. He hadn't said anything about love, but could this be his way of leading up to a proposal?

Then he went on. "Let me take care of you, Rosamund. I own a town house on Brook Street, but if it doesn't suit you, I'll buy you something else. You'll have anything you desire, a coach and horses, servants, clothing and jewelry, whatever you want. We can travel. I remember you saying once how much you'd love to see Paris and Rome. We'll go to France first, then Italy, and tour both countries, top to toe. And when we return, you can assist me with some of my cases. I realize it won't be the same as representing the clients yourself, but I'd value your insight and you can keep a hand in that way. You can still work in the law, only with me this time rather than your father and brother."

Her heart turned cold, her shoulders tensing beneath his hands. "So I'm to be your mistress—is that right?"

"No, you'll still be my lover." His voice changed, obviously sensing that he'd misstepped. "We just won't have to hide as we've been doing until now."

"And you'll pay all my expenses and find me a new place to live. How magnanimous." She pulled herself from his hold and went to find her remaining garments. "But you see, I already have a place to live. Besides, won't such an arrangement cause difficulties with your fiancée?"

"What do you mean?" he said guardedly.

"Oh, come, now, Lawrence." She gave a hollow laugh. "Let us not dissemble, not at this stage of our acquaintance. I read something recently that said you're all but engaged to Judge Templestone's daughter."

"I am not engaged to her."

"But you know her, do you not?" She turned and leveled a look at him. Her stomach churned to see the guilt on his face. "You've been courting her all summer long. All the time you've known me."

He dragged his fingers through his hair. "Look, it's a great deal more complicated than you think. I met her before I met you and at the time a match between us made sense. I suppose, on the surface, it still does."

"Because of her father? Of course." She thrust her feet into her shoes, then went to retrieve her gloves. "Given his position on the high court, I can see how he would be of great help to you and your desire to move into the judiciary."

"That was the original idea, yes," he admitted.

"And now?"

He met her gaze, his eyes haunted. "And now Templestone expects me to offer for her. If I don't, he says he'll make it his life's work to destroy not only my hopes to be a judge but my career as a barrister as well. She doesn't mean anything to me, Rosamund. It needn't have anything to do with us."

The breath went out of her at his confession, which was by far worse than anything she might have imagined. "So you thought to have us both; is that it? Miss Templestone and me?"

"No. Maybe. *Bollocks*, I don't know." He dragged

his fingers through his hair again, leaving it in an even messier disarray that somehow still managed to look attractive. He sank down on the edge of the bed. "I've been cudgeling my brains all week trying to think of a way out of this, but I can't. Not without . . ." His words dwindled into silence, hanging between them, heavy as a lodestone.

"Not without giving up the law," she finished.

"I suppose I could call Templestone's bluff, but I don't think he's bluffing. I think he really does mean to destroy me unless I marry Phoebe, and unfortunately he has the influence to do it."

He was right. Templestone was an extremely powerful and influential figure in legal circles. A positive nod from him could make a man's career. A blackball would end it.

Loving the law was what had drawn her and Lawrence together in the first place; losing his ability to practice it would crush him, even more so than it was going to do to her. But then, she'd always known she would have to give it up; being a barrister had never been anything more than a fancy. But for Lawrence, being cast out of the courts and unable to practice . . . well, it would be like a death.

As for any possible affection he might feel for her, it would surely die under the weight of such a loss. And if he were to choose her, he might well come to resent his decision—might even come to resent her. Hate her? And what then would any of it have been for?

Her heart splintered into a thousand jagged pieces, and suddenly she knew what she had to do.

"Marry her," she said in a dull voice.

His gaze swung up to meet hers. "What?"

"Marry Miss Templestone." She stared at the floor, blinking rapidly against the pressure building behind her eyes. "It's the only logical thing to do."

"But, Rosamund, I don't want to marry her," he said thickly. "I don't love her. I love—"

She put her hand over his mouth and silenced him. "Don't say it. You may feel that way right now, but later you won't."

He lifted her fingers away but didn't let go of her hand. "How can you be so sure?"

"It's only an infatuation," she lied. "One we'll both soon be over."

"And if it's not?" he asked. "I know I shouldn't ask again, but might you reconsider?"

Easing away, she moved to pull on her gloves. "Being your kept woman, you mean? I think we both know the answer to that. I've far too much pride for such an arrangement. What we've had these past few weeks, it's been like something out of an enchanted dream. But I could never abide being seen as your whore. So no, Lawrence, I will not be your mistress."

His eyes blazed with sudden anger. "I thought I told you never to call yourself such a thing. You would be someone infinitely precious to me."

"Maybe so, but the world would see it differently."

He sighed, his expression bleak. "Will I see you again?"

Picking up her hat, she put it on her head and tied the ribbons beneath her chin. "No, I think a clean break will be the best thing for us both."

He laughed but without any real humor.

"What is funny?" she asked.

"Nothing really. Only that I'm usually the one who says such things. I never thought I'd someday be the one on the receiving end."

She hesitated, then crossed to him. "Will you promise me something?"

He looked up from where he sat on the edge of the bed, his beautiful gold-green eyes very bright. "If it is within my power."

"Promise me you'll be happy, Lawrence."

Without giving him time to answer, she cupped his face in her hands and kissed him, pouring everything inside her into that last passionate touch.

Then, before she could change her mind about everything, she wrenched herself away and hurried to the door, unable to bring herself to utter that one final word.

Good-bye.

Chapter 26

For Rosamund, the next month moved past in a kind of fractured blur, some moments sharp and distinct, others barely acknowledged and forgotten only seconds after they had occurred. She went about her usual routine, presuming of course that there was anything remotely usual left of her routine, given the fact that she had lost two of its most essential parts within quick succession of each other.

First had come her breakup with Lawrence; then five days later she signed *Ross Carrow* on the documents for her last legal case and put an end to that as well. With dull eyes, she'd taken off her male garb, had it laundered, then folded all the garments neatly into a trunk. Her robe and wig had gone inside as well, since Bertram said he had no use for them; he was done with arguing cases before the court as well.

Afterward, she'd taken to drifting around the house like a ghost, quiet in a way she had never been. Often she would sit in a chair next to the window that overlooked the rear garden, a book lying open and unread in her lap. Bertram did his best to rally her, making sure she ate at least a few bites at each meal, offering her cups of tea and attempting to engage her in work or conversation. But she had no heart for any of it. Since losing Lawrence she felt as if she had no heart left at all.

She hadn't cried, not once. It was a pain that went far too deep. And at night, when she should have been sleeping, she would lie in the dark and think of him, wondering whether he missed her or if he was secretly glad to be free.

She remembered how she'd felt when Tom died, the boy she'd loved so long ago. Yet in spite of the depth of her sorrow then, it was nothing compared to this current loss. She'd known Tom very little really, their affection so innocent and carefree that she could now only marvel at its youthful folly.

With Lawrence, though, there had been nothing innocent or carefree about the experience. It had been raw and passionate, bold and maybe even a little insane. Knowing him, loving him, had been soul-altering, as if his touch had imprinted itself upon her and changed her in ways she was only now beginning to understand.

Perhaps worst of all, she simply missed him. Their quiet conversations and spirited debates, their mutual enjoyment of so many of the same things. At least once an hour she thought of something she wanted to share with him, or ask him, but she couldn't, not anymore.

Never again.

And so she pushed it all away, shoved it down deep

where she hoped she could keep it securely locked away so that someday she might find the strength to forget.

Then, on the morning of the thirteenth day, she saw it, the one thing that burst the dam wide. It was a tiny column in the *Morning Post*, only a few lines long, that relayed the information that Miss Phoebe Templestone, only daughter of esteemed justice The Lord Templestone, was lately engaged to be married to The Right Honourable Lord Lawrence Byron of London and Gloucestershire.

Bertram tried to keep her from reading the announcement, but she'd been alert enough to realize that he was keeping something from her. She'd demanded to see the paper, holding out a hand despite a protective part of herself that warned her to leave well enough alone.

She leapt from the table after reading it, racing for the nearest convenience in which she could be sick. She'd heaved until her stomach was dry, then let Bertram carry her upstairs to her room where she'd been put to bed. One of the maids had brought cold cloths for her swollen face and aching head, but nothing could stem the tide of the ragged sobs that broke through her like endlessly pounding waves.

She cried for two days straight, rising only to be sick again before finally she fell into a heavy, listless sleep.

Cook sent up strong beef tea and egg custards—two of her favorites whenever she was under the weather—but she left them untouched, preferring to huddle in a cocoon of oblivion.

On the third day, an extremely worried Bertram sent for the physician, who pronounced that she seemed to have suffered a nervous shock of some sort and advised repeated bloodlettings and immersion in a series of freezing cold, then boiling hot, baths.

Bertram kicked him out the door, Rosamund would later learn from one of the footmen, the doctor buoyed away on a stream of stuttered, but very understandable, curse-filled epithets.

It was Bertram who had finally broken through her delirium, forcing her at first to eat and drink, then later coaxing her to soak in a pleasantly warm bath, put on her dressing gown and come downstairs.

Yet even as she regained some of her emotional equilibrium, her nausea and vomiting continued, coming upon her most often in the mornings. It was at the start of the third full week when she realized the cause.

She was with child.

At first she was panicked and disbelieving, telling herself it couldn't be true, even though she knew in her heart that it was. She'd missed her menses right around the time she learned about Lawrence's engagement and had assumed it was her emotional breakdown that had caused the delay. But she'd always been as regular as one of the king's clocks, and when she still hadn't begun her bleeding eight days later, she began to suspect the real reason.

She thought back, reviewing her last few rendezvous with Lawrence, and realized that in the days leading up to the final night she'd spent with him, she'd forgotten all about taking the herbs he'd given her.

She'd run out of them several days before, and in all the anguished anticipation of their parting, it had completely slipped her mind to visit the chemist for more.

Or had it?

Had some unconscious part of her secretly longed for his child, despite the difficulty and potential shame a pregnancy would cause? She supposed she would never really know, and at this point it didn't much matter. She was pregnant and that was that.

Curiously a strange calm came over her, a clarity of purpose she hadn't felt in weeks. For the first time since she'd parted from Lawrence, a small glimmer of brightness lay on her horizon.

Still, she'd had to work up the courage to tell Bertram, anticipating how disappointed in her he would be. But if she were to make things work as she wished them to, she would need his support as well as his understanding.

To her surprise, though, he took the news with considerable aplomb, blinking a few extra times before he drew her into his arms for a long hug.

"You're k-keeping it, I presume," he asked as they sat together behind closed doors in the family parlor, talking over cups of afternoon tea.

She nodded. "Yes, but I'll need a story, something that will be believed by people we know, even if a few may still have their suspicions. I've been trying to think of a way, but so far I haven't come up with anything plausible."

Bertram drank his tea and fell silent. Then abruptly he set down his empty cup. "You'll go to our cousins in the north country."

"What?"

"Yes, we'll write and ask if you can stay with C-Cousin Ross and his wife. I reckon they'll be happy to have you."

She arched an eyebrow. "The same Cousin Ross I've been impersonating."

"Exactly. And don't worry, they know n-nothing of what you've been doing here in London and there's no reason why they ever should."

"But what will I tell them about . . . well, about the baby?"

"I've been thinking that through and I believe I have the answer." He paused and reached for the teapot to pour himself another cup.

"Yes?" she said impatiently. "And?"

His eyes went to hers. "Oh, you'll tell them you were recently married but your husband d-died shortly after the wedding. Accidental drowning or some such. You're so distraught that you need a change of scenery, can't b-bear to stay in London. Once there, you'll discover you're with child and ask to remain through the baby's birth. Fear of traveling and losing the child en route."

She frowned, considering. "And when I return here to London?"

"We'll tell everyone the same thing, only slightly rearranged. You went north to spend time with our c-cousins, met, married and were widowed while you were living away. As for the baby, you can claim he was premature. As you said, a few people may have their suspicions, but that's all they'll be. Most will accept the t-tale at face value, particularly if I lay the groundwork here at home with news of your letters telling me everything you've been through."

Slowly she smiled. "That's brilliant, Bertie. If we play this right, I think it just might work."

"I haven't the slightest doubt."

"You know, you really are rather marvelous at making up stories. Perhaps you ought to switch professions and write novels like Lawrence's brother."

She froze, Lawrence's name hanging in midair between them. It was the first time she'd said it aloud in over a month. Her smile fell abruptly away, her lighter spirits along with it.

"Will you tell him?" Bertram asked after a pause.

She didn't have to ask who or about what. "No. I've thought about it a lot, but I don't see the point. He's to be married, and telling him about the baby will only complicate things."

"Still, he's to be a father. Hasn't he a right to know?"

Guilt rose inside her, but she pushed it aside. "He didn't want a child. He made that more than clear when we were together. I doubt he'll care."

But even as she said it, she knew the words were a lie. Lawrence might not have planned to make a child with her, but if he found out he had, he would never turn his back on his offspring. Frankly she wasn't sure how he would react, and that was what worried her the most. He might offer her financial support—which she would refuse. Or he might wish to see the child as it grew, to have a relationship, which meant that she would have to see Lawrence—see him but never again be with him.

Worse, what if he wanted to take the baby from her? She doubted he would ever be so coldhearted as to rip a child away from its mother, but people did odd things when it came to their children. He might even suggest she give the baby up to Leo and his wife to raise. They had an adopted daughter now. Maybe they would want a son, assuming she gave birth to a boy. And since Leo and Lawrence were twins, it would be a simple matter for Leo to claim parentage.

Lawrence might also feel honor-bound to do the right thing and end his engagement in order to marry her. As much as she might love the idea of being his wife, she would never agree under those circumstances, would never countenance his jilting another woman, ruining his reputation and destroying his career out of a sense of obligation to her and their baby.

What a terrible way to begin a life together. What a miserable basis for a marriage.

So she would remain silent and swear Bertram to silence as well.

"This is *my* baby," she declared. "Mine to raise alone."

"Not alone," Bertram said gently. "He—or she— will have me for an uncle and I p-plan to spoil them quite shamelessly. The two of you will always have a home here with me, you know, no matter what may come."

Her shoulders sagged, a tear sliding down her cheek. "I don't know what I'd do without you, Bertie."

"Now, now, n-none of that. If you start blubbering in earnest, you'll quite put me off my feed."

She gave a weepy laugh and wiped her eyes.

"I'll get started on the letter to Cousin Ross while you decide what to pack." He smacked his hands against his thighs and stood. "And why don't you have a lie-down before dinner? I've heard expectant m-mothers need their rest."

She nodded in agreement and got to her feet, more relieved than she'd been in days.

Yet later as she lay in bed, trying to nap, she found herself worrying about everything that was to come, everything she would have to face without the one man she truly wanted at her side. Sliding a hand over her belly where their child nestled already, she let herself be with Lawrence the only way she could—in the private sanctuary of her dreams.

"You'd better find a way to wipe that hangdog look off your face. Otherwise, the whole family will be wanting to know who died and what you haven't been telling them."

Lawrence pulled his eyes away from the coach window and the passing Gloucestershire countryside long enough to cast a baleful glare at Leo. "I'll be certain to take that under advisement. In the meantime, why don't you go get buggered and keep your opinions to yourself?"

"As anatomically unpleasant as that prospect sounds, I think you're the one in need of having several sticks removed from a certain tender area of your person."

Rather than react to the fresh gibe, Lawrence returned his attention to the bare December branches on the trees and the frost-covered fields ranging beyond—a landscape that felt as empty and cheerless as his spirits of late.

For the first time in his memory, he was not looking forward to the annual family gathering at Braebourne, home to the Dukes of Clybourne and the Byrons for generations. Every year it was tradition for as many family members as possible to crowd inside the palatial country house, filling the large rooms and wide hallways with noise and merriment, and in the past few years, the high-pitched shouts and giggles of Lawrence's growing multitude of nieces and nephews.

Thalia and Esme, in fact, were riding in the coach ahead, nursemaids and babies in tow, including Thalia and Leo's new daughter, Julia. His brother-in-law Northcote had had the smart idea of traveling on horseback despite the freezing air and threat of snow. Lawrence wished now that he'd joined him, anything to keep himself distracted from the doleful thoughts that plagued him. Or rather the person whom he could not seem to shake from his mind.

He sighed and tried not to think about her, but it was impossible. She was the first thing he thought about when he awakened each morning and the last thing on his mind when he went to bed at night.

Concentrating on work provided him with some measure of distraction at least, so he'd begun to take on more and more cases, burying himself under a mountain of demands in an effort to keep constantly busy. Yet as his record of court victories increased, he found that he took little joy in the wins. His friends and fellow attorneys congratulated him, but it all felt strangely hollow without being able to share it with her.

Needing more, he'd increased his social engagements so that by the time he came home at night, he fell into bed, too tired some nights to even undress.

Then there were the women. He'd visited more than a few, determined to lose himself in their willing flesh only to end up feeling guilty and wrong afterward. The more of them he had, the more dissatisfied he became until he gave them up entirely, finding every one, no matter how skilled or seductive, unable to compare to the one he truly desired.

Yet despite all his efforts, he couldn't control the dreams, or his despair as he jolted awake, his body rigid with need, her name a soundless call on his lips.

Rosamund.

But she was gone, and in his past, and he would forget her.

He *had* to forget her.

Still, it had been five months and he was no closer to unshackling himself from her memory than he had been the day she walked out of his life.

He wondered how she was and what she was doing. Probably she was at home in London with her brother getting ready for the holidays. Since *Ross Carrow* had quite abruptly and unexpectedly packed up and returned north to his old home county, no one had seen or heard from the impressive young barrister. It was almost as if he'd never existed at all. As for Bertram Carrow, he was nearly as scarce as his *cousin*, no longer appearing in court and only rarely setting foot inside Lincoln's Inn and never when Lawrence was there.

He'd thought more than once about dropping by her town house, but what was the point? It would only reopen the wound and do nothing to change the fact that it was too late for either of them. For exactly as Rosamund had counseled him to do, he'd proposed to Phoebe Templestone, who had dimpled with graceful acceptance and cheerfully begun showing off her ring.

His family had been surprised by the news of his engagement but offered him hearty congratulations despite any private reservations they might have held. As for Leo, who was the only one who knew the full story, he'd been outraged, railing against Lawrence for being a stubborn, short-sighted, calculating fool who'd let ambition get in the way of his own happiness.

Lawrence had told himself at the time that Leo was wrong. That his twin had never taken the law and his career seriously and that no woman was worth giving up the professional strides and intellectual achievements of a lifetime. The work would nourish him, he'd told himself; need for the woman would fade.

But as he stared sightlessly out the coach window, he was beginning to think he'd been wrong. He was beginning to think he'd made the greatest mistake of his life.

But he was engaged and there was no longer anything to be done about it. Phoebe and her parents were coming to Braebourne for Christmas so they could become better acquainted with his family. She and her mother were deep into making wedding arrangements, although the only confirmed details so far were the date—June twenty-ninth; the church—St. George's, Hanover Square, in London; and the fact that half the Haut Ton would likely be receiving an invitation.

Even if things were different, Rosamund might well have moved on by now. If the men in her orbit had even the smallest amount of sense, at least one of them would have started courting her. Some up-and-coming captain of industry perhaps, a man with enough good humor and intelligence to see what a prize he had before him. If the fellow were smart, he would waste no time marrying her, wanting nothing and no one to stand in the way of claiming her for his own.

The idea of her in another man's arms drove him mad with jealousy, haunting him in ways he'd never imagined.

Had she taken a new lover?

Had she found someone else to love?

Assuming she'd ever loved him at all. The passion between them had been intense and undeniable, but maybe that was all it had been for her. And yet there were times when he thought he'd glimpsed something more in her eyes, a tender adoration that had been visible only when she thought he wasn't looking. An expression that could only have been love.

If only he could see that tenderness again.

If only he could see her.

He squeezed his eyes shut and pressed his forehead against the cold window glass.

God, what a shambles I've made of everything.

Leo was right and he had only himself to blame for not realizing in time how very much he loved her.

"You're not married yet, you know," Leo said quietly as if he could read his thoughts. "Until you've spoken those wedding vows, there is nothing that cannot be undone."

Lawrence looked at his brother with desolate eyes. "I'm honor-bound. I have to marry her."

"Yes, well, that is the gentleman's code. Then again, we Byrons are a lot of rogues and scoundrels who thrive on scandal and unconventionality. And really, is honor worth a lifetime of misery and regret? Think on that, brother. Before you commit, I ask you to think long and hard on that."

Lawrence stayed busy in the days leading up to Christmas. He helped cut and bring in the Yule log that would burn through the New Year inside one of Braebourne's massive fireplaces. He went riding in the mornings with a number of his relations. He participated in a daylong excursion to an old abbey that boasted particularly fine stained glass windows and ice-skated on a nearby frozen pond that proved a great success, especially with many of the children and the ladies. In the evenings after dinner, he joined the others as they all played cards and charades, sang and played the pianoforte, and listened to recitations of poems and stories that kept everyone well entertained.

Meanwhile, he worked at being an attentive fiancé to Phoebe—escorting her on walks through the snow-covered garden, showing her paintings of his ancestors in the portrait gallery, bringing her plates of sweetmeats for tea and partnering with her for games and holiday festivities. He listened to her musings and answered with his own, all the while contemplating what it would be like when she was his wife.

And exactly like the weather outside, he turned colder and colder by the day.

Leo had asked him to consider, and he had done so, his twin's words a constant nagging refrain in his mind.

He wanted to do the right thing.

But the right thing for whom?

Everyone gathered in the largest of the drawing rooms on Christmas Day to drink wassail, eat plum pudding and exchange presents. Lawrence did his best to keep up his cheerful facade, but the effort was quickly wearing thin.

On the excuse of refilling his drink, he got to his feet and crossed the room, hoping if he managed things right, he could slip out without anyone noticing. He couldn't stand the happy act anymore; he needed to be alone.

He had just reached the doorway when Phoebe appeared on the other side. Obviously she'd had the same idea as he and was only then returning from wherever in the house she had been. Her cheeks were flushed, one hand in her pocket as she pushed what appeared to be a letter deeper inside.

"Leaving, Lord Lawrence?" she asked.

"Yes, but for a few minutes only. I shall return before you even have time to notice my absence."

She gave a tentative half smile. "Everyone seems to be having such a lovely time."

"My family is known for their exuberance, particularly on holidays."

She nodded, casting a glance toward her parents, who appeared a bit wooden where they sat side by side on one of the sofas, decorously unwrapping their gifts.

The Byrons, on the other hand, were merrily tugging ribbons free and tearing off the tops of boxes, laughing and calling out their gratitude to one another while children of various ages raced around the room, playing with their new games and toys in the midst of the adults rather than being relegated upstairs to the nursery.

"Thank you for the gloves and perfume," she said. "They were most thoughtful."

Not really, he thought, since her mother had been the one to suggest them both, but hopefully they were things she would genuinely enjoy.

"My thanks to you for the book and the handkerchiefs. One can never have too many of either."

"Papa suggested the book. He thought it was one you might find interesting."

It was. Unfortunately he'd already read it, but he was too polite to mention that fact.

They stood, quiet in each other's company. Awkward in a way no affianced couple should be.

He was just about to murmur an excuse so he could complete his escape when there came gleeful calls from two of his nephews, the boys jumping up and down as they pointed at the door lintel above his head.

"You have to kiss her now," ten-year-old Maximillian said in a singsong voice.

"Ew." Zachary, Max's younger brother, clapped his hands and bounced up and down in place. "You've been caught, Uncle Lawrence, and have to pay the piper. That's the rule."

The boys whispered together, then snickered.

Looking up, Lawrence saw the green-and-white

mistletoe sprig hanging above himself and Phoebe. He cursed silently while Phoebe's eyes widened and her mouth rounded into an O.

"Actually, lads, Miss Phoebe isn't directly underneath it with me, so—" Lawrence began.

"Oh, go on," Jack called from across the room. "Kiss her."

"The boys are right. You and Phoebe have been fairly caught." Meg tossed a grin to her sons, her arms folded at her waist, which was still a bit thick after having given birth to a daughter, Bryn, only five weeks earlier. "Time to pay up, as Zachary so rightly said."

"What's wrong with you, Lawrence?" Ned declared. "I've never seen you reluctant to kiss a woman before, particularly your own fiancée."

Several of his other relations cheered their encouragement. Only Leo looked on with a frown, his arms crossed over his chest. And interestingly their mother, Ava, who watched with a troubled expression in her clear green eyes.

Lawrence forced a smile and turned to Phoebe. "Well, it would seem we're outnumbered. Shall we?"

Her cheeks turned pink, but she didn't move away. Bending, he touched his mouth lightly to hers, then straightened again.

"That's no kiss," Adam Gresham complained.

"Yes, do it properly," said Gabriel. "We all know you know how."

Good-natured laughter rang out.

Lawrence looked at Phoebe again, noticing that her cheeks had turned an even more vibrant shade of pink. He'd never actually kissed her before, not with a man's full passion, having shared nothing more intimate with her than another quick brush of lips after she'd accepted his proposal. Considering their relationship and his own womanizing reputation, he supposed it was a peculiar state of affairs.

Maybe kissing her was exactly what he needed?

Maybe it would prove so pleasant he would be able to put the memory of another woman's touch out of his mind for good.

Moving closer, he pulled her into his arms and kissed her—for real this time.

He did his best, closing his eyes and pouring himself into the act that he'd always before found so pleasurable. He kissed her harder, wanting to want her, suddenly desperate to lose himself in her embrace. But all he could think about was how wrong it felt. That this kiss was nothing more than a betrayal, worse in its own way than kisses he'd known with the other women he'd used in an attempt to extinguish his feelings for the one he truly craved. Yet no matter how he tried, those emotions, that love, could not be killed.

Rosamund is my love. The only one I will ever want, now and for eternity. Go to her and stop being such a blasted, idiotic fool already.

He broke away, setting Phoebe from him, as a quiet resolve settled over him—a peace unlike any he'd known.

Then he noticed Phoebe staring at him, her gaze strangely accusing. Around them, the room had fallen eerily silent.

"Who is Rosamund?" she asked, her voice low but firm enough to carry all the same.

"What?" Surely he couldn't have heard her right.

"You said *Rosamund* there at the end," Phoebe told him. "I heard it quite distinctly. So? Who is she?"

"Boys. Children," Meg announced as she held a pair of maternal arms wide as if to gather close every child in the room. "Let's go look at your presents again. You must all be eager to play."

"Yes, they must." Grace got to her feet, along with Claire, Mallory, Esme, Thalia and Sebastianne, who began gently guiding the young ones away from the scene.

The others stayed to watch. Leo, Lawrence noticed, was grinning widely. The Templestones, however, were not.

"This is an outrage." Lord Templestone stood, fists clenched at his sides. "What have you to say for yourself, Byron?"

Lawrence ignored him and turned to Phoebe, his voice gentle. "Miss Templestone, if we might find somewhere private, it would appear that you and I need to talk."

It took her several seconds before she nodded. "Yes, Lord Lawrence, it would seem that we do."

Chapter 27

The Yorkshire Dales in January were cold and bleak, the landscape composed of vast stretches of snow-covered ground broken only by clusters of bare-branched trees and rough stone walls that stretched off into the horizon as far as the eye could see. Yet in them Rosamund found something beautiful, a stark solitude that had the power to soothe the worst of the ragged edges of what remained of her heart.

Wrapped warmly inside a heavy brown woolen cloak with a bonnet on her head, thick gloves on her hands and a pair of sturdy boots on her feet, she walked as she had taken to doing nearly every day since her arrival last autumn. It was only during snowstorms that she remained inside for the whole of a day, the confinement wearing on her in ways it never had done in the past.

Her cousin Susan, a warm, grandmotherly sort of woman with kind blue eyes and a bun of thick white hair, worried about her "roaming the hills" and increasingly tried to convince Rosamund to remain indoors, especially now that her figure was turning round, the child she carried growing strong and steadily inside her.

But Cousin Ross had told his wife to leave her be. "Girl's grieving and needs to mourn. She'll come to no harm and the exercise will do her and the babe good."

And so she was left to walk and grieve, although not for the husband they thought she'd lost.

Her cousins had believed the tale she and Bertram spun, welcoming her with a generosity that had put her quite to shame. Never once had they questioned the truth of her story, the lie made that much more convincing by means of the gold wedding band she wore—her mother's once upon a time. When she'd revealed the news of her pregnancy to her cousins, they were happy and encouraging. The baby would be a blessing to her in the years ahead, they said. A joyful reminder of the love she'd shared with his—or her— father. A love she continued to feel despite all her efforts to drive the emotion away.

I am not going to think about Lawrence, she told herself as she walked, her boots crunching against the snow. Yet even as she thought the words, she knew them for the falsehood they were. It was a promise she made herself every day. And a promise she broke every day.

As if aware of her musings, their child moved inside her, a fluttery feeling that never failed to amaze and delight her.

No matter what comes, I have this. And Bertram.

Even from a distance, he had become a lifeline to

her old existence. He wrote her at least three times a week, keeping her abreast of all the happenings in London, telling her about legal acquaintances and colleagues, friends and neighbors and, to her pleased surprise, the novel he was writing. He was woodworking again too, building a crib for the baby to use when they came home.

He'd wanted to come north for the holidays, but the weather had been snowy and unpredictable, so they'd decided he should remain in London and plan a visit closer to the baby's birth sometime in April.

She hadn't had the heart to tell him yet, but she wasn't sure she was going to return to London. She'd thought it through and despite their plan, she didn't know if it was wise. Not only were there too many memories in the city, but there was too much of a chance that she might someday cross paths with Lawrence, and that was a risk she could not afford. They might not move in the same social circles, but he was a lawyer like her brother. What if word got back? What if he found out about their child?

So more and more, she was contemplating a permanent relocation and a fresh start. As her cousins would agree, Yorkshire was a fine place to raise a child. If only it didn't mean leaving behind everything she'd once held dear, including her beloved brother.

Realizing suddenly that the sky was turning cloudy and the air chillier, she retraced her steps back to the Carrows' house, her mind already looking ahead to the cup of hot tea and sweet biscuits she knew would be waiting.

She stamped her boots free of snow on the rear

stoop and let herself into the house. The warmth of wood smoke and the yeasty scents of freshly baked bread and currant buns greeted her in a delicious draft.

She'd removed her bonnet and gloves and was about to unfasten her cloak when Cousin Susan bustled around the corner into the rear hallway that was just off the kitchen.

Susan's blue eyes were particularly bright, sparkling with barely concealed news. "Oh, good, you are back." Her hands fluttered around herself in a surprisingly nervous way. "I was just about to send Morty out to find you, but he's still in the barn tending to the traveling chaise and team."

"What traveling chaise and team?"

The Carrows kept a single horse and a gig that they used for trips into Harrogate and to take them to services at the nearby village church on Sundays. Since retiring from the law, Cousin Ross saw no point in shouldering the expense to maintain a full team and coach, as he and Susan never journeyed more than half a day from home.

"A quite elegant one as it happens. You've a visitor, my dear," Susan said. "From London."

"Is it Bertram?" A smile came to her mouth. "Did he make the trip, after all?"

"No, it's not your brother. The gentleman said he's a friend. He's been waiting for you in the parlor for the past half hour."

Rosamund's heart began to race. "Did this gentleman happen to give a name?"

Susan frowned. "No, he said he prefers to surprise

you. I assumed he must be known to you and your late husband for him to seek you out like this, and in January no less. Was it wrong of me not to have inquired further?"

Rosamund shook her head and forced a smile. "It's quite all right, Cousin Susan. I believe I know who you must mean."

A look of relief moved over the older woman's pleasingly rounded face. "Oh, good. I already brought him tea. Shall I have a cup brought in for you as well?"

"No, thank you, not quite now. I doubt the gentleman will be staying overly long."

"Don't forget your cloak, dear," Susan said in a gentle reprimand as Rosamund started toward the front parlor.

But rather than stop to remove the garment, Rosamund drew it tighter around herself. Her pregnancy was only beginning to show, but if her surprise visitor was who she thought he was, she didn't want to risk revealing her condition to him. Then again, he must surely know already. What other possible reason could there be for him to have traveled all this way?

Forcing her hand not to shake, she pushed open the parlor door and stepped inside.

And there stood Lawrence, looking gorgeous and golden and even taller than she remembered. Dressed in dark, somber clothes, he exuded quiet elegance and an aristocratic sophistication that seemed markedly out of place in her cousin's modest house.

Despite the warning as to his presence, seeing him again came at her like a blow, robbing her of thought and breath. Blindly she reached out and grabbed hold of the doorknob, willing her knees not to buckle and give way.

At the exact same moment, he turned from the window where he'd been standing and found her, his beautiful gold-green eyes warming as they took her in.

"Rosamund," he murmured in his deep, dearly remembered voice.

Her chest grew tight at the sound, her throat closing so she was momentarily unable to speak. She stared instead, stealing a few precious seconds to drink him in, to memorize new images of him to refresh the old.

Yet it was only as she looked closer that she noticed the lines of tension around his eyes and mouth, the tired, drawn quality to his face that had not been there five months ago. He looked unhappy.

Is it because of the baby? Because he's learned the truth and feels honor-bound to take responsibility for something he had only ever wished to prevent?

She withered inside and looked away.

"Will you introduce me to your cousin?" he said, stepping away from the window. "I fear I was not as forthcoming with the good lady as I probably ought to have been."

She drew a steadying breath and released her hold on the doorknob to move deeper into the room, Cousin Susan following behind. "Of course. Lord Lawrence, pray allow me to make you properly known to my cousin, Mrs. Susan Carrow. Cousin Susan, Lord Lawrence Byron."

The older woman's eyes widened and she shot a slightly incredulous look at Rosamund. *"Lord Byron?"*

Rosamund decided not to correct her cousin's error

in addressing Lawrence as Lord Byron rather than Lord Lawrence. Neither, she was grateful to see, did Lawrence.

"No relation to *the* Byron the poet?" Susan asked.

"No, none at all," Lawrence said. "My family can't even claim him as a cheekily annoying distant cousin thrice removed."

"Well, good gracious me," Susan continued, "I had no idea that you were . . . well, who you are." She sank into a curtsey. "Forgive any offense I may have caused, Your Lordship. It was most inadvertently done."

"The offense is all mine, dear Mrs. Carrow, since I ought to have told you who I was from the start. You have been quite forbearing to play along with my little surprise and have been all that is kind and gracious while I awaited Mrs. . . . . Jones's return."

He arched an eyebrow to let Rosamund know that he was in on at least that much of the game. Before leaving London, she and Bertram had decided to give her fictitious dead husband a name. Paul Jones had seemed ordinary enough to suit the purpose.

"I am only sorry that your husband, *Ross Carrow*, has gone into Skipton for the afternoon. I should have liked the chance to meet him."

"He is expected back in time for dinner. You would be most welcome to join us at table tonight, my lord. I am sure he would enjoy meeting you too, since you did say you are in the legal profession. Ross is a retired barrister, you know."

"I am sure Lord Lawrence hasn't the time to stay for the evening meal," Rosamund interjected before

Lawrence had a chance to reply. "He has come to discuss business. Then he'll need to be on his way. Won't you, my lord?"

"Perhaps," he said. "My plans are as yet undetermined."

Susan looked back and forth between them, apparently aware of, but confused by, the undercurrent running between her and Lawrence.

Rosamund turned toward the older woman. "Cousin Susan, if you wouldn't mind, could you give His Lordship and me a few minutes alone please? As I believe he told you, he is a London lawyer. What he and I need to discuss is of a confidential nature. You understand?"

"Oh, of course. Yes, I see." Susan's expression cleared. "To do with your poor dear Paul, is it? I shall leave you both to it, then. Call me if either of you requires anything."

"We shall."

Rosamund waited until Susan closed the door at her back, her footsteps echoing softly away. Only then did Rosamund look up again.

"*Poor dear Paul*, is it?" Lawrence repeated. "You haven't really been married and widowed since last we met, I hope?"

She linked her hands in front of her. "No, as I'm sure you already know from having spoken with my brother. I presume he is the one who told you where to find me?"

"Yes, though it was not without a great deal of persuasion. He slammed the door in my face to start, then gave me a verbal hiding that would have put a fishwife to shame. He didn't even stutter when he did it. I believe he was so angry it drove the words straight out of his mouth. Maybe all he really needs in order to resume his career in court is a quiver full of righteous indignation. He's rather eloquent when he's got a head of steam on him."

"I told you he was good. It's only when he's anxious that he can't quite find his voice."

Crossing to the nearest chair, she sank down, abruptly weary in a way she hadn't been in weeks. She was careful to keep her cloak wrapped around her stomach, although it seemed rather pointless at this juncture.

She sighed. "He didn't have any right to tell you, you know, even if I'm sure he thinks what he's doing is for the best."

She looked up in time to see the hopeful light dim in Lawrence's eyes and the lines of unhappiness return. "He warned me how you might feel and that I would need to tread carefully as I made my case."

"Seeing that you excel at making cases, Counselor, I'm sure you'll have no trouble this time either."

"You might be surprised."

She looked up, startled as he knelt down beside her so they were nearly eye to eye.

"You've every right to hate me," he said, "and I can't blame you if you do. I've treated you shamefully and for that I offer you my humblest of apologies. What happened between us last summer was all my own doing. I pursued and maneuvered you, at first because I thought you were a rival, and then when I realized the truth of your deception, it was because I had come to desire you. But that is no excuse. I knew the kind of woman you were, the kind of woman you *are*, and still I seduced you without a scrap of conscience. I behaved like the veriest of cads."

Of all the things he might have said to her, this was not one she had considered. Had guilt driven him here to see her? Was he sorry for having had an affair with her and wished now that he could erase it? Erase her, from his past?

Of course he was. Because of the baby.

A chill settled through her despite the warmth of the cloak she still wore, ice forming even more heavily around her heart. Yet if it was absolution he sought, she would not deny him. She loved him too much to let him shoulder the blame, which truthfully was hers to bear in equal measures.

"You were never dishonest with me," she said softly. "The choice was mine and I made it freely."

He shook his head, a dark golden lock of hair falling over his forehead. She wanted to push it back but resisted the urge, the gesture one she would have made not so long ago without even thinking.

Then he was speaking again. "You believe you acted of your own free will, but as your brother quite rightly pointed out, I was the experienced one. The one who understood the rules and what might happen as a result. You were innocent, Rosamund, a virgin I led down the path of temptation in order to satisfy my own selfish desires."

Reaching out, he took one of her hands in his own. "Worse, I dishonored you again by wanting to keep you as my mistress, even while I contemplated marriage to another, and for that alone you may wish me to purgatory. I'll understand if you want me to leave, want never to have to set eyes upon me again. But before you decide, I beg you to hear me out just a little while longer."

She knew she should pull her hand away, knew she should be strong and tell him to go. Instead she left her hand in his, savoring the contact, the last she might ever have again.

"Rosamund, these past months without you have been nothing short of agony. I've missed you every single moment of every single day. I told myself it would get better, that my longing for you would fade and that in time I'd forget you."

She raised her eyes to his, her heartbeat turning erratic.

"But it's never going to fade," he said, "because I love you. And no amount of time will ever be enough for me to forget. I could as easily forget my own name or how to take my next breath. I know I've treated you abominably, but I pray you can forgive me and that it's not too late. Put me out of my misery, Rosamund, and say you'll be mine again. Say you will marry me and be my wife. If you will, I swear I'll spend the rest of my life striving to make you happy because, in the end, you are the only thing that truly matters."

Marry?

She knew she could not have heard him right. It was impossible.

And did he say he loves me?

Maybe she'd fallen outside in the snow earlier and hit her head. Maybe she was hallucinating right now and Lawrence wasn't even here, wasn't saying all these wonderful, fantastical things the likes of which she'd only ever dreamt.

"But you can't marry me," she said.

"Who says I can't? Only you have the power to refuse."

"But what of your fiancée? I saw the announcement. I know you're engaged."

"I was but not anymore. Miss Templestone and I have gone our separate ways."

"B-but what? How?" Rosamund stuttered, knowing suddenly how Bertram must have felt all these years.

"Our engagement is done. I told her at Christmas that I could not honor my pledge because I loved someone else. We talked and she agreed to release me rather than suffer the stigma of a public jilting."

"But the scandal . . . her father . . ."

"Yes, the judge was furious to say the least. He was even angrier, or so I'm given to understand, when Phoebe ran off to Gretna Green a few days later with a young man she has apparently loved for years. They grew up together, but her father wouldn't approve the match. The boy is the eldest son of one of her father's clerks and hasn't the pedigree or wealth to make him a suitable candidate for her hand. But I guess not even her father could stop them from writing to each other in secret."

He gave a wry smile. "When I told her I wanted to break off our engagement, she looked so relieved I thought she might laugh, or worse, cry. She said she liked me a very great deal and was flattered by my attentions during the Season. To please her parents, she had even convinced herself for a time that she wanted to marry me. But after our engagement became official, she saw it for the mistake it was, and that despite trying her hardest to feel more for me, she just didn't. I told her how sorry I was for everything, but grateful that we could part with no bitter feelings between us. And that, as they say, was that."

"So the judge won't ruin your career if you don't marry his daughter?"

Lawrence shrugged. "He may; he may not. We shall see. Frankly, though, I've come to realize that my career isn't nearly as satisfying or all-important as I once thought it was."

"But you love the law and you're so good at it," she protested. "You're too excellent a barrister to quit."

"You love it. And you're good at it. And you're every bit as excellent a barrister as I, and yet you had to give it up and for no better reason than the fact that you're a woman. If I have to give the law up as well, I will be sorry but it won't be the end of the world. I don't need the money and there are a host of other interesting things I can do with my life. The only thing that would be the end of my world is if you tell me you won't marry me. If you tell me you don't love me when I ache from loving you."

"Not love you?" She freed her hand and laid it against his cheek, finding it warm and memorably rough with a day's growth of whiskers. "I have loved you from the day we first met, even if I may not have recognized it then for what it was. Why else do you think I let myself be drawn into your web despite all the warnings? What other reason would I have had to give myself to you, an acknowledged rakehell, if not for love? Of course I love you. These past few months haven't been hell only for you."

His eyes glowed from within. "So you'll marry me?"

"I will, assuming you're sure I'll make you a proper wife. I'm not an aristocrat and your family may object."

"My family will adore you. Leo's been needling me ever since we parted, telling me what an absolute fool I was to let you go and to hurry and get you back."

She chuckled. "I like your brother. It's only that . . ."

"Yes? Only what?"

She tucked her hand back into her lap, her forearm resting against the small swell hidden underneath her cloak. "You really don't know, then? Bertram didn't tell you?"

His eyebrows drew tight. "Tell me what?"

She fidgeted a little in her chair. "Because originally I thought you'd come here strictly out of duty. That you knew the truth and were only trying to do the right thing."

"The truth about what? Rosamund, please just tell me what you mean, because at the moment you're not making a great deal of sense. What is it I don't know?"

Reaching for his hand again, she drew it beneath the edges of her cloak, then pressed his palm to her gently rounded stomach. "This."

He stiffened, his shock unmistakable. "Rosamund, are you . . ." Pushing open her garment, he stared, moving his hand across the slight bulge as if to better define the shape.

"Yes," she said. "I am carrying your child."

Myriad emotions flashed across his face—surprise and confusion warring with pleasure and elation before moving on to frustration, then anger.

He got to his feet, towering above her. "You weren't going to tell me." It was a statement rather than a question. "Didn't you think I had a right to know?"

"Of course you did and I thought about telling you. You don't know how badly I wanted to tell you. But by the time I became aware of my condition, you were engaged. I didn't see the point in telling you then. In coming back into your life only to ruin it again. You made it clear you didn't want a baby. I couldn't shackle you to me like that, couldn't force you to give up everything you held dear just so you could do the honorable thing."

He crossed his arms over his chest. "So you were going to keep me from my child? Never even let me know of its existence?"

Sadness fell upon her again as she shook her head. "I fear I'm the one who must beg your forgiveness now. If you no longer wish to marry me, I'll understand. Even if you do, it will cause a dreadful scandal. I'm nearly six months along, so there'll be no hiding it and no claim of a premature birth. Your family will be justifiably appalled."

Tears stung her eyes. "Please don't hate me, Lawrence. I'm sorry. I only did what I thought best. I didn't know what else to do."

Silence fell. Then before she knew what to expect, he reached down and pulled her up and into his arms. "Don't be a goose. As if I could ever hate you. It's impossible or haven't you realized that by now? I love you and I love our child and I am only sorry that you've had to bear this burden alone all these many months. I should have been with you. Then again, I should never have let you go in the first place."

Gathering her even closer, he crushed his mouth to hers and kissed her. She kissed him back, putting everything into their joining as she let all her love and longing pour forth, her worry and heartache, her joy and relief, as their touch formed the bridge that healed the pain of their separation.

At length, he drew away, untying her cloak and tossing it aside before taking her place in the chair and nestling her gently across his lap.

His mouth found hers again and neither of them came up for air for quite some time.

"A baby, hmm?" he said, running his hand over her stomach again in slow circles. "Of all the things I expected, that wasn't one of them."

"I may have forgotten the herbs a few times there at the end," she admitted. "I'm sorry."

He smiled. "Well, at least we won't have to blame the chemist."

"So you aren't angry?"

"About the baby? Not a bit. As for what my family will think, they'll be delighted." At her doubtful look, he laughed. "Believe me, you don't know the Byrons well enough. We all thrive on scandal. It's about time we had some fresh fodder with which to shock the Ton."

She couldn't help laughing in return, then sobered as a new thought occurred. "Heavens, what am I going to tell my cousins? They both think I'm a respectable widow, not the pregnant lover of a wicked aristocrat."

"Shortly to be his wife. I plan to wed you as soon as I can lay hands on a special license."

"Bertram will be relieved."

"I think that's the only reason he didn't kill me when I showed up on his doorstep. I told him I loved you and planned to marry you as soon as I could convince you to have me."

"There was never any doubt about my answer."

"Oh, I'm not so certain. I think he thought it could go either way."

She grinned again and kissed him. "But about my cousins. I suppose we'll have to tell them the truth. They've both been so good to me. It seems only fair."

"Leave it to me. We'll tell them enough. I presume you don't want to admit to your cousin Ross that you borrowed his name and bar affiliation for a few months of exceptional legal work in London over the summer."

"No, I'd rather not. I think he and Susan will be dismayed enough by news of you and the baby without heaping on more."

"Then me and the baby it is. I had wondered about this Paul Jones fellow. Seemed rather shabby of the man to marry you, get you with child, then stick his spoon in the wall all within a couple of weeks."

"Two months."

"Ah, that long, was it? Maybe Leo can use the idea in his next novel."

"I think Bertram has beat him to it."

"Your brother is writing? Good God, how many novelists will there be in the family?"

"More, it would seem, than lawyers."

His expression grew serious. "Do you miss it? The law?"

"Sometimes. It was exciting and I'm glad to have done it. But I missed you so much more."

"I meant it when I said there's nothing and no one more important to me than you. You're my heart, Rosamund Carrow. My very breath of life. Now kiss me again before your cousin Susan comes in, worried I'm holding you for ransom."

She threaded her fingers into his hair to bring him close. "You can hold me for ransom anytime you like, my lord, because I never want you to let me go."

"And I never will." He grazed his lips against hers. "I promise."

Don't miss

Happily Bedded Bliss

Available now from Signet Select.
Continue reading for a preview.

Lady Esme Byron hiked her sky blue muslin skirts up past her stocking-clad calves and climbed onto the wooden stile that divided the vast Braebourne estate from land owned to the east by her family's nearest neighbor, Mr. Cray.

Cray, a widower near her eldest brother Edward's age of forty, was rarely in residence and never complained about her trespassing on his land; since her childhood, he'd let her traipse across it almost as if it were her own. Not that Braebourne didn't provide plenty of beautiful vistas to explore—it did, especially considering that her brother owned nearly half the county and more besides—it was just that Cray's land possessed a lovely natural freshwater lake that sat at a perfect walking distance from the house. The lake attracted a rich variety of wildlife, so there was always something fascinating to sketch. Plus, no one ever bothered her there; it was quite her favorite secret place when she was looking for an escape.

She jumped down onto the other side of the stile,

taking far more care of the satchel of drawing supplies slung over her shoulder than she did of her fine leather half boots. She wobbled slightly as they sank ankle-deep into the mud, then stared at her ruined boots for a few seconds, knowing her maid would give her a scold for sure. But as she was always able to talk dear Grumbly around, she shrugged away any concern.

Grabbing hold of the fence, she unstuck herself one boot at a time, then scraped the worst of the mess off into the nearby grass. Turning with a swirl of her skirts, she continued on to her destination.

As she walked, she angled her face up to the sun and sighed blissfully.

How good it was to be home again after weeks in London.

How wonderful to be out in the open once more, free to roam wherever she liked, whenever she liked.

A tiny frown of guilt wrinkled her dark brows, since technically she was supposed to be back at the estate helping entertain the houseguests visiting Brae-bourne. But all seven of her siblings and their families were in residence, even Leo and his new bride, Thalia, who had just returned with celebratory fanfare from their honeymoon trip to Italy. With so many Byrons available to make merry, she would hardly be missed.

Besides, they were used to her penchant for disappearing by herself for hours at a time as she roamed the nearby woods and hills and fields. She would be back in time for dinner; that would have to be enough.

An exuberant bark sounded behind her and she glanced around to see her dog Burr leap the stile and race toward her. She bent down and gave his shaggy golden head a scratch. "So, you're back, are you? Done chasing rabbits?"

He waved his bright flag of a tail in a wide arc, his pink tongue lolling out in a happy grin. Clearly, he was unapologetic for having deserted her a short while ago so he could hunt game in the bushes.

"Well, come along," she told him before continuing toward a stand of trees in the distance.

Burr trotted enthusiastically at her side.

Nearly ten minutes later, they reached the copse of trees that led to the lake. She was just about to step out of their protective green shelter when she heard a splash.

She stopped and motioned for Burr to do the same.

Someone, she realized, was swimming in the lake. Was it Mr. Cray? Had he returned home unexpectedly?

Soundlessly, she peered through the leaves and watched a man emerge from the water—a man who most definitely was *not* Mr. Cray.

But who was most definitely *naked*.

Her eyes widened as she drank in the sight of his long, powerfully graceful form, his pale skin glistening wetly in the sunlight.

A quiet sigh of wonder slid from between her parted lips, her senses awash with the same kind of reverence she felt whenever she beheld something of pure, unadorned beauty.

Not that his face was the handsomest she had ever glimpsed—his features were far too strong and angular for ordinary attractiveness. Yet there was something majestic about him, as if a dark angel had fallen to earth. His tall body was exquisitely proportioned: wide shoulders, sculpted chest, long arms, narrow hips and sinewy legs, even the unmentionable male part of him that hung impressively between his heavily muscled thighs.

Clearly unaware that he was being observed, he casually slicked the water from his dark hair, then walked deeper into the surrounding area of short grass, which she knew was periodically trimmed by the groundskeepers.

She caught her lower lip between her teeth, her heart pounding wildly as she watched him stretch out on his back across the soft green carpet of grass. With a hand, she motioned again for Burr to remain quiet. She did the same, knowing that if she moved now, the mystery man would surely hear her.

One minute melted into two, then three.

Quite unexpectedly, she heard the soft yet unmistakable sound of a snore.

Is he asleep?

She smiled, realizing that was exactly what he must be.

Of course she knew she ought to leave. But even as she began to ease away, he shifted, his face turning toward her. One of his hands lay on his flat stomach, one ankle tucked under the other at an elegant angle.

And suddenly she couldn't leave.

Not when she was in the presence of such splendor and grace; it was as if the universe had decided to give her a gift.

I simply have to draw him.

Without considering her decision any further, she sank quietly onto a fallen log nearby that provided her with a sheltered, yet excellent view of her subject. Burr settled down at her side, laying his chin on his paws as she extracted her pencil and sketchbook from her bag and set to work.

Gabriel Landsdowne came abruptly awake, the late-afternoon sun strong in his eyes. He blinked and sat up, giving his head a slight shake to clear out the last of the drowsy cobwebs.

He'd fallen asleep without even realizing. Apparently, he was more tired than he'd thought. Then again, that was why he'd come here to Cray's, so he could spend a little time alone, doing nothing more strenuous than taking a leisurely swim and lazing away the day. He could have done the same at his own estate, of course, but visiting Ten Elms always put him in a foul humor.

Too many bad memories.

Too many unwanted responsibilities on behalf of a place that had never brought him anything but pain. For the most part, he left Ten Elms' management to his steward, since he rarely set foot over the threshold, but invariably there was some matter or other that would crop up requiring his attention. There was also his house in Cornwall and his town house in London, both of which put claims on his time and attention, but he never minded seeing to those properties. They were his and his alone, with none of the taint of the past to sour his habitation.

Yet he'd grown tired of his usual haunts of late—and his usual companions and their seemingly insatiable craving for debauchery.

Even the devil needed a holiday every once in a while.

When his old, and far more respectable, friend Cray mentioned that he was going hunting in Scotland—an activity Gabriel did not enjoy—Cray offered Gabriel the use of his house in his absence. Knowing that Cray House was a place none of his regular crowd would ever think to find him, Gabriel had accepted. He'd actually left London without so much as a word to anyone, instructing his butler to take the knocker off the door and say only that the master was away at present and not receiving.

Wouldn't his ribald set of cronies laugh now to see him doing something as prosaic as taking a solitary afternoon nap? Then again, he was out of doors, stark naked, so they would most certainly approve of that.

Smirking, he stood up, brushing an errant blade of grass from his bare buttocks. He was about to cross to the stand of bushes where he'd left his clothes when he heard a faint rustling sound behind him. He turned and stared into the foliage.

"Who is it? Is someone there?" he demanded.

The only answer was silence.

He looked again, scanning the area, but nothing moved; no one spoke.

Maybe it had been the wind? Or an animal foraging in the woods?

Suddenly a dog burst from the concealment of the trees, its shaggy wheaten coat gleaming warmly in the sun. He was a medium-sized mix of no particular breed, part hound, possibly, or maybe retriever. He seemed well fed, so it was doubtful that he was a stray.

Then again, mayhap he was skilled at poaching birds and rabbits from the bountiful reserves of game in the area.

The dog stopped and looked at him, eyes bright and inquiring but not unfriendly.

"Who might you be, fellow?" Gabriel asked.

The animal wagged his tail and barked twice. Then, just as suddenly as he had appeared, he spun and disappeared into the trees once more.

In that instant, Gabriel thought he spied a flash of blue in the woods.

A bird?

The dog must have sensed it and gone off to chase.

Gabriel stared for one last long moment, then shrugged and turned to gather his clothes.

The Rakes of Cavendish Square

by Tracy Anne Warren

The most devilishy dangerous rakes in all of England
are no match for the bewitching and beguiling
women who capture their hearts.

**Find more books by Tracy Anne Warren
by visiting prh.com/nextread**

"Tracy Anne Warren delivers...A truly
satisfying romance."—*The New York Times Book Review*

"Deeply moving."—Fresh Fiction